Note:

This is the second annual anthology of weird, wacky, outrageous, off-the-wall short stories. We're now accepting submissions for the 2020 edition.

For Authors:

If you would like to submit any of your stories, we would love to see them. For the details and submission requirements, send an email to:
anthology@bouldawards.com
and you'll get an auto-reply with all that information.

# The 2019 Bould* Awards Anthology

*Bizarre, Outrageous, Unfettered, Limitless, Daring

Edited by Jake Devlin

These are works of fiction.

Any resemblance to actual persons, living or dead, business establishments, events or locales, including public figures, is entirely coincidental.

All rights reserved. No part of this book may be used or reproduced in any manner whatsoever without written permission, except in the case of brief quotations embodied in critical articles and/or reviews.

Copyright © 2019 Jake Devlin
(aka R. J. Hezzelwood)

Individual Stories

Copyright © Respective Authors

Preface

I challenged authors around the world to think and
write outside the box, WAY outside the box
(we do NOT recommend that for cats with diarrhea)
and submit whatever they could come up with.
The more bizarre, outrageous, unfettered,
limitless and daring, the better.
I hope everyone who reads this finds it both
enjoyable and perhaps thought-provoking.

The stories were selected anonymously
by an independent panel of judges.

If you're an author and any of the stories
you read in here inspired your own off-the-wall
creativity, I'd love it if you'd submit for the
2020 edition. Check out the info on the very
front page of this book for that information.

Jake

CONTENTS

Bitch and Chips - Maddi Davidson -1060 words

A Walk In The Park - Francis Hicks - 490

A Man Without His Word - Lise de Nil - 1848

Honor Amongst the Rigid – Wil A. Emerson - 2980

Clarity - Francis Hicks - 720

In the Octopus's Garden – James Dorr – 2400   jamesdorrwriter.wordpress.com/

Take Nothing For Granite - John Clark - 1170

When I Think About - Gary R. Hoffman - 450

Teacher's Pets - Kat Fast - 1990

Teagan's Special Sand Castle - Jake Devlin – 1300   JakeDevlin.com

Note Found Near Scattered Human Skeletal Remains - Jack Ewing - 1840

Oh Henry – Wil A. Emerson – 2990

Bait – Eve Fisher – 2700

Zero-Sum - Cheri Vause - 1500

Chemo Queen – Tom Barlow - 2970

The Sadist - Jimmy Summers – 750

In A Town Mostly Forgotten – John Clark – 2060

The Purloined Pickled Peppers - Herschel Cozine - 2400

Eggboy and the Drunk - Lise de Nil - 2990

The Price You Pay - William A. Rush IV - 1850

Henry The Butler - Francis Hicks - 500

The Mystery of the Missing Albino - Steve Shrott - 2800

A Shifting Plan -Elizabeth Zelvin – 2500   elizabethzelvin.com

Input From A Serial Killer - John Furutani – 2570

Confession of a Serial Killer – Jake Devlin - 500

The Cat - Robert Petyo – 2100

Deer Juj - David Hagerty – 850

The Society - KM Rockwood – 2200   kmrockwood.com/

Something Wacky This Way Comes - Karen Phillips – 2000

Pinning Ceremony – John Clark – 2670

Drip-Dry and Wrinkle-Free – Lesley A. Diehl – 2440

Mr. Happy Head – James Dorr – 2700

Preincarnation – Eve Fisher – 1000

To Die a Free Man: The Story of Joseph Bowers – KM Rockwood – 2790

The Suicide Bureau – Robert Petyo – 1700

The Silkie – Elizabeth Zelvin – 2900

Meeting on the Funicular – Kaye George – 735 kayegeorge.com

Cold Snap – Maddi Davidson – 640

Euthanasia – Karen Duxbury – 260   karenduxbury.com

An Apocalyptic Micro Short Story – Jake Devlin – 20

3rd Place

Maddi Davidson

The 2019 BOULD Awards Anthology

Bitch and Chips

Maddi Davidson (~1060 words)

The skier was off-piste in a heavily wooded section of Baldy when he collided with a Douglas fir. The only one to witness the accident, I skied over to where he lay. He was dead, his face smashed in like day-old road kill. I noticed he was wearing one of those high-end ski outfits with heating and cooling systems built into the jacket, bib, boots, and gloves. Obviously a rich guy, but stupid: he'd not been wearing a helmet.

Even now I can't tell you what I was thinking when I pulled up his right sleeve and sliced out his financial chip with my survival knife. I left the body in the trees and skied down the hill. The next day I flew to California: I'd always wanted to see the Pacific Ocean.

I'm a Nobotech (No body technology). My long departed parents were part of the migration of '32, when those unwilling to accept government biosensor implants were ordered to move to one of the "Left Behind" states, as many called us. I've spent my entire life in Hailey, Idaho, at the foot of the Sawtooth Mountains, living without electronic implants and paying cash or bartering for what I needed. In this state, God and guns are revered and the national guv'ment despised.

With the dead guy's chip taped to the inside of my wrist and covered with a big bandage, I was now able to travel outside the state, paying for flights, hotels, and food with a swipe of my arm. Each day in Los Angeles was a whirlwind of activities as I had limited time before the chip was shut down. The skier's biosensors would have instantly registered his death and transmitted the information to a U.S. Department of Health & Human Services (HHS) database. I was counting on ordinary bureaucratic ineptitude and the incompatibility of the government systems with private financial systems to give me a week or two before the banks became aware that purchases were being made by a corpse. If I didn't return to Idaho by the time the dead man's accounts were frozen, I'd be trapped in LA with no way of paying for anything since the forty-eight enslaved states no longer accepted cash—not that I had more than a few dollars.

But I didn't want to go back; there was nothing for me in Idaho. I wanted to travel, to see the Grand Canyon, the Great Lakes, Manhattan, Niagara Falls, and all the sites in between.

I needed financial chips.

My targets became rich, old men. Finding my victims at country clubs, coming out of doctor's offices, or dining at five-star restaurants, I'd follow them home and concoct a way of approaching them. Being a relatively attractive woman in her early thirties, they never saw me as a threat. Before shepherding the silly, old codgers to the great beyond, I'd spend at least twenty minutes stroking their male egos. I was doing them a service by ensuring they didn't suffer the progressive atrophy of the mind and dissolution of the body that attend senescence. The quid pro quo was ten days living off their savings. Seemed like a fair exchange to me, not that they were alive to dispute it.

Robobank was the first institution to recognize the pattern of murdered old guys and plundered accounts. Someone at the bank leaked the discovery to a Denver reporter who aired the story. All hell broke loose. Thousands, then tens of thousands fearing imminent death had their chips removed. Shirts emblazoned with "Chip in my wallet" sold like hot cakes and the only firm still manufacturing wallets—located in Wyoming, the other Nobotech state—acquired a six-year backlog nearly overnight.

By that time, I was in Pigeon Forge, Tennessee, visiting the Alcatraz East Crime Museum. The display of arcane murderabilia was a rich source of new ideas and the mango margaritas at a nearby fusion restaurant were to die for.

The public berated the police forces for the ineptness of their investigation. For the past several decades, crime rates had declined dramatically, particularly offenses against persons. Since biosensors provided the exact location of anyone and everyone at the time of a crime, old-fashioned detection skills had atrophied. Only police in Idaho and Wyoming were trained in traditional investigative skills. When asked by the Feds for help in catching the serial killer, Wyoming's governor replied, "When bison fly, buttheads"—a sentiment echoed by Idaho.

The FBI called in long-retired agents to develop a profile of the murder suspect, which they released to the public. No better than drivel, all the character sketch got right was my intelligence and resourcefulness. The bit about a grandiose ego was insulting; I maintain a healthy respect for my innately superior abilities.

It was pure dumb luck the police caught me.

An over-protective mother at Disney World spotted me alone, waiting for the "It's a Small World" ride. She feared I might be a child kidnapper in search of a victim. Instead of just keeping an eye on her own children, Madame buttinski felt compelled to report her concerns. When I stepped out of the boat Snow White and Dopey, aka Disney security, accosted me and muscled me backstage. They checked to see if I carried a chip record of criminal behavior and discovered I didn't have any biosensors. I did, however, have a financial chip for the recently deceased Brennan Houseworth III.

Fifty years earlier I would have been given the death penalty. Instead, I was sentenced to experience one simulated death for each person I had killed. Tied to a bed and covered with electrodes, I've felt the chest-crushing pressure of a heart attack, the tearing and burning of my lungs while drowning, the agony of multiple gunshot wounds, and the excruciating pain and acrid smell of burning skin. As a special treat, my simulated death always ends with the razor-sharp pain of a financial chip being torn from my wrist as I draw my last breath.

I've lost count of the exact number of times I've died: more than ten but less then the twenty-three the government knows about. After the last death, I'm supposed to be incarcerated for twenty years; plenty of time for a genius like me to escape.

I've always wanted to see France.

END

The 2019 BOULD Awards Anthology

Edited By Jake Devlin

The 2019 BOULD Awards Anthology

Walk In The Park

Francis Hicks (~490 words)

A sky, dark like cobalt glass, taps my window, daring me. "Come out here."

Work will wait.

The park is a slice of wilderness nearby; a fast walk to where my mind is free. I lengthen my stride until my left foot drags. Searing pain slices through my head.

"Ernest, you all right?"

A stranger, dressed like a runner, stares at me.

"Ernest, say somethin'."

Who're you?

"Maybe you should sit down."

I slump to the path. The cobalt sky grows darker.

The stranger is on his cell. I realize the man is my neighbor. *Chuck, who're you calling?*

"He can't talk right and he sorta collapsed."

Chuck ignores me. Damn cell phones.

"What can I do for him?"

I look up at Chuck. *Why do you need to do anything?*

"Yeah, I'll stay until the EMTs come."

Chuck. I'm talking to you. I try to stand, but fall sideways. *I just need a hand.* I try to raise my arm. Nothing happens.

Chuck holds his phone to his ear as he looks down at me. "Hang on, man. Help is on the way."

I try to straighten myself, but there's no feeling in my feet, legs, stomach. My arms don't respond. I flop onto my back and stare straight up into the once deep blue, now almost-black sky.

"What happened?" Chuck asks.

Edited By Jake Devlin

The question grates on me. *Nothing! I was walking and then... I don't know. And then you were here. Dammit, Chuck. Help me!*

"Talk to me."

I am talking to you, dumb ass.

"I'm goin' to meet the medics. Hold on." Chuck jogs off.

Unable to move, all I see are trees and the inky sky.

I can't feel my neck, mouth, tongue. The tissue surrounding my windpipe sags, giving in to gravity. Every inhalation makes a buzzing, gagging sound. Each breath becomes more labored.

My muscles don't respond to my urgent, then panicked demands. Tears form. I crush my eyelids closed in despair. *Dammit, I'm going to die.*

I hear footsteps scrape on the caliche trail. My eyes shoot open. A heavy gold chain dangles from the neck of a young man in a knit cap.

"Gotta roll you, dude. You're chokin'."

My head clunks on the hard trail as he rolls me onto my side.

"I ain't a doctor or nothin', but sometimes my clients don't cut the shit before they cook it, and they seize. So, I hadta learn how to do this." He grasps my chin with both hands and pulls.

My throat opens and I suck in greedy breaths.

"I see EMTs comin' up the path. You'll be awright. But I cain't stay." The young man glances around nervously and heads back down the trail.

I can't feel my body, yet in the total darkness of the moonless sky, relief floods my mind. Until I realize, my mind, all I have left is my mind.

END

The 2019 BOULD Awards Anthology

Edited By Jake Devlin

The 2019 BOULD Awards Anthology

A Man Without His Word

Lise de Nil   (~1850 words)

"I have decided," he said, "to eat you."

He was a hulk of a man, rolling a joint, his green eyes glowing, jaw set. Thick and massive, he was a boulder of flesh in a small room she knew not where.

She thought about the sharpness of his teeth. Perhaps she should have taken the drugs he had offered. It was not too late but if she did, how would she escape? She needed to stay awake, make a plan.

But she hurt so badly—she was bitten, bruised, scratched and scraped.

He had gnawed at her breasts, chewed her throat, broken the flesh on her face, her mouth was swollen, she could taste blood. The insides of her thighs stung raw, the breath of air was a slap of cold steel.

She looked back at him, and said nothing.

She was tied to the bed, itself a torture, the fabric rough beneath her, her wrists hurting, muscles aching.

"Are you sure," he said, "that I can't get you something to ease the pain? I would hate you to get all sensitive on me now."

Again she did not reply. She wondered where they were. Was he not concerned that her cries could be overheard? There was no electricity in the cabin, it was cold and rough. Suddenly she remembered, he had mentioned a buddy of his had a cottage way up north, it was out in the middle of nowhere he had said, with no running water or electricity, she would like it he had said, he would take her there one day.

"A man without his word is nothing," he had also said.

"That's the one thing my father taught me. A man without his word is nothing."

And so, true to his word, he had brought her to this place in the middle of nowhere.

She was tired. Impossibly tired. It must have been days before that he had taken her. Why was no one looking for her? Why had they not found her? Had they, inconceivably, thought that this was what she had wanted? Surely not? But they had all said that they knew little of her and that they were sure she had a wild side and that they had not known what she had seen in him from the start, that they hoped she would see, sooner rather than later, what it was they all saw.

The smell of hash filled the room. She licked her swollen cut lip and raised her head, looking down at her stomach. It too was bruised and crushed.

And there I was, thinking this was true love.

He came over to her and covered her with a hand-knitted blanket, white with a red maple leaf, soft, old. Lay down next to her, put his arm around her, slept.

She lay still, breathing, in and out.

She knew when he woke.

"I'm hungry," he said and lumbered naked over to the table where he opened a can of beans.

"You still think I'm fat?" he asked, "not that I care what you think."

He raised a bottle of orange juice in her direction, as if toasting her, and he drank, spilling juice down his chest. He rubbed the mess with a hairy paw.

"Nice and sticky," he said "You want me to give it to you now, are you ready for me to give it to you?"

"All things in good time," he continued, "first it's time for me to do some coke, I'd offer you some but I know you'll say no."

He bent his head over a plastic tray with yellow sunflowers.

Then he rolled another joint and inhaled deeply.

"Time now," he said "to give it to you, you want that, don't you? You've always wanted it, right from the start. People have no idea about your dark side, you walk around all professional like in your little accountant suit, nice high heels, getting everybody's payroll worked out but you like this, don't you? I know you do. Who knew it was the carpentry guy you wanted, someone who could nail you?" He laughed at his own joke. "Nail you! Get it?"

He approached the bed and she forced herself to relax, it would hurt too badly if she didn't. She wondered, as he pounded inside of her, why this brought him such pleasure, he seemed to resent every thrust. It was hard for her to breathe, he held her head down on the pillow, his hand twisted her neck sideways, he pushed her down and pulled her hair.

He came, grunting hard, a bowel movement sound, nearly painful.

"I'm just getting warmed up," he said and climbed off her. He unscrewed the cap off a bottle of water and cleaned himself with a dishtowel.

He cracked open a beer and drank deeply. He belched and farted loudly, smiling in a self-congratulatory way, so proud of himself.

"I have no idea," he said, "what you ever saw in me."

Annihilation. That's what she saw. The ending. The exit sign to normalcy. The end of the pretend game, the social niceties, the lets-play-nice rules of civilization. It was the end that she had welcomed in him.

He came over to her, leaned down by the side of the bed, his face close to hers and held her head in his hand.

Edited By Jake Devlin

"Do you have any idea how I feel about you?" he asked. "You have no idea, no idea. I watch you... I watch you... I love you, I love you."

He untied her and washed her, the water cold, facecloth rough, inside her legs, her buttocks. He leaned down and licked her, softly, like a cat, his tongue lapping her.

Then he bit her, hard. She jerked back in sudden horrified surprise, she screamed, arched away, and twisted as far away from him as she could.

"I told you," he said "I am going to eat you. A man without his word is nothing. I told you, I am going to eat you."

He bit harder, his impossibly sharp teeth cutting into her. She lost consciousness, sliding away from the pain.

When she woke she was throbbing. Insanely hurt. She cried without opening her eyes. Her heart was broken. She pressed her legs together hoping to ease the pain. She felt sticky, torn. She pulled her legs up to her chest and leaned her head on her knees. She cried wetly, sobbing.

He came over to her and unfolded her almost patiently, inevitably. He straightened her out on her back, smoothed her hair, rubbed her arms. Tied her up.

"I had done better than my parents had expected," he said conversationally. "I had a good job, a partnership at work, a normal life, a truck, no prison record, enough money to make it okay. I was doing okay.

"But then you came along and I don't know what it was, why I couldn't just walk away from you, god knows I tried. I knew from the start how different we were, you couldn't seem to see it, but I could. I didn't know why you wanted me. I thought we could have some fun, I still don't understand where it got so complicated. I told you from the start, I am a simple guy, you told me you were complicated, but I had no idea how complicated you are. How manipulative, you really are a piece of work. I've been told I am controlling but you, you take the cake. If I said left you'd say right - only you'd find a way to get me to say right so that you could say left. I don't even know my left from my right any more. All I wanted was for you to behave yourself and to have no expectations from me. But whatever I did, you expected something else. You wouldn't leave me alone, and then you slighted me out of nowhere just when I thought we had reached an agreement."

He stopped, got up and went over to his backpack. He pulled out a large knife, and he twisted it in the fading light, the steel gleaming.

He came back and sat down again.

"You like knives, don't you?" he asked "You said you did. Here, let's see how you like this one."

He drew a line down her body, from her neck all the way down, a thin string of red. Sharp cold wet.

"So I decided to take you with me," he said, "and finish this once and for all."

"I can't go back now," he said, his mouth close to her ear. "It's all gone now. I don't know where I'll go when this is done and I don't care. I always knew it would end like this, one way or another. This is the way it was meant to be, I just didn't know it would be with you, that's all, I didn't know you would be the one."

He climbed off her and went back to the plastic tray. She felt like a raw wound, open from head to toe. It had grown dark and he lit a candle.

"Must be careful," he slurred, "not to start a fire."

He was drugged, out of control and he staggered and crashed into the table.

"Pardon me," he mumbled and focused on setting the candle

down carefully.

"I am so hot," he said. "Don't you feel like it's so hot in here?"

He lay down on the floor, splayed out, hirsute, immense, and fell asleep.

She was cold, uncovered, shivering. Her teeth chattered, her jaw ached. She couldn't tell one area of pain from another. She must have dozed off because when she woke she was covered with the soft old blanket, and he was beside her, his head buried in her neck.

She dozed again and woke to find him gone, he was bending over the plastic tray, mumbling to himself. It was getting lighter. She felt feverish, covered in a cold sweat. She was shaking uncontrollably.

"Ah, now," he said, he came over and hugged her awkwardly. "Don't be like that, we're still going to have some fun you and me."

He straightened her out again, with difficulty, she was jerking uncontrollably.

"Lie still," he said irritably, and he lay the weight of his body on hers.

"Do you want me, need me or love me?" he asked her.

She knew the answer to this one.

"I love you," she said.

He smiled.

"And now," he said "I am going to eat you, just like I said I would."

He stared into her eyes for a instant, his lashes long and guileless, then he turned his head away, his unshaven cheek sandpaper on the soft pale skin of her chest. He lingered for a moment, as if he were considering, then he sank his teeth deep and ripped off her nipple. A quick fluid bite, and then he came back for more.

A man without his word is nothing.

END

The 2019 BOULD Awards Anthology

Edited By Jake Devlin

The 2019 BOULD Awards Anthology

Honor Amongst the Rigid

Wil A. Emerson (~2980 words)

"The eclipse will come soon, Beguile. When it does, my fellow Rigidites will be ready to depart. One more journey, perhaps two, is all I have lft. You must acquire all the Legacies you deserve."

"Seven is enough. Stay with me. Do not venture beyond the perpendicular. Infinity may well be altered by the next Thermal rise. Please, loyalty has been a gift we share. Stay with me and our seven."

Honored Cornic lifted his taut chin. Faded blue eyes darted toward the mass of white clouds floating above the unfettered graphite ceiling. Yes, he considered, Beguile may have surmised the ultimate fact. The atmosphere has changed since the last eclipse. Ten degrees warmer with each lunar phase. Too rapid, he thought. It could surely accelerate the Solid. He and the older Rigidites would lose their flexibility sooner than the Inevitable Plan. First a digit, two, three, more, then an entire hand. If Thermal increased another five degrees, they all risked the onset of Brittle in arms and legs. Heart and Brain would soon follow. Solid before the expected twenty-seventh Cast-a-Shadow.

Cornic rubbed his hand and then his arm. Did it feel different? He raised his bare arm above his head. Flexed his leg and rolled back his shoulders. Perhaps if he imbibed another premature earthling. The gray mass, the spleen, the marrow. Give the pituitary gland, the heart and cortex to Beguile. It would provide the diverse cellular proteins to give another Legacy a strong and hardy constitution. Beguile then would have the minimal Eight lifelong Cares the Master Breviary proclaimed Sufficent until Solid took his loyal to Designated Eternal.

Edited By Jake Devlin

Perhaps at his side? Cornic shook his head. A foolish notion indeed. Only Earthlings believed in an Eternal Place where Loyals rested together. A substandard ideation. A folly of primitive nature that no other Orbit shared.

Cornic recognized the first sign of his inevitable Solid more than a cycle ago. Seldom did the stiffness start in the twenty-fifth cycle. A review of the Chronicles confirmed his acquired affliction had no remedy. Silicon had not lessened the pain nor increased flexibility. Yet, he kept the secret buried in his heart. And would do so until he insured Beguile had more than the necessary Legacies. He had to address the Plan.

"You need ten Legacies. That is the requirement to achieve Most Beneficent Offspring Standard. Tomorrow I will contact Prevail the Stronger and designate his life sperm for the next Legacy. It does appear that our last union did not bring a Foster. And if I fail with Igniting the Earthling Mass I bring back from Earth, Prevail will take my place at the Over-Seed until ten are achieved."

"But your sperm is all I desire." Beguile placed her hand on Cornic's heart. "Your blood runs in my veins. Pure Sperm has filled my void with The Life seven times over. That is enough. With hearts together, our Devine Legacies will always be devoted to us. Please, I beg of you. Stay and let us evolve as we are until Solid replaces the softness of our hearts."

"Mine will turn long before yours. That is meant to be. Yes, our Legacies are devoted but eight is Minimum and ten is Beneficent. We have never settled for minimum standards. It is my honor, my duty to insure your safety."

"With permission, I will spill four millimeters of tears. I cannot bear to hold this pain inside and yet, I must make room for the joy you bring me."

Cornic nodded. Of course, his Loyal should be allowed this

one diversion. In the fifteen cycles they had been together, Beguile had never spilled. She was soft, pliable in form and nature and never had reason to spill over the Inevitable.

If only my bank sperm had not dried so soon, Cornic thought. Beguile could have had fifteen Legacies before my departure to Solid if she so chose. I could have fostered all the storage Earthling Masses for Steady Guard with my Vigor. But the last test, the yearly deposit, had been deemed too weak by the Holy Master Naturalist for inclusion in the bank. It was doubtful if cell life could be ignited even in fresh mass, Master said. A secret more profound than any he'd share with his Loyal.

Yet, the Holy Master Naturalist said Cornic might gain two more cycles from outside the Orbit if he infused their stronger amino acids directly into his veins. Outsider's Flow might enhance his weak Foster. Was he strong enough to withstand the anaerobic plunge into Earth Outer? It would be a major risk with the rising Thermal. The affliction of premature Solid might be attained before he returned. His Loyal, with a heart so soft, would be alone to withstand Rigids outside his sphere.

Did Cornic really have a choice? Eight Legacies were the Minimum. Yet, he wanted ten Legacies to protect Beguile no matter the Thermal increase or decline. Cornic would travel to Earth Outer. It must be done. Even if it cost his remaining cycles. He would contract Prevail the Stronger for a Master Fold.

When Cornic garnered Prevail the Stronger the next moonfall, their talk ended with a commitment. A serum contract to Foster one Legacy with Beguile before Cornic left for the journey. Thus the Minimal attained. Beguile and this eighth Legacy would see the light together. Eight as a Minimal but not Satisfactory and definitely not Beneficent. However, as the Highest, he had to make concessions. He could not change what Naturalist had decreed.

Edited By Jake Devlin

If Cornic returned safely and could Over-Seed fresh Earthling masses as protective Folds, though, he could at least ease into Solid with a clear conscience. If Cornic did not return, Prevail would be allowed to Fold with Cornic's lifelong Loyal and experience Pleasure Reward until Tenth Legacy arrived.

It was a high price to pay, much at stake, but Beguile's future had to be considered. With the pulse of his heart, Cornic knew his decision would cause stress for Beguile. However, there was no truer Loyal than Beguile and she would faithfully endure a Fold for the Minimum with Prevail the Stronger if Cornic were at her side.

As per decorum and the laws of the Holy Masters of Natural, Beguile and Prevail would Harness in a Master Fold in full view of Cornic and two chosen fellow Ancients in their last stage of Solid to serve as Holy Witnesses and confirm Ordination Spill.

There must be no doubt in anyone's mind that Cornic's Loyal did not betray him or the duty of High Order over which Cornic ruled.

The Ordination Spill decreed an emotionless Harness for Beguile. Prevail the Stronger, too, would be prohibited from expressing pleasure, but it had to appear that Beguile welcomed the Fold as he entered the Void so Performance could be maintained. A Strong would only relinquish Seed for honor and duty. Beguile's acceptance would be induced by Elixir Sublime and consumed moments before the Harness to mask her Frowned Heart. If pleasure arose with the Orgasmic Rise during thrust, the Sublime would also release Beguile from the memory of indulgence. Then she and Cornic, thereafter, would rightfully celebrate another Legacy who would bear their name. Their name alone.

However, the night before the Harness, Beguile's eyes began to spill without Permission. She clung to Cornic and pleaded Forgiveness but the spills grew stronger.

"I am weak of heart. It feels as if my vow of Loyalty will be forever broken. I cannot Harness with another even if you demand an eighth Legacy. So I do not dishonor you, I will drink the Demon Juice of the Hemp tonight to rid me of my shame."

Cornic, who had never spilled, wiped his moist eyes. "I cannot bear to see your pain. And I cannot let you leave our Legacies before you are brittle. You must do as I say. My Failure shame is greater than your heart pain."

"Then let us drink together," Beguile pleaded. "Why wait for Inevitable?" Beguile continued to spill harder. Pure saline crystals covered her cheeks.

Cornic had been challenged in many battles. Men of Conviction, Men of Deceit, Men without Soul. His heart had always held strong, led him to the highest level of Honor. He would give his life in battle for Beguile but how could he let either one die the Unnatural.

"Leave my sight. Give me the Peace," he commanded.

An hour later, Cornic knelt before Beguile, "True to Loyalty, we have traversed this universe with dignity. Yes, I cannot let you go to Solid in my sight. The Holy Masters may condemn me for not giving you Minimal before I go on a treacherous journey but I will postpone the Harness with Prevail until my return." His lips went to her hands. "As I command on return, you will prepare then, in your most honorable manner, for the duty of Harness. Not the Minimal but Ten Legacies for Beneficent. That is my decree."

Cornic and Beguile shared the Master Bed that night and although they were unable to engage the Desire Fold as Loyals, late into the evening they touched each other's cheeks and wiped away each other's fresh spills.

When Cornic and his Journeymen returned from Earth Outer after the third Lunar, Beguile saw the strain on Cornic's face. She read the pain behind the lines under his eyes, felt stiffness in his limbs. Her desire to Spill grew in equal proportion to not embarrass Cornic again.

To him she let her heart speak first, "Let this time away prove our Core serves us well. Seven Legacies, we are rich with Heart."

"You will honor my Heart with Beneficents. Your needs fulfilled."

"Please, dear Cornic, let us try again to foster after consumption of Earthling Mass. Sperm at hand; love to guide us. In perfect Loyalty, fill my Void. We can surely bring to life Ten Legacies together."

"Dear Beguile, the most perfect Loyal of all the orbits, it is not possible. Hard has failed. It is time to accept the fade, the Solid of my Soul. Fate writes my story. In one light or two, my limbs will be Brittle, my body will be Solid. Before I leave, I must guide our Legacy sons into the Master Naturalist vault. In good time, our sons will cover Earthling Mass with their banked sperm and guarantee another evolution here and on Earth Outer. Dear Loyal, we may Fold in our hearts but this body no longer lets me take the Orgasmic Rise with you. I cannot protect you for all your eternity."

Her pleas did not serve the night well. Cornic sheltered in the Master Manor without the good night blessing with Beguile.

Beguile slept in the Shadow of Doubt. Her thoughts resisted the commands of her Loyal. When the light of Day fell on her face, though, Beguile resolved that Duty demanded submission and would bring bliss to her Loyal. She would Fold with Prevail the Stronger. Beguile spilled eight millimeters without seeking Cornic's permission and thanked Master Naturalist her Loyal did not witness the last drops fall.

The next night, Cornic appeared in Beguile's chamber.

"It is time to call Prevail. While you prepare for the Fold in the morrow, I will take my place at the High Throne. First Officer will sit at my right side, his Loyal will offer you the Sublime Elixir. Second Officer will prepare the Life Document and his Loyal will attend to your cleansing after the Fold.

"As you wish, Loyal Cornic," Beguile said with a faint smile.

Cornic kissed his Loyal's hand. "Then, my dearest, we share Hearts until the end of my existence."

They walked together clothed in white linen shrouds, hand in hand, down a wide, long hall that led to the Most Sacred room in their citadel. The walkway had been cleared of all servers and Legacies. Golden bowls of Pomegranates were placed in ten side tables, Lotus flowers in full bloom filled ten tall vases. The aroma of Star Anise filled the air. Ceilings were opened so the blue sky of Eternity could shine on the Holy Master's Sacred ritual. The initiation of Life.

Prevail the Stronger opened the door to the Master Fold, a platform at the level of a tall man's eye. The Folding bed was surrounded by glass walls with two doors. Prevail held the ornate wooden door open for a moment where he could not be seen. He smiled at Beguile who entered at the same time to take her designated place at the head of the Folding Bed. Prevail released the handle and slowly moved forward. His Performance groomed and in view.

With tight lips, he whispered, "You are the most beautiful Loyal in all the orbits. More deserving of The Stronger than a Brittle Loyal."

Beguile drew in a breath and covered her mouth with her hand. She spoke in a soft whisper, "You have broken the order. You must not speak or show pleasure. Your duty is only to fill my Void."

"I made a commitment with My Sperm when I first laid eyes on you. The High Cornic has given me the best Gift. When he is Solid, you will be my wife and we will Harness for eternity."

Barely able to breathe, Beguile said. "I will never depart from my Loyal."

Her eyes went to her devoted Loyal as he sat on the High Throne with his two favorite Ancients in front of him. Their ears farthest from the chamber to block the sounds of Initiation into the Void.

Beguile took her place on the Folding bed, the long white gown covering her neck, her breasts, her arms, her finger tips and the skirt hem falling to the floor. First Officer's Loyal approached from the far door and gave Beguile the first sip of Elixir Sublime as required by Holy Master. Beguile's eyes strayed from the crystal cup to Prevail the Stronger's face. Two, three more passes to her lips.

"Loyal of First Officer please take your place at the side of my Loyal Cornic. Touch his hand as my Void is filled. Compassion will flow from your heart for what he cannot do." Beguile looked into the eyes of her Loyal for one moment, lay back and then raised her Seed Tunic. "Duty in an Honored Place."

Prevail let his tunic fall to the floor, turned to reveal to Witnesses he had achieved the Proper Dimension. His Force conformed to the requirements of Duty. He edged onto the Fold bed, his knees first, his hands inching closer, his Force full and direct. With deliberate motion, the Performance began with controlled Duty action.

Beguile smiled before the entry. Elixir Sublime had altered her emotions as the Master Naturalist had assured. As she listened to Prevail count each sanctioned thrust, she kept her Honored Loyal in sight but did not meet his eyes. Ecstasy, the work of the Unknown Gods, soon took flight as Beguile's body succumbed to the thrusts of the duty-bound Force as Prevail's Performance heightened during the Fold. While Elixir Sublime masked sorrow, Holy Masters of the Natural had never been able to tame the unwritten laws of nature.

Body Nature would climax and be final proof of Prevail's

ability to provide a thorough, fertile Fold. But the Harness for Prevail the Stronger itself could not go beyond the Master's decreed time. Moments or minutes, infinity or never, Prevail did not know. He had to decide when it was best to release or be deemed a Failure and never allowed to Fold in Duty. Now or More? His face lit with joy. Another moment and a bell rang.

As the Stronger withdrew from Beguile, he whispered again with clinched teeth, "You and I will share the Master Fold again and again. I will take you to Orgasmic Rise a dozen times over."

Beguile's Heart Pain could not be fooled by Sublime Elixir nor did her Void yearn for another entry from Prevail.

As Beguile slipped the pristine white Seed Tunic below her hips, Prevail the Stronger took a stance at the base of the Master Fold and bowed to her Loyal Cornic. His uncovered, decreasing Force confirmed his ceremonial duty had met its end.

Cornic raised his right hand in salute. "Duty is a high Honor."

Beguile leaned forward, her pale hand shaking, "Prevail the Stronger, you shamed my Loyal by speaking as you entered my void. You whispered the Longings of Your Loin and have brought dishonor to the Master Fold. For this I do my duty."

Beguile straightened her dress and in doing so, drew a thin, long dagger from the hem of the Seed Tunic and thrust it in the center of Prevail the Stronger's back. A quick twist and the knife tore into the artery leading to his Lustful Heart.

Cornic gasped, the First and Second Officers stood up abruptly and drew their weapons. The Ancient Witnesses rocked back in their chairs.

Beguile smoothed the wrinkles of the Seed Tunic and quickly stood to face the collective witnesses who had taken an honored place by their Highest Officer. The Master Fold bowed his head and closed his eyes. Betrayed by a Strong, a diligent servant, he could no

Edited By Jake Devlin

longer trust his judgement. Beguile bowed to Cornic, to the panel of Ancient witnesses and smiled.

With hand to her heart, she said, "Dear Loyal, your desire has always been my Honor. Prevail shamed you, and thus, only seven Legacies will carry your name. I now must receive the punishment of Eternal Solid for causing Death to Another."

The Loyals of the First and Second Officers covered their mouths.

Again Beguile spilled without permission.

"Shame will never divide Loyal hearts." Beguile fell to her knees in submission as crystals of emotion rolled down her smooth cheeks.

END

The 2019 BOULD Awards Anthology

Edited By Jake Devlin

Clarity

Francis Hicks (~723 words)

Anguished terror in the voice screaming through the phone cut the paralysis of sleep. "You gotta come. I need you."

"Samantha?" I said, but the connection had been severed. I threw on shorts and a t-shirt and sped to the hospital, bewildered that she'd called *me*.

I knew her from biology lab. She was pretty, but we seldom talked before yesterday when she asked me to eat lunch with her. She was full of energy, talking a mile a minute. We spent the afternoon together, making love in my dorm room. Before she left, she held up her phone and said, "Only special people get in here." Then she put my number in. It was an amazing afternoon, but still, I hardly knew her.

At the hospital I ran through soggy air toward the emergency room. Samantha shuffled out the door as a gurney was being wheeled in. She stumbled past an ambulance, then slumped to the curb. Her head sagged between her legs. Insects buzzed around her in the yellow light.

"Why are you out *here*?" I asked, standing over her. She smelled like rubbing alcohol. "What happened?"

Samantha raised her head. Vacant eyes stared from sockets so dark they look bruised. Tear trails on her cheeks reflected the harsh light. Dried saliva crusted a corner of her mouth.

"Samantha?" I said. I bent down, putting my face level with hers. "What do you need? How can I help you?"

Her eyes drifted towards me. "Why..." she said, and wrinkled her brow. "...*you*?"

An ambulance pulled up to the entrance. Red and blue lights

colored the pale bricks of the building. The attendants ran to unload their cargo. Urgent shouts erupted from inside as the hospital doors slid open, then faded as they shut.

"You *called* me," I said.

I sat down beside her and pulled her into me. Her body responded like a sack of flour, boneless, dense, not like yesterday. I rubbed a drop of blood from her arm. "Why are you out *here*? You can't just walk away, can you?"

"They drugged me," she whispered into my chest. Warm tears soaked through my t-shirt. "They're erasin' my memory. Pretty soon I won't be me any more." Her head rolled to the side. Unfocused eyes looked up at me. "But, why're *you*...here?" Her mouth fell open. Her eyes rolled back in their sockets.

"Hey," someone shouted. "What're you doing?" A man and a woman wearing dark blue scrubs jogged toward us. "You can't just take her outside," the woman said. "She could have a seizure."

They pulled Samantha up by her arms and dragged her into the hospital. I followed them into the harsh light and chaos. They laid her on a stretcher in the hall. Nurses surrounded her, attaching sensors and putting in IV lines.

A tall, tired-looking woman approached. "I'm Doctor Johnson. I saw you with her outside. How do you know her?"

"She's in one of my classes," I said. "Why is she here?"

"I can't talk about her condition, but I need information in order to treat her. Does she use drugs? Does she have a history of mental illness?"

"I don't know anything about that."

"Why are you here?" she asked.

"She called me, screaming that she needed me. But I hardly know her."

"Hmph." The doctor shook her head. "She was pretty upset

when the police brought her in. She called someone before we sedated her. I guess that was you."

"I guess," I replied.

The doc shrugged her shoulders. "How'd she have your number?"

"She put it in her phone after we... before she left my dorm."

The doctor pulled Samantha's phone out of a plastic bag laying on the stretcher. "What's your name?" she asked.

"Danny. Danny Grable."

Her thumb slid down the phone's screen. "Amanda, Annie, Betty," she said, scrolling through the contacts. "Charles, Chris, Daddy, Dan- Oh." She glanced at me, then tapped the phone's screen and raised it to her ear.

"Yes sir," she said into the phone. "This is Doctor Johnson at University Hospital. Do you have a daughter named Samantha?" She smiled and nodded. "We have her here, in the ER. She's had a bad night, but she's safe. Her friend, Danny, is here with her, but who she really needs is her daddy."

END

Edited By Jake Devlin

The 2019 BOULD Awards Anthology

IN THE OCTOPUS'S GARDEN

James Dorr (~2400 words)

I remembered -- pain. Red pain.

A sound of thunder crashing around my ears.

Blackness and brightness. Words and expressions -- I tried to make sense of them. Desert sand. Beaches. Desalination. Meetings in darkness.

Meetings at nighttime, and . . .

Over and over I heard a name, "Gallagher." Which I recognized. Which was my own name. Then clankings and scrapings, as if on a concrete floor. Metal on concrete. A weight -- a chain. Heavy. My legs. Wrapped around them. My shoulders. Another chain.

Blackness and brightness, as if a long tunnel, stretching, endlessly, through a dark void, yet leading to brightness. A warmth and a joyous feel of completion. I knew of this, somewhere, of where I was. What I was. . . .

But, then, a splashing sound.

Then darkness.

Nothing.

#

I woke to this new darkness, swirling about me.

A phrase sticking in my mind -- "Lazarus Syndrome." What happened to people when they had died, but, for some reason, some lack of death's completion -- some not-finished business -- had rejoined the living. But there should be doctors. Others around me, to help pull me through. But all there was was darkness and a dull, background pain. Chafing against my flesh.

Had I felt chains before?

Memories were fleeting -- somewhere I thought, perhaps, I had been a doctor. Or maybe a chemist. A specialist of some sort, maybe, but memories were drifting from me. I tried to hold them back.

Had I been killed then? I tried to hold that back, that single thought. That I, perhaps, had been killed, shot in the head maybe. That was the thunder. Shot from behind when I'd gone, at night, to an assignation. A meeting with someone. The docks of a city, or -- no, not the harbor, but farther, closer to its private beaches, the town's water plant where the ocean was cleaner, the salt removed from it, the chemicals put in, a place of shadows, of secrets and crannies. And assignations.

I tried to hold to the thought -- who was I meeting? But, always, the water.

The place sloshed with water. I heard the water. The place of the meeting. The place where I was now, a new sound of water. And memories went from me. I tried to hold on. If I hadn't died, I was here for a reason.

I felt muscles stiffen as, then, I realized -- who said I had not died? And yet I was here, feeling the gases of decomposition begin to slowly collect in my body. I felt my bowels loose, smelling the stench in the water around me. I felt my eyes bulging. My eyes were open.

And far above, far ahead, there was a new light, but that of a morning's sun on the sea's surface. Around me, as light came, I saw brilliant colors, pinks and oranges of a coral reef, blues and aquamarines and purples. The greens of sea plants, the crystal delicateness of medusas -- transparent jellyfish -- drifting toward the shore at the tide's turning.

And somewhere an itching. A sort of tickling. I didn't know what from, but at least I knew this:

That I had been dumped, to rot, in the ocean.

\#

I slept. I woke. I felt gases swell in me, then burst forth from my ears and my anus. I, still weighted down with iron chains. I felt no sense of time. Not of its passage.

Time works differently here in the ocean.

But only of cycles.

Only beginnings.

As that of the beach that bordered the ocean. The swimmers by bright hours, from the resort beach. The one closed to townspeople. I recognized human forms, male and female -- despite my death I was still human-formed too! At least for those first cycles, even if covered with deep blue-green blotches, enlarging to pustules. Spreading to blisters, the flesh tingeing purple. Day-cycles, week-cycles, we dead keep no count, except, on what seemed its own regular cycle too, one female form, in a red thong bikini, would swim above me, frolicking in the warm ocean water.

And one time I realized I had an erection -- then felt more tickling, the tickling of before, when I realized. A fish was devouring me! Sucking fluids out of me as, far above me, the cherry thong glistened, separating white, pumping buttocks as she swam on her back, little realizing what watched below her. And also my lips, my eyelids, my tongue, were plagued by the tickling, and this time, straining, I saw the tiny crabs crawling sideways across my splitting flesh. Watched as skin loosened. Peeled.

And I saw from crab eyes, myself eat my own body in tiny nibbles. Week-cycles. Month-cycles. Crabs, too, sense no time, but I, in an act of will, learned to project my self into these crabs' minds. Into the shrimp that browsed the putrescence that had been my fingers, loosening the nails to get at the soft meat that lay beneath them. Never in anything that didn't taste of me, but in those things that did . . .

#

One crab, many crabs, fleets of crabs I became, crabs and

shrimp and schools of bright-colored fish, brighter than even the thong bikini that still, on its schedule of surface cycles, would visit my ocean.

And then I knew fear again. Once a dim memory. A dim, lost memory of what may have been, before. But now, with crabs' minds, a devouring panic as shadowed spokes, wheel-like, blotted the ocean floor.

Chittering, screaming as crabs might scream, I dispersed my multiple-bodied oneness, then stretched my mind out to those fish that had tasted too -- one in particular that I remembered well -- seeing, above now, the reef and its carpet of brightly-twisting tentacled polyps. And more of tentacles as, from below, I felt as a human, above I saw as a fish, as a crab felt terror all-encompassing -- the octopus, wheeling, darting, feeling the shredded flesh remnants of myself as human corpse. Then darting further. Propelled on a water-stream out of its mantle. To strike out at crab-kind.

And I learned the law of ocean creatures: To eat and be eaten.

The law of all living things.

And felt myself devoured in myriad crab-bodies -- and felt myself dart up toward the surface, radiating fourteen-inch tentacles sweeping through the water behind me. Myself as king, king of this part of the ocean! Small, yes, in human terms, but of a world of miniature crab and shrimp, fish no larger than Irish shillings, eight-inch sea-anemone forests that carpeted the living, cragged coral, an emperor of giants indeed.

And saw, amazingly, out of an eye that was even more sharply developed than human, the white female form in its cherry-red thong swimsuit paddling slowly across the surface.

And I recognized her!

#

A day-cycle, week-cycle, now as the octopus, eater of eaters, I recognized her. Came to remember her. Came to recall her form straddling my own as we wrestled together, human on human, lips pressing lips and chest against chest on sweaty sheets in an apartment bedroom. Looking up, seeing the slowly turning fan on its ceiling, radiating its own octopus-limbs.

But after that – nothing.

Except that I knew now my fascination -- the thong suit I'd bought her. Fascination even as octopus, wondering if I might reach with a tentacle, press it where once hands pressed. Where –

But I couldn't . . .

Wondering, if as crab, I might pinch where once my human fingers had pinched her. Gently. Excitingly. And knew I couldn't.

Unless . . .

I concentrated all thought I could gather, into a single ball, into my old body, into an act of will, willing myself to rise out of the chains whose weight still pressed me to the bottom. I felt muscles tearing -- what was left of muscles -- bones scrape against bones -- slowly -- searingly -- even as tendons, what were left of tendons, disintegrated into the water. I felt myself as a cloud of bacteria rising like smoke to the ocean's surface, just as I heard a scream. Felt its vibrations. As hands, strong man's hands reached from a boat's side to pull her up, from my grasp.

Felt a voice –

"Jesus! Is that where you dumped him? My God. The stench!"

Felt another voice answer.

"The tide must have pulled him out. Caught the body against the reef somehow. But don't worry, Magda, even if someone does find him at this point there's not enough left to identify who he is."

And now I knew her name.

#

Now I remembered it. Magda. My Magda. Dark, curly hair. Legs sinewed and supple. Sheets twisted around us.

And now, in my human flesh, what was left of it, I felt myself also as feasting microbes which, through my will's action, I formed once more into the shape of a human. I felt flesh-memories, of larger fish eating my legs. My stomach. An eel twisting into the space of my ribcage.

And these I brought to me, using my will to have them swim for me, to follow the boat's shape past the city's desalination plant where I'd been murdered -- that memory came back too! The memory of meeting -- of Magda's panicked call, begging me to meet her at the plant, in the deepest of the shadows of its maze-like corridors, her lips on mine there. Whispering of threats. Of information. Of foreign secrets. Of payments, and yet . . .

Of other payments, too, as she pulled from me, as I heard the thunder. As metal crashed through my spine -- pain above pain!

And yet, unfinished business as, spinning, I saw a man's hands grip a pistol, smoke from its orifice, strong, man's hands lowering it to a table, then calling other men who came with heavy chains.

The first man, kissing . . .

And I recognized him.

#

I do not remember the circumstances -- who was in who's pay, which was which nation, who were the "good guys" and who the "bad guys" as I remembered now that we once used to say. None of that mattered. None does when one is dead. Communists. Neo-communists. Fascists. Running-dog capitalists. Right- and left-wingers. These are just phrases.

Like desert sand. Beaches. Shifting in wind and water and tide. Not in time, but beginnings.

Like death in its cycle.

But unimportant -- not the incompletion that brought one back from death. Even when it was too late for the body to be revitalized, when it was weighted and thrown in the ocean. To rot. To disintegrate. To wash, in pieces, the beach of a whole city, baking in sunlight during its day-cycles, moonlight at nighttime. Of tourists and swimmers.

His name was Hansen, the one who had shot me. The one who had paid Magda to betray me. I'd known him also, when she'd introduced him. Claiming to me that he was her half-brother.

And I knew who'd paid him -- and that didn't matter.

Nor did it, either, that he was fucking her now instead of me. In my own bed, in my own apartment. Under the ceiling fan. That his strong fingers explored what was once mine -- oh, yes, I recalled how she looked at him then, after he had shot me. While others wrapped chains around my body, to keep it from floating. The kiss.

The whispers.

And even that might have allowed me to die in peace, but one thing did matter. That I had trusted.

And on the ocean's floor my octopus form fought a small shark that dared to invade its anemone garden. And almost defeated it.

And I knew then what I had left to do.

#

One cycle. Two cycles. Magda no longer swims in the ocean, not in this part of it, but at the public beach I have seen her. As flying fish, eaters of flesh-eating shrimp, I have skimmed the water. And, as the last of my human-form carrion dissolved in the ocean's cleansing current, mixing in water and minerals and microbes, in salt and bacteria, memories grew stronger: The desert. The sand. The city between the sand and the ocean.

The infrastructure -- the piping and conduits -- once, in a past

Edited By Jake Devlin

existence, apparently I had made maps of these things.

The beaches. The harbor.

And all of me, still one. A chemical form now, still held by strength of will. Unfinished business.

#

I thought as an octopus.

#

As I had seen between the beach and the harbor, a screened duct, too small for fish to swim into, but not for microbes. And in a long pipe, as dark as the void of death, water flows through chlorine, purifying it, courses through filters and chemical baths that desalinate it, yet no process ever takes everything out.

Especially not the will, once of a living man, that once even took into its own grasp the nervous system of a small shark, causing it to swim and thrash, and to dart at swimmers at the public beach, sending them panicking out of the water. Even then following into the shallows until it, itself, was destroyed on the shore.

One more betrayal.

And one more re-forming as pipes once more widen to tanks for cooling. A will recoalescing -- an unfinished business -- that courses to brightness, a warmth, a promise of final completion. A taking of water throughout the city. And eyes, above, scouting, those of sea birds that live eating small fish.

A will that may force any animate being, once it is ingested, to do what it might have: Even to tear itself limb from limb -- however obscene the thing. To tear a lover. Betray or betrayal, to eat or be eaten. To eat and be eaten.

However obscene the thing.

As -- a flash of red -- thong against buttocks -- a screaming -- a running -- all in a mind's eye I see, encompassing, realizing well that no creature living can not drink water –

I search, first, for Magda. **END**

The 2019 BOULD Awards Anthology

Edited By Jake Devlin

The 2019 BOULD Awards Anthology

Take Nothing For Granite

John R. Clark (~1170 words)

"They're shutting us down? You gotta be friggin' kidding. I just mortgaged my soul to get my kid through his last year at Maine Maritime Academy."

Delmont Bechard shrugged, maintaining eye contact with his friend and best driver. Lambert wasn't telling him anything he didn't already know. "It sucks for all of us, except Durwood. Lucky bastard's probably enjoying his half interest in that Nicaraguan fishing lodge he lucked into. If I didn't know better, I'd swear he must have known things were going to hell and decided to cut the cord."

"How in hell did he manage to scrape enough money together to go halves on something like that?" Lambert Wilkins tipped the bottle of Narragansett straight up, draining it without his throat seeming to move. Under normal circumstances, nobody at the Somerset Cement Works would even think about sneaking a drink on the job, but the news that the plant was going to close in three weeks made this anything but a normal Monday. While the statewide unemployment rate was negligible, folks up in the real Maine knew that was more because everyone was working at least two jobs instead of the economy booming. Lambert had no illusions that finding something that paid anywhere near what he was making as a cement truck driver were promising.

Delmont took a pull from his own bottle. "Got even better news if you're ready for it," he grimaced. Drinking any kind of alcohol wasn't something he liked, but this Nastygansett was barely above the town water which tasted, at least to him, like a mix of chlorine and dishwater. "Once word got out that we were shutting down, I got a call from some know-it-all at the Augusta office of the Department of

Transportation. It seems that we've been violating at least two state regulations for years and if we don't do something, they're gonna fine the hell out of us."

"Why not go after the owners?"

"Because we were dumb enough to sign off on that profit sharing agreement six years ago. If any of us had read the damn thing carefully and realized we were actually getting pieces of this corporate disaster instead of real cash money, we'd never have gone down that road, but we did. The way the weasels at the main office tell it, since we work at the plant on a regular basis, we're more liable for their screw up than they are."

Lambert looked at his empty bottle and sighed. Whatever was coming was just another scoop of crap to add to the already overflowing poop sandwich they were all facing just down the road. "Don't sugarcoat it. What are we gonna have to do?"

"Dismantle the slag heap and truck it to Norridgewock. Christ, just thinking about it gives me hives. That thing has been building for twenty-five years and it's gonna be a bitch to break up. Screw it, no sense in wasting a perfectly good misery, let's grab the rest of the crew and get rip roaring drunk."

****

Delmont, Lambert and the other three who worked at the plant were in pretty sad shape the following morning. Only Penny Halliburton was anywhere close to functional. She had the other four go sit in the crushing room and drink whatever amount of coffee was necessary to sober up while she maneuvered the heavy duty rock drill to the bottom of the slag heap. There was a technical term for the twisting swirling monstrosity that had been formed by countless cement mixers discharging remnant loads before washing out the mixing tank, but nobody could remember it. Slag worked as good as anything.

She had a double line of holes drilled by the time her co-workers felt somewhat human. Nobody suffered from the delusion that one round of blasting was going to break up the entire mountain of discarded concrete, but they had to start somewhere. Granted the thing was almost level with the edge of Route 19, but nobody on the crew could think of a compelling reason why some asshat at the DOT would care whether it stayed or went. Even so, with job prospects being what they were, the thought of having to pony up fine money, especially to those fat cats in Augusta, rubbed everyone the wrong way.

Penny was the only one licensed to use explosives because most of the materials used to prepare and mix concrete loads were already crushed before being unloaded in the giant bins beside the tower above the shed. The others watched from the mixing shed while she prepared the blast holes.

"Don't spare any expense," Delmont yelled as she was finishing up. "Anything left over after we shut down sure as hell ain't gonna be ours, no matter what the agreement we signed might say."

"Ice your skivvies, boss. I've made sure we'll get our money's worth." Penny gave him the finger before walking over to where she would detonate the explosives safely.

The other two crew members were sent up to the roadway. They were to signal when no traffic was coming in either direction. Regulations stipulated that traffic was to be stopped a safe distance from the blasting zone, but Delmont was in a hurry to start loading and removing the broken concrete and given his mood, regulations, unless they were critical, could go hang.

Delmont got the go ahead from Tim and Roger up on the roadway, relaying it to Penny as he and Lambert took cover behind the mixing shed, earplugs firmly in place. Even so, the detonation left them with ringing ears while they waited until the dust cloud blew past them.

They came up behind Penny who was staring, slack-jawed at the mound of rubble. At least half the slag heap had broken apart, but that wasn't what had caught her attention.

"Son of a bitch! Are you seeing what I think I'm seeing?" Delbert pointed at what looked like half a dozen mummies lying amid the debris. A couple were intact, while the other four more closely resembled things they'd seen in horror films and news clips of major disasters.

Lambert pointed at the closest one. "That sure looks like Oscar Minton, the guy the boss said quit without notice last summer."

By the time Delmont and the others had regained enough composure to call the county sheriff and had taken a more careful look around, they'd discovered ten bodies and had been able to identify nine of them. All nine had been former co-workers and every one was supposed to have quit suddenly and left the area. Since the cement plant was seasonal work, nobody had thought much about turnover, but now that they were staring at the carnage in front of them, it was becoming clear just how Durwood Briggs had been able to afford a half interest in that Central American fishing lodge. After all none of the deceased had been likely to collect severance and vacation pay.

END

The 2019 BOULD Awards Anthology

Edited By Jake Devlin

The 2019 BOULD Awards Anthology

Edited By Jake Devlin

The 2019 BOULD Awards Anthology

When I think about...
or Never Trust a Nearsighted, Dyslexic Tattoo Artist

Gary R. Hoffman (~450 words)

When I think about...

God, what was her name? I can see her, but that doesn't help.

Why do people say things like that? If I can see the person, is that supposed to give me their name? If that's true, then I should immediately know the name of every new person I meet. I can see them—I must know their name. Is their name written across their forehead? Might help.

I walk up to a woman in a bar and try to visualize her name written on her forehead. Only one name comes to mind. "Hi, you must be Harvey."

"My name's Jennifer, asshole."

Well, so much for knowing a person's name when I see them. I also made a mental note to scratch that as a pickup line. But I really might like to know someone named Jennifer Asshole. It could be interesting. Wonder what her middle name would be? The?

Now when I think about...

Noel. That's it. Noel. How could I forget that?

She did have her name tattooed on her forehead. She had her eyebrows removed by electrolysis and replaced with her name in small block letters spelling out her name.

And come to think of it, she also had her name tattooed on the bottoms of her feet.

On her left foot, her name was tattooed in red. On her right foot, her name was tattooed in green. That probably explains why she would take off her sandals around Christmas time and stand on her head a lot. While standing on her head and pointing her toes in

Edited By Jake Devlin

the air, she wanted to present a Christmas message to the world.

    N N
    O O
    E E
    L L

After she had the first foot done, she had to wait to get the second one finished. Two reasons.

    1) no more money,

    2) her newly tattooed foot was sore and swelled to the size of the belly of a pregnant woman who was carrying quadzillits.

By the time she saved up enough money to get the second foot done, the man who had done the first foot was no longer tattooing. He was now painting pictures of huge-eyed, crying kids on velvet.

Unfortunately for Noel, the tattoo artist who put on the second message in green was nearsighted and a bit dyslexic. When Noel stood on her head, the message read,

    N L
    O E
    E O
    L N

Of course, anyone who was around and named Leon got a nice, colorful Christmas greeting. The rest of the people usually just got a puzzled look on their faces.

When I think about Noel, I think I'd rather be associated with Jennifer Asshole.

END

The 2019 BOULD Awards Anthology

Edited By Jake Devlin

The 2019 BOULD Awards Anthology

Teacher's Pets

Katherine Fast (~1990 Words)

Doc's head took a swan dive and then snapped back up. He stretched and tossed the graded papers into his briefcase. Four more to go. In-class essays were a pain. Some handwriting was almost indecipherable. He yawned and smiled. He'd saved the best for last. As he spread the pages out on the coffee table, he noticed how different the handwritings were. The scripts actually *looked* like the students. One had sharp, penetrating angles, another lovely curve-like waves. The third was a picture of control and reserve, while the last writing was almost illegible with thready connections that slurred letters together in haste.

He removed his glasses, rubbed his eyes and patted the cat next to him on the couch. Marbles, named for her three-colored fur, purred softly and placed an ownership paw on his leg. In seconds, Doc's head lowered to his chest, his breathing deepened, and his pencil slid to the couch.

Slowly the letters on the four papers on the coffee table came to life. The squared off printing moved one letter at a time across the paper. The pointy, angled letters darted from left to right. Next, rounded letters yawned and rolled over and on the fourth paper, random letters twitched and bobbed about the page.

"I need to make a list." Arcade prided herself in being organized. She looked longingly at the pencil on the couch.

"It's hot in here! I'd like a dip in the pool," Garland said, before turning over her round vowels.

"Let's slip out and go for a swim." Squig shook his letters, slid them to the floor and wove erratically toward the door.

"Out of the way, Squig." Angle made a chevron formation of

his letters like a vee of geese flying south. "Follow me."

"Wait!" cried Garland, rearranging her letters to best advantage.

"Forget it. I don't like spur of the moment nonsense." Arcade's printing remained rigidly lined up.

"Chill, Arcade," Squig called as he struggled to realign his letters behind Angle.

Arcade sighed and ordered her letters.

They formed a curious parade behind Angle's chevron. Squig's letters danced to different rhythms behind, beside, and sometimes in front of Angle, and Garland, lethargic at first, became more animated as she moved and swayed. Arcade's orderly string trudged along behind.

Angle headed straight to the double doors leading to the pool. They slid under the door and tripped across the patio to the pool deck. "Turn on your auras, it's dark!" commanded Angle.

As Squig connected his letters, they emitted a changing rainbow of colors.

"Awesome," whispered Garland watching him. Slowly she began to glow a deep magenta.

"You'd think he could decide what color to be." Angle whipped his letters into shape and turned a cold slate blue, but he was secretly envious of Squig's ability to be whatever color he wanted to be.

Arcade's aura was moss green. She didn't approve of flashy colors.

Garland giggled and made a few false starts toward the water, giving the others ample time to admire her rounded forms. She waded in, splashing, hoping to entice others to follow.

Angle dove into the deep end and began swimming laps, alternating between crawl and butterfly. Sidestroke was for sissies, and the breaststroke—well, the name spoke for itself.

Squig dangled a few letters into the water. He whistled and searched for the Big Dipper in the night sky.

Arcade dragged a float to the pool. She felt safer with a buffer between herself and the water.

Squig's expression of wonder suddenly changed to concern. "We'll never change. We're just a snapshot of our masters' thoughts and personalities, captured on a page."

"Oh, get off it! Live a little," Garland retorted, but she stopped splashing and began to tread water.

Angle, who never listened seriously to Garland and was too impatient for the deliberate truths of Arcade, aborted his time trials. "What do you mean?" he demanded.

Arcade spoke up. "He's right. Our masters who wrote us will change, but we'll remain just as we are, the written evidence of who they were this morning."

They fell silent as Arcade's truth sank in.

Squig sighed. "I'll never write the great American novel."

"Not fair," wailed Garland. "I just got my period. I'm meant to have babies. I'll never know them or who their father was ..." She looked longingly at Squig.

Embarrassed, Squig changed colors. "You know the four of us are stereotypes, don't you?" Squig arranged his letters in a question mark and shook his period. "Most kids don't have such clear auras or consistently shaped connections between letters. That's why Doc likes us. We're so quirky we get his attention."

"Off in Neverland again," said Angle.

"It's true. Look at you, Angle. No curves, only straight lines and sharp points. You even *act* pointy. Your aura is a cold, manganese blue," Squig persisted.

"So?" Angle, resisted the impulse to grind Squig into the pool deck.

"So, you're impatient and assertive. Now, Garland doesn't have sharp edges. Her letters all connect at the bottom and look like graceful waves. She's empathetic and a bit on the romantic side."

Garland's letters heated up.

"Back up, I'm confused," Arcade objected.

"Typical, Arcade. You need the big picture first so that you can sort and analyze everything." Squig ignored Angle's feigned yawn. "When you're not printing, your letters connect at the top and look like a row of little boxes."

"You forgot my aura."

"See? You want every scrap of information lined up neatly, and I forgot your aura. It's a deep leaf green with earth tones on the lower letters," he said.

"Booooring!" blurted Angle.

"Don't be rude, you'll hurt his feelings," interjected Garland. She edged a few *a*'s and *o*'s closer to Squig.

Arcade turned on Squig. "If we're so pure, what the heck are you?" she challenged. "You're all over the place, like charcoal dandruff on a page."

Squig laughed and shook his letters. They radiated like a prism and then turned into a golden halo. "I'm anything I want to be. I slur and merge letters, and if I'm in a hurry, I sometimes leave out a few."

"Together, we'd have all the abilities ..." mused Angle. "I could use a little Garland softening, and Arcade's organization would come in handy. Even Squig's imagination would help." He eyed Garland and grimaced a smile. "Let's experiment. Garland, may I have this dance?"

"Dance? There's no music." Garland looked to Squig, but he was distracted juggling consonants.

"So what?" Angle retorted. He covered a few of her letters with his, darted to the left and then lurched to the right.

"No, no!" cried Garland. She smiled and patiently showed him how to move. Soon Angle's blue and Garland's magenta hue blended into a lavender aura.

Squig thought about asking Arcade to dance, but quickly reconsidered merging his aura with hers. Why sully his theories with her organized facts? He glanced at the dancers. He slid behind Angle and tapped him on the shoulder.

"Beat it, kid," Angle snarled.

But Squig's interruption caused Angle to miss a beat and stumble. Garland slipped from Angle's grasp into Squig's. As they danced across the pool deck, their auras became a kaleidoscope of colors with a rosy overtone.

Arcade arranged her letters in a line and inched toward Angle.

The telephone rang inside.

They froze. Through the window, they saw Doc walk through the hallway toward the kitchen.

"What if we can't get back?" gasped Garland."

"We flunk! Turn off your auras!" whispered Angle, fading as he spoke. He formed the chevron and surged forward with Arcade close behind. Garland and Squig scurried to catch up. They slid under the door.

"I don't know you from a toad." Doc hung up.

"Telemarketer," whispered Arcade.

They raced across the rug and stacked their letters in a ladder to reach the top of the coffee table. Suddenly, Marbles sprang and batted Squig's letters, sending them flying. Squig quickly corralled a few and spelled, "HEP!"

Angle saw Squig's plea, but also heard Doc's steps in the hallway. No time! He made himself into a dart and speared the cat's paw. The cat jumped a foot in the air, puffed up twice her size, turned sideways, and spat.

"Guess you don't like those callers either," chuckled Doc. He looked about. "Where the hell did I leave my glasses?" He sighed and trudged back toward the kitchen.

"Hurry!" Angle whispered. "I've got the cat." He poked and jabbed at Marbles from different directions to give Garland and Arcade time to reach their pages. He did well until the cat charged and flattened his capitals under her paw. Doomed!

Just then Squig danced across the cat's tail, wiggling and weaving in a seductive string no cat could resist. Marbles released Angle who made a beeline for his page. The cat leaped and batted at Squig who danced and twirled around the room. Suddenly Squig held still, baiting her. Marbles wiggled her backside, tail switching. Pounce! Missed! Squig vaulted to his page before she could regroup.

On her paper, Arcade sorted her letters logically into words and sentences. Angle climbed into the deep grooves he'd carved into the paper, and Garland rounded into her soft indentations.

Squig dashed about frantically without a clue where his letters should go. When he found a fit, he popped in a letter, but it was taking way too long. Doc shuffled back into the room, glasses in hand, and sank into the couch. Squig had to abandon a smudge of letters on the corner of his page.

Donning glasses that he'd found in the refrigerator, Doc picked up the last four papers. He expected them to be wildly different, and he wasn't disappointed. The first one was the longest. She never left anything out. She ticked off her points, building her arguments to a logical conclusion. Organized and thorough: A+.

The next paper was spare and to the point, written in efficient and powerful prose. Sometimes the boy took a wrong turn and derailed himself, but not this time: A+.

He picked up the third paper and smiled. He took a moment to clear his mind of the image of the lovely young girl who wrote it. He was intrigued by her ability to empathize and to understand the underlying emotions and motivations that drove people to act: A+.

Finally, the last paper. He squinted. The letters seemed to move. He took off his glasses and rubbed his eyes. He was exhausted, but he really wanted to read this paper. He re-focused and was rewarded by one of the most creative interpretations of the subject he'd ever read. Out of left field, but plausible, even possible.

Marbles jumped up and head-butted his arm. He patted her absently. Lacking her deserved attention, the cat jumped onto Squig's paper. Stray letters in the corner moved. She batted them to the floor and jumped down for a little sport, madly chasing the letters about.

"Lost your Marbles again?" Doc chuckled.

He returned to the paper. Inventive theory. The kid couldn't spell, but the ideas were brilliant: A+.

Doc hesitated as he was about to toss the four last papers into his briefcase. He walked to the study and made copies of them. He put the copies in his briefcase and saved the originals in his file cabinet. He shuffled to bed. Marbles jumped up and nosed under the covers.

#####

Inside the file cabinet, the pages came alive.

"A+. Just what I needed," said Angle.

"So what? We can't grow up," said Garland.

"I know. 'You've just got your period …'" Arcade chided. "Get over it. We are what we are."

Squig intervened. "She's right. We'll be the same tomorrow. But, when he leaves the file cabinet open, we can—"

Edited By Jake Devlin

"What if he throws us out? Or shreds us?" Garland shuddered.

"He won't," Squig reassured.

"How do you know?" challenged Angle.

"Easy. Look at his tiny writing. He saves everything."

END

The 2019 BOULD Awards Anthology

Edited By Jake Devlin

Teagan's Special Sand Castle

Jake Devlin (~1300 words)

(First published in Perflutzed, © 2019 Jake Devlin)

"Quit bothering us, Teagan," Mom said, opening her fifth beer of the morning. "Go play down by the water, build a sand castle or something." She turned to her boyfriend, Bill, and smiled seductively.

"Get going, you little twat, or do you want another whuppin'?" he sneered at Teagan.

The five-year-old grabbed her plastic bucket and shovel, scampered down the beach to the surf line, looked left and right, headed north about forty feet, then paused, cocked her head, walked back maybe ten feet south, cocked her head again, walked about three feet back north, and settled in.

Bill pulled a small baggie from his pocket, extracted two pills, gave one to Mom and swallowed the other with a few gulps of his seventh beer. Within five minutes, both were lying back on the sand, either asleep or passed out.

Teagan filled her bucket with wet sand and upended it, slapped the sides and top and pulled it up, leaving a perfectly formed round turret, then repeated the process over and over until she had a rough sand castle about four by four feet by three feet tall.

"Peter, do you see that?"

"What?"

"The little girl there in the pink bathing suit."

"Building the sand castle?"

"Yeah."

"Yeah. What about her?"

"See the bruises?"

"On her arms?"

"Yeah, like she was grabbed and maybe shaken."

"Yeah, it does look like that."

"I've gotta get some pics."

"Oh, Janice, remember, you're retired."

"Hey, Peter, once a cop, always a cop."

"Okay, okay."

Janice pulled out her phone and started snapping pictures.

"Can you tell where her parents are? I don't see anyone paying attention to her."

"Uh, lemme – no, can't see anyone who might be supervising her."

"Oh, look; she's got a black eye, too." She snapped a few more pictures.

Teagan started making a window in the castle, carefully and with great concentration.

"Teagan," a voice whispered, so quietly that only Teagan could hear. "Teagan."

Teagan looked closely at the window.

"What? Who's there?"

"It's me, Teagan. Don't you recognize my voice?" The voice quietly hummed a few bars of a lullaby.

"Nana? Nana, is that you?"

"Yup, it's me, Teagan. And your dad is here, too."

"Hi, Princess."

"Daddy? Oh, Daddy!"

"Yeah, it's me, Princess."

"I miss you both so much."

"And we miss you, too, Princess."

"I wish you were still with me."

"And we wish we could be with you."

"Mom and Bill are so mean to me."

"We know, Teagan, we know."

"He hits me and Mom doesn't even try to make him stop. I hate them!"

"We know, Princess. It's terrible."

"I wish we could all be together."

"So do we, Teagan, so do we."

"Can't you come back from the farm?"

"The farm?"

"Yeah. They told me you're both living on a farm somewhere, but they'd never let me visit you. How did you get in my sand castle?"

"This is where your dad buried my ashes, and your Aunt ZaZa buried his ashes here after your mom and Bill murdered him."

"Ashes?"

"Yeah, Teagan. We're both dead."

"Noooo!"

"Afraid so, Princess. We --"

"Murdered?"

"Yes, Princess."

"Not on a farm?"

"No, Teagan, no farm."

"So I can't visit you? Nooooooo! I wanna be with you."

"I know, Princess. I wish you could be with us, too."

"Can't I do that?"

"Well, Princess, I don't --"

"Please? Pleeeaaazze?"

"Momma, do you think --"

"Maybe we can find a --"

"Oh, pleeeeaze! I wanna be with you, both of you!"

"Really, Teagan?"

"Oh, yes, yes, yes, Nana, Daddy! I'm sure."

"Okay, then. Let's try, see if it works."

Two pair of wispy, smoky arms extended from the sand castle toward Teagan.

"Take our hands and maybe we'll be together."

Edited By Jake Devlin

As Teagan reached out for the hands, Janice and Peter and everybody near the castle sneezed. But Janice's finger tapped the camera button.

Whoosh! Teagan was pulled into the castle. But instead of winding up with a face full of sand, she wound up in a magnificent modern throne room, dressed in a purple velvet robe with white sable trim, a diamond-studded tiara on her head and all her bruises and black eye completely healed.

"Hi, Princess."

"Daddy!"

Teagan ran to her father, throwing her arms around his neck, then her grandma joined in the hug, as all the men and women in the crowd cheered, as did everyone in the kingdom, watching on their implanted personal video devices.

"All hail, Princess Teagan! All hail, Princess Teagan!"

As Teagan settled in to her new life, she was taught how to work the meal manifestor, how to train her android, Iva, how to run a teleporter, and when she was a teenager, how to fly a car and work a time machine, a 5-D printer and her very own cloning device. She did have some trouble mastering her anti-gravity boots, suffering a few bumps and bruises around her tenth birthday, but as usual, she healed quickly.

Most importantly, she learned how to *govern* the kingdom with a light touch, not *rule* it with an iron hand, and when she turned 21, she married the prince from the neighboring kingdom, and they became king and queen of the merged kingdoms, beloved by all their citizens, and lived happily ever af- – well, as happily ever after as two married people with strong personalities and opinions could. They argued occasionally, but reconciled quickly.

When Janice stopped sneezing and opened her eyes, she stared at where Teagan had been, astounded that all she could see was the bottom of her pink bathing suit sticking out of the middle of the sand castle. No one else had seen how the little girl had disappeared, seemingly into thin air.

Janice looked all over for the parents, and finally someone pointed to Mom and Bill, but Janice couldn't wake them up. So she called 911.

When the cops arrived, Janice identified herself and showed them the pictures on her phone, discovering the last one, which was very fuzzy, but showed Teagan's ankles and feet sticking out of the sand castle. The cops dug into the castle, but all they found was the pink bathing suit.

When they were finally able to awaken Mom and Bill, they interrogated them at length, after which they were arrested, tried and convicted of child abuse, child neglect leading to death or grievous bodily harm, public intoxication, multiple drug charges, resisting arrest with violence, and after further investigation, the murder of Teagan's father, and sentenced to life without parole.

As they were being led off the beach in handcuffs, two wispy, smoky adult right arms came out of the flattened remains of the sand castle and waved a sardonic goodbye.

Then they twisted around and gave two middle finger salutes, high-fived each other and disappeared back into the sand.

END

Edited By Jake Devlin

The 2019 BOULD Awards Anthology

Note Found Near Scattered Human Skeletal Remains

Jack Ewing (~1840 words)

Growing old is a bitch.

Body parts wear out.

Illnesses linger.

The mind wanders to other times and places.

79 years are long enough to live. I'd rather leave this earth while I'm still somewhat in control of my physical and mental faculties, while my memories are still sharp.

The means of my self-extinction has taken considerable thought. I've eliminated, for personal reasons, swan diving from a height or staring into oblivion down the barrel of a firearm. I won't carve myself or swing from a rope. (I'll leave it to forensics experts to determine my method, if you find enough of my corpse to examine after nature takes care of it.)

Once this message is signed, sealed and delivered, I'll hike one last time into the mountains, make myself comfortable, and sign off.

But until then, there's work to do.

Let me clear a flock of cold cases with this simple declaration: I am the most prolific solo murderer in history. Discounting my own forthcoming death, I have killed exactly 13,013 men and women. I averaged about 260 corpses per year for a solid half-century, at the rate of about one every normal workday. Murder was my job, and I was very good at it: as death's most enthusiastic employee, I never missed a day, never took a vacation, even worked on weekends sometimes.

Edited By Jake Devlin

I'm egotistic enough to hope my record will stand for some time.

Wherever my carcass winds up, this document—written on nearly indestructible paper and preserved in a waterproof container—will serve as explanation. Hidden within the narration is a cipher, which took me six months to compose and went through about twenty drafts before I was satisfied with the message. Careful inspection of the text will reveal a chain of clues: find the key code word, and the entire message will neatly unravel.

Is it worth your time to solve this verbal puzzle? You decide.

You'll get precise directions to a weatherproof subterranean depository. It holds information that could be of incalculable value to law officers, statisticians, estate lawyers, insurance companies, perhaps even psychologists.

Figure out the code, and you'll learn how to open my secret vault. Inside, you'll find my will (I have a considerable estate, which will boost the prospects of a number of worthwhile charities).

You'll also discover detailed journals of my activities over the past fifty years.

There's photographic proof of my misdeeds.

There's a stack of topographic maps, with precise, GPS-calculated locations of each cadaver I created. (Some victims left in remote areas may have remained undiscovered, while other individuals disposed of in water—rivers, lakes, oceans—may have sunk or floated away from the spots where I initially left them.)

Before you get to work, let me give you a preview, so you'll know my lethal claims are legitimate.

I never shot anybody (too noisy, too impersonal), so you can eliminate bullet-ridden bodies from consideration as my handiwork.

I preferred to work up-close. Though I varied my approach as much as possible—scaldings, applications of caustic chemicals, poisons found in nature and other exotic means—I had my favorite methods of dispatch. More than half of my victims were stabbed (2,614), strangled (1,865), or bludgeoned (3,478). I often used weapons of opportunity: icicles, shards of broken glass, rebars, bricks, tree branches, hammers, liquor bottles, lengths of chain. I once beat someone to death with a frozen leg of lamb, as an homage to Roald Dahl and Alfred Hitchcock. Some of these deaths were probably not counted as murders. it would be difficult, for example, for a medical examiner to tell how somebody died after a 100-car freight train has ridden over a body left on the tracks.

I've thrown people out of high-rise windows (65), tossed them off roofs (44) or balconies (26), dropped them down dry wells (5) or played-out mineshafts (12), and pushed them off cliffs (89). That naked parboiled body in Yelllowstone's Norris Geyser Basin in Yellowstone? That was mine. So were the three bodies found roped together off Point Imperial at the Grand Canyon's North Rim.

Many folks I encountered wound up drowned, especially in the Pacific (642) and Atlantic (473) oceans and the Gulf of Mexico (279). Such deaths were often considered the results of accidents or suicides.

I've been an equal opportunity murderer, without regard for race, religion, sexual orientation or any other factor, because I believe that worthless humans come in every shape, size and color.

I never killed anyone below the age of eighteen (though in my professional opinion some children should be eliminated early) or over eighty (I know: some of us geezers really don't deserve to live).

I never molested anyone before or mutilated anyone after death.

I never took anything from any victim except a life—and a snapshot of the corpse.

Why did I kill, you ask? I wished to do humankind a service.

Edited By Jake Devlin

Credit where it's due: Mom and Dad are ultimately responsible for my actions. They combined genetic material to produce me.

They made me believe I could do no wrong.

They pampered their only child, and catered to his every whim.

They provided a superior liberal education that collapsed my moral boundaries yet simultaneously instilled a fierce intolerance of stupidity.

Finally, they furnished the means to operate: I inherited a great deal of money after my parents died tragically—events, ironically enough, I had nothing to do with—on either side of my twentieth birthday.

One thing the folks never gave me was ambition.

For years after graduating from college, I traveled widely if aimlessly, trying to find myself.

I painted in Rome and Venice.

I studied music in Vienna and Prague.

I scribbled stories and poems in Paris and Brussels.

I dabbled in theater in London and Dublin.

It was all a waste of time and money. I found I had no particular aptitude for anything creative. After returning to the States, I involved myself in various enterprises, but could not connect with a trade that captivated me.

My investments profited, though I had no interest in business. I used my fortune to acquire vast lands in western states. I hired contractors to build several luxurious cabins—one in high desert, another beside a lake, a third perched on a mountain ridge—as permanent home bases. Then I bought a fully equipped, customized mobile home (regularly upgraded until at the end I piloted a luxurious RV equipped with top-flight GPS to improve the accuracy of cadaver placement) and set out to explore the Americas.

What came from my journey of discovery was a revelation: among people I encountered were some who did not deserve to live. A glimpse was all it took: I could intuit, as though watching their histories unfold in a blink, which exhibited high potential to harm others because they thought only of themselves. These individuals needed to go. The world would be better off without them.

What was needed was an agent of destruction. Who better than I—no relatives, no intimate friends, unlimited funds, no time demands, no built-in grudges—to act as impartial judge, jury and executioner?

These were just unformed, directionless notions until one day they crystallized into action. I was driving through the Midwest along a busy freeway when a low-slung sports car flew past, twenty miles above the limit. I jotted down the license, and watched as the driver tailgated, wove from lane to lane, and committed other risky moves with impunity. It wasn't difficult to track the offender —George Simmons—to his home.

One night I lay in wait on the dead-end street where he lived. As he exited his sporty little car, I came out of the shadows to greet him.

"Who are you?" he asked, straightening from the car, arms full of groceries.

I didn't say a word, just took a quick step forward and cracked his skull with the hammer I'd found in his garage. Even with George, my debut murder, I arranged his body on the driveway, and took a photo. I left George with his head haloed by spilled oranges and scattered onions and pooled blood.

In case psychologists are interested, I felt nothing at his death, beyond the sort of self-satisfaction you get when you dump trash in its proper receptacle instead of cluttering the gutter.

After the first time, I researched more and planned better.

Edited By Jake Devlin

Successive murders became easier. I finally had a cause I could believe in. I became skilled at my new avocation.

At the start, my standards were high. I went after offenders flouting justice: spouse abusers, pedophiles, bullies, hotheads, firebugs, thugs, junkies, road hogs, and other assorted lowlifes breathing the air of decent people. I also got rid of several corrupt politicians and many unscrupulous businessmen. (You're welcome.)

I wandered the country, an anonymous tourist, watching and listening for those whose removal would be a relief, like shaking an irritating pebble out of a shoe.

Before long, I lowered my sights. There was much work to do.

I suffocated a nasty lady who potentially infected a busload of passengers by neglecting to cover her mouth when she sneezed.

I clobbered a disgusting man who spit on the sidewalk.

I stabbed a young guy who refused to turn down his stereo.

I whacked a staggering drunk pissing in an alley.

I strangled an infected prostitute.

I murdered theatergoers who talked through the movie, obnoxious clerks, cell-phoning drivers, rude waitresses, chatty barbers, unsympathetic bartenders, gum-chewers, nose-pickers, know-it-alls, loudmouths, windbags, sponges, goldbricks and similar annoyances.

Above all, I hoped to make the world a better place to live; I believe I succeeded. (I don't crave fame, but a little recognition never hurts—I wonder what nickname the media will give me after they discover the good I've done. I have a modest suggestion: the king of the killers.)

It was easy to find victims: wherever I went, there was a surplus of those who deserved to die. In fact, I think I showed remarkable restraint creating only 13,013 bodies. [Note to aspiring record-breakers: There's no shortage of material out there.]

Now I'm almost finished. One left to go.

This life is ending just in time.

Arthritis has weakened my grip. It takes longer to choke the life out of a spiteful woman or beat a worthless man to a bloody pulp with a blunt object.

My lungs are deteriorating. The exertion of wrestling bodies into aesthetically satisfying tableaus winds me.

I'd better get to my final chore before I lose resolve, before a new target of opportunity presents itself to distract me from my purpose: my own murder. After all, as the greatest lone killer in history, I deserve to die.

Who better to perform the execution than yours truly, the world's best life-snuffer?

What better place than here?

What better time than now?

So long, everybody!

Here goes nothingness.

END

Edited By Jake Devlin

Oh Henry

Wil A. Emerson (~2990 words)

Fluorescent lights illuminated Henry Weinstein and the stainless steel cart he pushed down the long black and white tiled corridor.

"I've got a bone to pick with you, Henry."

Trudging along, he kept his head down. Carlotta managed the surgical ward; Henry managed his own activities.

Well, I've got a bone, too.

If he responded, he'd wet himself. Something he'd rather do while Sweet Lady Jesus Sheryl Crowe wailed in his ear.

All I wanna do is have a little one, two, three, four, fun with you.

He hummed his favorite melody when he wanged off to her sultry voice. Shades pulled, doors locked, alone and happy.

"Henry, did you hear me?"

"Of course," Henry responded under his breath. Of course, Carlotta missed his answer. Truth be told, her twang struck like a hot poker. The first time, he shivered. That was before his eyes took a full length gander at the lusty supervisor. Thereafter, heat raced through his limbs like a freight train with no place to dump its cargo before it hit a firewall.

Tonight Henry had to keep Supervisor Carlotta far from thought. He rushed toward the elevator.

A few feet and out of reach. In his mind, the lights were off and he was already out of sight. He sniffed hard to dislodge a nagging mass stuck in the back of his throat. A few hours in the hospital corridor's stale air that hung like a London fog left his nasal cavities stuffed like a cabbage roll. Cool air ahead. The elevator opened and Henry's stubby fingers curled around the stainless steel bar on the portable table with its fat black rubber tires. A hard push between the sliding doors. With perfect timing—finger on the down button, he'd disappear before she caught up. He practiced each time he delivered specimens to their final destination—the bowels of the hospital.

In the nick of time, the doors cut down the center of throaty, sensual Carlotta. Henry stood tall, well beyond her reach. Carlotta, hot-bodied, smart-ass, wouldn't interrupt him tonight. No, by god,

Henry had cargo to deliver. Fresh cargo on this mission.

The elevator hummed to the sub-basement, carrying him to his sacred work place. Final destination for parts and parcels where souls unwillingly wandered. When the doors parted, frosty air struck Henry's nostrils. He rolled his cargo to a metal door, pulled a lever and a long tray slid out. Henry drew in a deep breath of antiseptic oxygen and formaldehyde vapors. Distinct aromas brought momentary relief for clogged sinuses so he honked off a big wad of green goo into the wastebasket, then flared his nose for a re-uptake. In a short time, he'd be at his locker where he'd swab Vicks Vapor Rub* up each hairy portal. Two hours before dawn's early light and home again. Fresh air on the walk but not the scents he savored.

No barbeque pork, roasted peanuts, no hot cinnamon buns. He tolerated Detroit's carbon monoxide fumes and garbage strewn streets, overflowing trash bins, puddles deep with spit and grit. On one corner, urine rose from the curb as if a herd of buffalo ran loose. Beyond cracked sidewalks and unoccupied buildings, Walton Boulevard awaited. Fresh air. A block with a community center and Rosemont Assisted Apartments. Sanctuary. Brush and John-R were far from thought as he crossed the threshold where he and special friends had apartments. Sterile, dry hospital air far from his lungs. Nothing here to clog his nose.

Within the blue painted rooms, Henry listened to music he loved. Well, even at the hospital, music played in his head. Day or night, her tunes wrapped warm arms around Henry and he was nothing but blissful. At home, he danced with Sweet Lady Jesus Sheryl Crowe, too. Whether Mother liked it or not, Henry had his space, his music, his kind of people and the city, too.

Away from depressing Lutheran Green Acres where Mother insisted they kept him *healthy*.

Three squares a day. Meat, potatoes and vegetables.

With a bunch of loonies who didn't know one day from the other. Full bellied loonies. He couldn't be forced to stay anymore. Twenty-one, no harm to himself or others. That's what the lawyer said.

An apartment, the hospital, bones, Sweet Lady Jesus Sheryl Crowe.

You can't tell me what to do, Mother.

Honestly, he'd tried. It only led to trouble.

Henry doesn't cooperate. Really?

His case worker introduced Dr. Ralph Winston, who sponsored Henry in Center City Hospital's Outreach Program. Arms wide, Henry thought. What advantage was there in an 'Outreach' program?

What about Wild Wings or Cramer's Sports? They'd leave him alone, wouldn't they? But living close to a hospital had its rewards.

Doc Winston, with shaggy brows and coffee breath, never walked down the smut laden corridors, or asked personal questions or visited his apartment. If he did, he'd not let Sweet Lady Jesus shine over the kitchen sink, kneel at his bedside, sit over his commode or wail Sweet Jesus tunes all day. Old Doc Winston, with his big words, wouldn't understand how Sweet Lady Jesus Sheryl Crowe took away sights, sounds and smells that made Henry feel like

Edited By Jake Devlin

shit. Glorious Sheryl let Henry's mind travel far from the life of ordinary people. After Doc Winston's six months of scrutiny, shaggy brows and coffee breath, though, he'd found a friend. Doc didn't work at night. For that Henry rejoiced.

Instructions not needed from doctors, nurses or parole officers. Sheryl's songs brought peace.

Sweet Lady Jesus gave her blessings. At home and at work.

The shiny steel chambers of the morgue provided peace, too. In gray silence, music in his head, his voice could soar like a concert singer. Madison Square Garden. Bose speaker quality. Baritone warbles bounced off metallic surfaces with superior reverberation. Henry rolled into a personal rendition of Sweet Lady Jesus Sheryl Crowe's pithy tune, *The First Cut is the Deepest* as he attacked his favorite chore. In practiced style, hand to mouth, the microphone of imagination at his throat, echoes bounced off the ceiling. This audience didn't wag a finger or make cruel jokes or drown out his songs. Henry belted loud and clear as magnificent as a TV star.

"Gonna have me soooooo mmmmmuuuuchhh funnnn. I ain't the only one".

Sheryl, long-legged Sweet Lady Jesus, soulful temptress, kept a steady cadence as Henry

counted off the rules of song, rules set by Old Doc Winston, what everyone else expected, too. Routines with Sheryl were a joy. Write name on the chalk board, add patient's ID number, put specimen in cold storage tray, add number to the green log book. One, two, three, four, then one more. One, two, three, four, then one more.

Yes, after Old Doc Winston cut him loose, Henry added an uncensored step to the routine. No over the shoulder coaching, excitement began. No eyes, no reports. And sassy, wet-mouth, big lipped bitch Carlotta wouldn't spy on him, either. Enter the morgue at night? Not in her job description, she'd said again and again.

Not Carlotta, even when she ragged her old refrain.

Henry, I have a bone to pick with you.

Henry eyed the instrument cabinet. Don't touch sterilized equipment on the exam table. Don't touch open razors. Rules to follow. But a package from the clean stock cabinet wasn't on the *No* list.

Clean or dirty? Clean supplies were under the white linen cloth Old Doc Winston arranged on his work table. Henry's job was 'dirty'. After Doc used his tools, Henry put them in the dirty wash room. Brooms, mops in the dirty closet. Henry's supplies were dirty. Don't mix clean and dirty. Dirty this, dirty that. Don't ever touch *Clean*.

Henry slipped the sharp blade from its paper case and walked over to the fresh cargo table and faced the specimen he'd brought from the surgical ward. Knew her name, where she'd come from, where she'd been. He knew how she had been connected and how she'd been taken apart. His chest went lump, bump, lump. A whisper from heaven drifted into his ear.

Sweet Lady Jesus are you speaking to me?

Why don't you have soooommmmeeee moooorrreee fuuuunnnnn.

Henry could handle this part. Parts and parcels were better than the whole. No eyes to stare. No sneering lips. No nasty wagging tongue, no pointed finger, no breasts to flaunt, no butt to swing, no dirty dark hole to poke. Remnants, bones. Parts and parcels. Finger, arm, leg, toes, skulls, jaw bones. Bones.

Carlotta Gonzales, I have a bone for you.

Henry gazed at the package. Angels of mercy carefully wrapped what doctors cut away. Henry slipped the sharp razor under the first layer of soft white tape. Round and round, they secured the remains as though they'd swaddled a baby. Or wrapped a gift? My Christmas present, Henry grinned. No red bow, no green holly. Henry unrolled the layers, one, two, three, one more. A sacrament inside.

The first cut. How deep should it go?

Henry continued to unroll the gauze. Why did the bloody, dissected waste need yards of white gauze? Not smart to waste supplies. Did nurses think someone would slip a finger beneath the first layer and steal the grizzly remains of the surgeon's cut? If it fell out? So what, it would end up in the fires anyhow. Nurses didn't make Henry's job easy. It wasn't in their job description. They did what they wanted to do and didn't consider what Henry needed to do.

But Henry, you have the patience of a saint.

What was that sound? Carlotta? From his head, behind the nape of his neck. Underneath his eyebrow, beside his ear?

What takes you so loooooonnnnng? She never asks nurses what takes them so long.

Wrap and roll, unwrap and unroll. With a steady eye, Henry worked to unleash the bondage.

Flesh and bone. Part and parcel. A part of the whole. The whole of the part.

The scalpel felt warm in Henry's hand. One, two, three, four. Slip, nip, slice. Less one, less two, through each layer. Ouch, ahhh. The binding fell away. Henry's fingers shook. Steady, he thought.

Steady, Slow. Part and parcel. A perfect present. A feast for patient eyes. Thank you, Sweet Lady Jesus.

Does she look like you? Never so pure.

Henry had read the surgical posting. Amputation. He couldn't pronounce the big word but understood what it meant. Strange words all over hospital walls. On chalk boards, doorways, lapel pins, packages, on instruction sheets. Doc Winston pointed his crooked finger, "Learn a new word every day."

One a week was enough. A week, a month, two months, more words. How many words did one human need to know? Six months later, Henry understood every word on the packages he carried out of the surgical ward.

Below the knee. BTK. Left or right. L or R. Female or male. F or M. He knew the difference between F and M.

Henry gazed at the bundled contents. A rush of anxiety started on his scalp where hair stood on end and ran to the end of – well, to the end of his bone. Perspiration beaded his forehead. He arranged the edges of the surgical cloth around the mass of flesh and held it high to the light.

This I give to thee. Lamb of God. Sweet Lady Jesus of the Light.

Cocoon gone, the flesh exposed, he gently replaced it and gazed at the specimen, the parcel the surgeon had rendered, and wondered if nurses gasped aloud when the cut, the dirty deed, was done. Or did they accept the fruit of the doctor's labor? Necessary work -- instructed by a divine power.

The first cut. Body and blood. Take this and drink from it.

Henry cradled the sampling. The large fragment sparkled like white porcelain. Milk bone, crystals from Mother's broken dishes. Small pieces tinged with juice from the vine. Sweet Jesus Blood. Take this and drink from it. He ran his hand along the pallid calf, over bruised shin, along the bony notches of a once smooth, curved ankle. He felt the spongy, crinkly mass where muscle and bone gave stability to a woman who'd ran as fast as a gazelle.

Henry Weinstein lingered over the limb.

Spineless twit, you'll never run again.

Oh Henry. Why would you think such a cruel thing?

Tears spilled down Henry's cheeks. Large, salty tears. Henry knew this woman. Wasn't she just like him? Didn't they share the same story? Misfortune, pain, misery, now in a hospital and no other place to go. Other people controlling bodily functions. Others deciding what you should eat. Food cooked in big steel pots. Even what to wear. Uniforms made you look crazy. She had to wear a pale gray hospital gown, couldn't walk again and sat in a chair with locked wheels.

The world -- one big cruel boiling pot of festering stew.

Henry could escape the big pot. He could operate in this world. He knew how to protect himself.

Why wasn't this girl-less-one leg more careful?

Henry's gloved fingers worked the margins of the glistening wound. He peered at the waxy, gray string of artery that carried life's force from the center of her heart to the tips of those blunt toes painted in slut hot pink. He poked a finger into a web of crushed, thin fiber. Piece meal, mush. Blood dripped from the spider veins underneath the flaccid muscle. Blood from the empty heart of a whore.

Henry placed his hand over his heart. Yes. I'm alive. Thump, da-lump, thump, lump. A pure heart pushes blood to the core of the body. To the end of his big bone. Thank you, Sweet Lady Jesus.

Focus on the sacrament. Repeat the refrain Sheryl sings so well.

The last cut is the cleanest.

The sun comes up on Walton Boulevard. Sun shrines on his throne.

A sigh of sympathy. A woman without this leg. Sorrow clutched his throat. Even an untrained eye knew the fracture would never heal. It must be used for the greater good. Yes. Henry would keep it out of the sight of those who would abuse it. Or be tempted by wicked ways. Dirty secrets, dark places. Parts and parcels.

Henry looked at the wall clock's round face with its twelve eyes and two long arms. A spindly limb in the middle, limp, up, down, around. Then remembered what Carlotta had said a half hour before. 'I have a bone to pick with you, Henry.'

Oh really? Bone. Bones. What did Carlotta know about bones?

I have a bone to pick with you, Carlotta Gonzalez.

Henry glanced at the door. One, two, three, four. A minute more. He slipped the edge of the scalpel into thin, pallid skin. Slit, slice, expose. Probe, dig, dislodge—one small morsel. One translucent pearl, a nugget of good fortune for his rosary. Henry sighed.

I have a bone.

Henry's hand rested momentarily at the band of his green scrub pants before it darted in and grasped the bulge of his intact bone. One, two, three, four. A minute more. Sweet Lady Jesus Sheryl whispered in his ear. A pearl in Henry's free hand and stroked in three quarter time.

I give this up to you.

No. What did she just say? He shook his head.

The first cut should be deeper. No. The first cut is deep enough. One, two, three, four. A minute more.

How many minutes before the elevator pinged to announce its return to the third floor? One?

No more.

Henry pushed the empty stainless steel gurney back to surgical floor.

Carlotta Gonzales came from behind her desk, eyes flashing, a clipboard in her hand. Her head tilted toward the clock. "Henry, didn't I say I wanted to talk to you? What takes you so long to get to the morgue and back?"

Henry noticed the rise in her chest. That stance he saw too often. Carlotta huffed again. Henry kept his head low.

Would she write a discipline note again?

Edited By Jake Devlin

If she did, Henry wouldn't get another job.

Henry darted into the supply room and put the gurney in its usual place. An orderly room is a functional room. One, two, three, four.

Carlotta followed, "Listen, Henry, when I say I have a bone to pick with you, it means we need to talk. I don't explain myself well, do I? No need to be afraid of me. It's my job to see that you get your job done. Do you understand, Henry?"

Henry Weinstein edged toward the window where the golden glow of daylight had just begun to rise off the earth's floor. "Yes, Miss Carlotta. I know. I have a bone to pick with you. Yes, I know. One, two, three, four."

Carlotta Gonzalez rubbed her hand over her weary face. She agreed to take Henry on as the night orderly at Doctor Winston's urging. A man didn't need a high I.Q. to push a gurney back and forth, pick up the trash and clean up after a sloppy staff. This man just needed a gentle hand and a measure of kindness behind every direction. Be patient, Carlotta thought, in good time Henry will follow orders. If she used her leadership skills in a humane way. What better place than a hospital to care for those who are not capable of caring for one's self.

"Next time, Henry, don't take so long. You're needed here."

Carlotta returned to her desk; head bent over a pile of hospital charts.

Henry smiled as he looked out the window. Lady Jesus Sheryl delivered the sun. He rolled the small white fragment of bone between his fingers. The Mason jar on his kitchen counter was half empty. If full, he'd have enough for a rosary.

One more hour and home.

No bone to pick with Carlotta Gonzalez, I have my own.

END

The 2019 BOULD Awards Anthology

Edited By Jake Devlin

The 2019 BOULD Awards Anthology

Bait

Eve Fisher (~2700 words)

I took to the sea from my cradle. Born on the brine in Downings and rocked across the waves with my mother, to good old Nantucket, east of the Manhattoes. Ye gods, what a town. Soaked with sea spray, reeking of fish. The cows themselves eat fish heads for dinner. You don't need cod in your chowder here, all you need is milk, and a bit of salt tack and onion. That's what they do down at the Try Pots Inn and the sailors pack themselves full every night.

I've thought of working there once or twice, but they'd never hire me. Not now, a widow, and <u>his</u> widow to boot. It's just as well. I'm tired of sailors. If ever I marry again it'll be to a man with two legs firmly planted in solid earth. A grocer. Or a banker. My mother laughs when I say that.

"Sure and you can't escape the sea, my darling," she says. "It's in your blood for the generations, my dark one."

And I am dark, dark hair, dark eyes, black Irish, small and neat and sleek-skinned. My family came from the islands off County Donegal, where the birds and the seals and the people all meet in one big happy family.

Myself, I swore I'd never marry a sailor, a fisherman, a whaler. There's enough salt in our blood, no need to add more. And then, they're such a hearty dull lot for the most of them. Brawny and broad-shouldered, curly hair smelling of bay rum, and the reek of the spirit strong on their breath. Pretty lads, all of them, good for a dance and a kiss, but none of them to make a girl howl like a banshee on a full moon night.

I shouldn't have said that, should I? A young, tender, dark-eyed girl, now she shouldn't be thinking such thoughts, should she?

Edited By Jake Devlin

Flowers and quilting and shuddering at storms she should, not gulping down darkness like fiery wine. But I did. And yawned at all the tall sunflowers nodding their heads at me.

And then he came. Ahab. Sure and his mother must have nodded off in church the day that lesson was read. "'Tis from the Bible," no doubt she said at the christening, and everyone too horror-struck to tell the poor old cow no. Ahab. White scar like a lightning bolt from crown to foot, and the other stumped off to an ivory peg. Dark he was, dark and seared and the salt spray and the raw spirit smelled different on him.

He came to pay a call upon my mother; my father had shipped with him seven years ago to die of a quartan-ague in the South Seas. My mother wasn't one to hold a grudge, and welcomed him with seed cake and a tot of rum. "Ye'll remember my Nancy?" my mother said, as he sat in our parlor, stiff as a mast. His eyes rolled over me, and I swear the waters swirled up and around me, bubbled and frothy and churning as they did around my grandmother Shelagh when she went down in the waves to never come back, for home she'd gone at last. I listened to the roaring in my ears as my mother pried a recital out of him -- it was like opening an oyster -- of my father's disease and demise. The shrieking of the laundress in the basement spared us his burial, for my mother jumped up and ran, leaving us alone.

"'Tis laundry day," I said. "A fine mess of steam and water, and the whole house at sixes and sevens for the week. You manage it better at sea, I hear." No answer. "Would you be having more rum?" He nodded, briefly. I poured his drink, and sat down again, all quiet as he toted his peg. But I had seen the slight tremor when my dress brushed past.

After a while -- for the silence was smothering -- I tried again. "My father was a grand one for writing letters," I said. "He could write so you could see the waves roll under you. He wrote of all the birds and fish and whales he'd seen... I remember one he wrote of, 'A white-headed whale with a wrinkled brow and a crooked jaw.'"

His eyes blazed, his voice was an earthquake: "The beast that dismasted me!" His voice lowered, cunning and dangerous to rise as he went on: "Brave men have clapped their mouths shut as with iron bands before they dared to speak of him to me, and they did right. And am I now to hear my razing made parlor talk? Made 'Come, tell me of thy shame, but lightly, to pass the time!'? By a dark girl in a dark room?"

"Neither shame nor light," I replied, my voice steadier than my belly before his wrath. "But simple true desire to hear of the dangers you have passed."

His eyes dropped away, like soundings in the sea. "You cannot pass the present, living in the flesh. I have met Elijah, and he spoke the truth, that I would be dismembered." And then, almost to himself, "What can mortal man do against prophecy?"

I answered with my hand, reached to his.

It was a three months' courtship, and then we were wed in the Whaler's Chapel, his face set like burning flint, his voice rumbling like thunder as he said "I do". There was no bawdy at our wedding breakfast; only solemn toasts, muffled whispers, uneasy glances. I had married Nantucket's madman, and all there were pitying and curious and dying to get home where they could talk it to death over a cup of grog. And go home they did, with indecent haste. Captain Peleg was the last to leave, and as he left he kissed me on the brow, murmuring, "A sweet resigned girl." A master of physiognomy to be sure. Then, "Take care of her, Captain." My husband bowed stiffly, and we were alone.

We spent our honeymoon in my mother's house. My mother, with rare access of tact, had taken herself off to New Bedford to visit my aunt for a fortnight, where I knew she would spend her time in fear and trembling, for she'd never been a great truster of men, and Ahab seemed more of a sidhe than a man to her. All things considered, I thought it a grand idea for her to leave us alone at our starting. Still, the missing her took me as much by surprise as did the apprehension when he stumped up beside me in the dark.

"Behold, thou art fair, my love; behold, thou art fair..." His voice rumbling through the empty house, my hair falling like water through his hands. "Fair as the moon, clear as the sun, terrible as an army with banners..." His voice muffled, his arms like iron.

My mother returned, thankful that I was whole and well. I was thankful I'd had time to burn the sheets.

"Well, and what of him?" she asked. My husband was out on the wharf, looking over his ship, for he was leaving soon to go whaling.

"What of him indeed," I said, pouring the coffee. "He'll do for me."

Mother nodded. "Well, and it makes sense. You always were for the odd ones."

"He's no more odd than any other man who's been half eaten alive by a fish. Sure and I'd say Jonah had a few odd moments himself once he was belched back on shore."

"Sure and you're mad for him, I can tell," she sighed. "Does he sleep well?"

"You'll hear him breathing deep tonight."

"Good. I was worried about him, not being kin and all."

I set down my cup. "Don't be starting that up with him," I said. "He doesn't need to be hearing all the tales told of our family."

My mother eyed me as a cow would her errant calf. Then she reached out and took my hand, crooning "My dark one, my sweet one, my darling..."

A week more, and he was gone. I was glad of it, mad as I was for him, for I needed time to sort things out. A whaler's wife gets lots of time. Off he sails, waving his hat or his kerchief, everyone crying on shore, and that's that. Years pass, two, three, five or even more, until the face is dim and the touch far dimmer, and then he's back, loaded with wealth. A month or two, he's off again. If you like your own way in your own house with your own things about you, it's a good life.

Ahab was back in six months.

Sickness said he, and I was sweetly flattered. I sent my mother back to New Bedford so I could tend my husband's fever without distractions. But it was no quartan-ague, no pleurisy, not even a winter's cold. It was a terrible lack of sleep he had, from the nightmares that crashed over his slumbers as soon as the waves started crashing into his ship. Drowning dreams, the waves roaring and foaming, the legs kicking and the lungs burning and the clothes hanging wet and sodden and heavy as shot, dragging him down to where a great white bulk was waiting, deep in the dark green bottoms. He fairly kicked the bed to pieces, fighting his way up. And when he beached, gasping, he shook his head as if the water still clung to it, and the sheets were no paler than his cheek.

"Hush, cushla," I said, taking him in my arms and rocking him. "'Tis dry, 'tis safe. All's well. Hush, cushla, sleep."

Sleep he did, and well. Until the next night. And each night after. I'd never known the dreams to take such tight hold of a man. I wrote my mother, who replied with five pages, crossed, most of it nonsense and superstition. The only thing that made sense was a reminder that kelp soup was a grand thing for bad nights. So I went down to the kitchen and made some, dark and rich and hot, and served it that night for dinner.

The sea boiled in our bellies, seeped in our veins, mulled in our heads. I slept and dreamed I was back in County Donegal, with all my friends and family about me. The seagulls were squalling overhead as we lay out on the rocks in the warm sun, the waves crashing, the foam just touching the tips of our feet. I rolled over onto my back in the warm sand, and fanned myself with one long dark hand, drifting away in the heat and the sound of the waves and the little shivers of cold spray.

"Nancy!" my mother barked me awake. I rolled over and looked at her. She nudged me to look across the strait: "Your man over there, he's not looking at all well."

And there was Ahab, alone in a whaling boat, looking at us, his eyes dark with rage. He rose up, a harpoon in his hand, and as he rose, beneath him rose a wave as big as an island, swelling white and smooth, raising him up swift and smooth so that he never even noticed until suddenly the wave rose over itself and flipped him and his little boat and sent him, shrieking, into the deep green waters.

I dove, swift and sleek. Down, down, down, the bubbles flying past my dark eyes, dark hair, dark body. There was Ahab, thrashing in his heavy clothes -- the line to the harpoon tangled up around him so that soon he could never struggle more. I had it dragged away from him in a moment, diving deeper with the line in my mouth, and as I swam below him, I looked up at those thrashing, kicking feet -- both feet, no ivory peg and -- shame though it is to admit -- I thought of having just the wee little nip of him, just for fun, just to get him going. And beneath me something large and white rolled in delight.

Himself woke me up. Ahab standing in a corner of our bedroom, shouting the house down while I tried to remember where I was and find my bathrobe. "For the love of God, husband, what's wrong?"

He drew a shuddering breath and said, croaking like a coffin lid, "Who <u>are</u> you?"

"God and Mary and St. Patrick be with us, and I'm your wife,

Nancy," I said. Thinking, sure and he's gone mad completely now.

"I saw you," he said. "In the sea, swimming like a --"

"'Tis the kelp soup," I interrupted. "Sure and I shouldn't have given it to you so late at night –"

"You were there!" he roared, and the windows rattled with it.

"Well, and if I was, it was only a dream you were having," I said reasonably, sitting on the edge of the bed. "You're taking the whole thing much too seriously." I looked at his peg leg and added, "You know, the poor beast wasn't trying to kill you at all. He was all for saving your life. It was just afterwards, there you were in the water, kicking like a fool, and he couldn't resist --"

He howled like a mad dog. I scrambled back to the other side of the bed. He leaned forward, his face stretched out like Lucifer's and said, "Speak to me of the unreasoning brute as if it were the reasoner? What lies behind that mask of yours, wife? What thing is it that you carry in your belly? What creature speaks through the mouldings of your features? <u>What are you</u>?"

"I am your wife," I repeated, and stood tall to say it. "Nancy, and it's your son I'm carrying in my belly."

"I did not ask you who you were," he croaked. "I asked you what you were, that I saw you lying on the rocks among your brethren creatures, a seal among seals."

"Oh, that," I said, and waved my hand. "That was the other branch of my family."

Ahab bounded out of the house as if the devil was at his heels.

I believe he told Captain Peleg something of our conversation, for the next day the good Captain paid a visit upon me, to commiserate with me upon my husband's sad fancies.

"I think the only thing for him is a long voyage," he said. "If he stays here, in the state he's in…" I nodded. "He must surmount

Edited By Jake Devlin

his fears," he continued, "and to do that he must face them, not shirk them here on land." He looked discreetly at my swollen body. "I would for your sake -- and for his -- that he could be here for the birth. But you will be well provided for. And hopefully, he shall return, much improved." I nodded again, and he left.

My grandmother Shelagh -- and she should know -- said, before she went back home, that it was a dangerous thing to save a drowning man. It's little thanks you get for it, and some turn wicked after. She also said that a drowning man, once saved, should never return to the sea, for the sea will claim its own. Myself, I think it's the ingratitude that calls it home on you. And Ahab, of course, well, he was certain the universe was personally after him, Himself.

Oh, but I do miss him, you know. That dark fire suited me well, it did, and I never minded the madness. He wanted a sense of humor, is all. I can still see him in the deep water, those two legs kicking away like minnows. I tried to tell him, there was nothing malevolent, or even personal about it: he just looked like bait.

And bait he did become.

Ah, well. So, would you care to be joining me for a quick one down at the Try Pots? It's clam tonight, clam chowder, and the grog is very good.

END

The 2019 BOULD Awards Anthology

Edited By Jake Devlin

The 2019 BOULD Awards Anthology

Zero-Sum

Cheri Vause (~1,500 words)

'Nothing happened today.'

If Harold Poy owned a diary, he could have written those words on every page. If he was a painter he would use the dreary colors of a shallows to illustrate the stagnation of his life. But he wrote those words on the back of an envelope, fully intending to crumple and throw it away. And yet, he didn't. He held fast to it, as if it were a valuable resource to convince his creeping soul that he existed behind a poorly oiled hinged door and must exit.

Thoughts swam like deep sea creatures through his mind. How he wished to escape the stultifying existence in his humdrum apartment, of cell phones, of the banality of clocks and employers that demanded obedience.

He longed to be free, but he needed a manifesto, something delineating a path to his future. Emptying the totality of his mind, he drew a blue inked circle on the opposite side of the envelope.

He pondered the nature of the shape. Was it really an O or a circle? Or could it be a zero? There was a definitive difference in subject and meaning between the three. Horrors existed within the tall devourer, the alchemists' snake, *Ourovoros Ophis*, or could it be the beautiful beast of eternity? Yet, the simplicity, the absoluteness of that simple circle was beautiful.

"Perhaps I've created something new?"

As he stared at the curved line, he realized the shape was both empty without and within. Only the blue line existed.

"Zero-sum," Harold announced, laughing heartily. "Is this the world where I am finally the master?"

Whatever he could think, would it be so? He laughed, again.

Edited By Jake Devlin

As a fence it would defy him, though whatever was in there could be kept from breaking out, but it would also keep him out.

"Does it oppose me?" *No*, he thought. "A prison more likely."

His brain teemed with possibilities.

Yet, his job, the garrote of the day, ensnared him in exhaustion. Reluctantly, he climbed into bed, picked up a book, and eyed the first sentence of the first chapter:

"'There is a taint of death and malignancy to lies,'" the words unrolled before him.

"The lies we tell ourselves ..." Yet, he couldn't advance, for he was caught on the lip of the O in the word, to. He reread the sentence again, pausing once more on the word, to. Reading was useless in the light of his discovery.

Wasn't there a touch of violence in discovery? It upended what came before it. Or could it be enlightenment? He had to admit that sometimes it was both. And neither. And an amalgam. He closed the book and his eyes, searching for that dark moment when sleep would creep in. At last, he dreamed his body drifted on a cloud, inching closer toward the blue circle below him.

In that moment, the zero magnified into astounding proportions, as if he were floating ten thousand feet above it. The blue monstrosity was ruthless, acquiring a vaulting ambition of its own. The cloud lowered him to the ground, and he stood at the base, watching it curve away from him, and rise hundreds of feet into the air, until it disappeared into the clouds.

In awe of his creation, he began to understand his magnificent zero. It was the dark spot on an X-ray, the mass in the MRI, the looming explicable blotch that terrified and repulsed. Life and death in an eternal struggle was magnified on its inky line.

Sliding his eyes over the smooth surface, it seemed to drink in the light. Extending his hand, he deigned to touch his creation, to connect with it physically. Yet, the frigid surface forced him to jerk his hand away before it could be burned. He stepped back, and back again, and again, in an attempt to view the top. But he was unable, for the creature was impossibly huge. Yes, it was a creature.

The creature was not tied to a number, nor the absence of one, but the terror of all those on the outside of it. His mind burned with the definition of the life existing inside that circle. He ran around the wall until he could no longer stand.

Morning jarred him awake, and yet, he was both mentally and physically exhausted from his dream. He rose from bed, brushed his teeth, ate breakfast, showered, and dressed for work. Just as he started for the door to leave, his eye was drawn once more to the zero.

A voice could be heard saying that he should stay, "You didn't define the physical laws that would govern this universe."

It was true. He hadn't. He merely sought to find what it was. How would he live before he could discover that?

"But I need the money," he pleaded.

When he raised his eyes to the door, breaking eye contact with the zero, that zero-sum world suddenly transported itself from the paper into the apartment. The blue wall blocked him. He attempted to move around it, and in the process, the wall grew, forcing him to step all the way back to the window to avoid being crushed.

"You created me."

"Am I your god?"

Suddenly, he was no longer in the apartment, but inside the circle. Harold surveyed the area around him. Everything was an emptiness, both above and below. At the edge of the stark landscape was the blue curved wall.

"You're beautiful."

Still, there was a part of him frightened by his own creation, terrified of its possibilities.

"Are you an abomination?" he said, in a heightened pitch.

A voice replied, "You declared me beautiful, perfection. Now you call me abomination."

"If I'm your god, how can you defy me?"

Only silence followed. He began to hate his perfect zero. The thing did have a voice, a life of its own. Was it sentient? Or was it Pandora's Box, with nasties and furies nesting inside it?

He had created and trapped himself inside a perplexity. Was there a part of himself willing to do this, to ensnare his own mind and body?

He screamed, loosing his emotions into the empty space around him. Holding his face between his hands, he heard the scream echo, then disappear into the void. He had created his own hell.

Though terrified, he still managed to force himself to focus. First, he was outside. Then, when he desired it, he was transported to the inside of the zero.

"Could it be that simple? Whatever I think, is."

Somehow, that was wrong. Everything that happened was not a result of himself, but the sentient creature that was running amok.

"Get me out of here!" he screamed.

Yet, Harold Poy was completely alone, the sort of man who was null and void, who roamed through life as a listless vagabond of musts and obedience. Now, he was lost inside a trammel of nothingness.

#

Mrs. Campbell stood wringing her hands in anguish, her voice rising in desperation, "It's been a month, and no one has seen Harold. He hasn't shown up for work, and he missed his deadline for the rent."

"But, Mrs. Campbell—"

"Listen to me," she cut him off. "I know Mr. Poy. He's quiet and reliable. He's never missed a day of work. He pays his rent on time every month, even a few days early. Something has happened to him. Something terrible. I know it."

"I'm sorry, Mrs. Campbell, but we've looked everywhere. He's just disappeared." The policeman shrugged his shoulders. "Some people do that, become fed up with their lives and take off."

"He has be somewhere. What about the hospitals?"

"We checked. Did he leave a note for you?"

"This is all I found." She handed the officer the white paper with the blue circle and a strange, discolored blot.

The officer turned it over and read, "'Nothing happened today.'" He wrinkled his forehead. "What's this supposed to mean?"

"Somehow, I think it's important, a clue."

The officer wrinkled the paper in his fist and tossed it into the trash. A tiny shriek sounded in the distance. "What was that?" He cocked his head, listening for the sound to repeat.

"It sounded like a scream," Mrs. Campbell said.

The officer shrugged his shoulders again, closed his notebook, and took one last look around the room. "Give me a call if you hear anything," he offered his card, and strolled out the door.

Mrs. Campbell eyed the trash receptacle, staring at the paper the officer tossed there. She bent over and drew the paper out. Stepping to the table, she slowly smoothed it with the edge of her palm.

Harold Poy screamed, "Help!"

She startled, but listened for another scream.

"Help me!"

She shrieked, dropping the envelope, and fled the apartment, stepping on it as she ran out.   **END**

Edited By Jake Devlin

Chemo Queen

Tom Barlow (~2970 words)

Andrea cursed as she attempted to shave the back of her head. She dare not nick herself, and since everything in the mirror was transposed, when she tried to move the razor left it went right. It would be so much easier if she could use the electric razor she had stolen from her ex when she moved out, but it would leave stubble.

She longed to apply some makeup; at 41, she could still pass for someone 10 years younger with a little foundation, eyeliner, lipstick, but for now she needed to remain as pallid as possible.

The trailer was in dire need of cleaning, there were dishes to wash, sheets to change, clothes to iron. Instead once she was done, she snorted an oxy, put on her headphones and hit the recliner, allowing her iPhone to feed her some perky Taylor Swift.

***

The church was half-full when Andrea arrived. One of her ex-boyfriends had given her a blue handicap mirror hanger for Christmas one year, and she used this to park near the front door.

Reverend Bond was greeting parishioners in the narthex of the church as he always did. She always spent time talking with him; he'd been the one who first took up her cause, using his considerable reputation to cajole the rest of the community into donating.

"How are you feeling?" he asked as he gave her a brief, very gentle hug. She had warned everyone the week before that her bones could become brittle due to the radiation.

"Hungry," she said. "It's kind of hard to hold down food."

An old couple, Rose and Harold Barrett, smiled as they circled the two of them to enter the church. Someone in the congregation had given twenty-five grand to her fund over the past six months, anonymously, and it could be them, so she returned the smile.

"How is your daughter? I haven't seen her in years," the pastor said.

"We don't talk much. She has a job in Columbus, something in insurance. And a boyfriend who drives a truck."

Three more couples had lined up behind her, giving her an excuse to break off the conversation. She took a pew in the front so that she didn't have to catch every glance, wondering with each if the onlooker was questioning her illness. Thank God for her mother Patti, who had been a rock upon which the church thrived until her death four years earlier. The parishioners owed quite a karmic debt to her, which Andrea was allowing them to repay.

The Wednesday night service was unexceptional. She put on her stoical face as they sent the collection plates around a second time at the end of the service for donations to the fund they had established to help cover her medical expenses.

***

She returned to the trailer, but she was edgy, energized, and most of all, lonely. She dared not let anyone spend too much time with her for obvious reasons, but she hadn't had any fun in months. Around 11 p.m. she snapped. Makeup, her new blonde wig, her best top and miniskirt, the nice Alexander Wang pumps she bought on a splurge in Columbus when she got the first donation check. She had to belt the skirt; she'd dieted hard to lose weight as a chemo patient would. She was pleased by her appearance as a blonde.

She drove north an hour and a half to a nightclub on the south side of Columbus, well beyond the distance any locals in Crockett would travel for entertainment; she would be shocked if she saw anyone she knew at Kickin' It. The cover charge made quite a dent in the contributions she had received at church that evening.

Before she entered she did a couple of lines of the cocaine

she had been saving for a special occasion.

The place was packed, the air dense with sweat and lust. She found a lean at the end of the bar, the atmosphere of the club merging with the coke and the remnants of her last dose of oxy to set her mind free. When she was like that, her inhibitions disappeared and she soon glided onto the dance floor, whirling by herself in time to the band's tune until a cowboy took her hand and followed along.

She was not particular; she hadn't been with a man in eight months, not since she sent Glenn packing after she intercepted a call from his other girlfriend. This guy was not bad, either. Young, for sure, maybe late 20's, on the thin side, long face, large rough hands; he worked with those hands. She was able to forgive his stained teeth; he obviously chewed, but so had her father, and in her eyes he had been perfect. It was too loud to talk but he kept her hand between songs, and drew her close when the band started a slow number.

The heat of the place, the friction of his body plastered up against hers, the dope, all set off hormones like fireworks and they ended up in the bed of his truck, parked conveniently at the far end of the dark parking lot. She was on top of an old blanket he kept in the tool chest, and he was on top of her, when he grabbed her hair and her wig came off in his hand.

He stopped. Exasperated, she explained that she was a chemo queen. She couldn't see his face in the dark, but she could sense something was bothering him.

"How come you still have pubes?" he whispered.

"It's not that kind of cancer."

He thought this over a moment. "You OK to do this?"

"Would you just shut up and screw me?"

To her relief, he dropped the inquisition and went back to the task at hand.

***

Edited By Jake Devlin

She was in the shower shaving her cooter the next afternoon when someone knocked on her door. She scrambled into shorts and a tee and answered. Standing outside was a perky blonde, no more than 25, made up, in a red button-down top with an NBC logo. Behind her was a very short black man about twice her age with a television camera on his shoulder.

"Mrs. Apple? Andrea?" the woman said. "I'm Olivia Hayes, Channel 4, Columbus. I was talking to your pastor about a freeway interchange project that plans to take his farm when he told me about your struggles and what the community has done for you. That's the kind of story we like to run to reassure people that there is good in this world. Can we talk?"

Andrea thought frantically, looking for a way out, but could see none that would not cause suspicion, and she certainly didn't want that. She let Olivia cool her heels outside for a few minutes while she dressed for an interview, something tasteful, yet casual. A Wal-Mart sun dress fit the bill, periwinkle blue to accentuate her pallor.

Fortunately, the reporter soft-balled her questions. Andrea played along, vague on questions about her illness, enthusiastic when explaining what the charity of the people of Crockett meant to her. The whole thing took only 15 minutes, and after the fact Andrea felt rather proud of the way she'd handled the situation. Perhaps, she thought, it might even inspire wider giving.

***

It didn't take long for her mistake to become clear. A couple of days later, when she returned from Portsmouth, where she had scored some more medicine from the pain clinic, she found a familiar pickup in her driveway. The driver was asleep behind the wheel, a cowboy hat cocked to cover his eyes.

He woke when she parked beside him. As soon as he righted

his hat she recognized him from Kickin' It and cursed Channel 4.

She whipped on the ball cap she had come to wear whenever she went out into the sun and stepped out of the truck. He met her by the front door. "Hey, darlin'. Aren't you going to invite me in?"

"It was just a drive-by," she said. "We're not in love."

He reached over and raised the bill of her cap so he could look into her eyes. "I'm not here for sex. Although I wouldn't turn it down."

She unlocked the door and, with trepidation, waved him in.

He took a seat at the table and threw his feet onto the adjacent chair. "You have any coffee?"

She poured what was left from breakfast into a cup and stuck it in the microwave. "How did you find me, anyway?"

He gave her a reassuring smile. "When I recognized you I took a picture of the TV screen. The guy at the gas station in town was more than happy to take a twenty in return for directions to your place. You're kind of tucked away out here in the woods."

She'd gone to high school with Donnie Shonk, the guy in question, and was not surprised he'd been so cavalier with her info; he was still peeved she'd turned him down for a date to the prom.

She handed him his coffee. "So why are you here?"

"My sister is a nurse. She said if the hair on your head is totally gone, the rest of your body hair should be too."

"And from that, you figured, what?"

"According to that TV report, you've received over 40 grand for your cancer treatments. You seemed pretty lively at the club for a woman with cancer, so I got to thinking this might be a con."

"You think I'm conning people? Look." She raised her sun dress and hooked a thumb into the waist of her panties, pulled them down to show her smooth mons Venus. "It was just a matter of time."

"That was fast," he said, leaning over to run his forefinger across it. "Got a little stubble there though."

She knocked his hand away and lowered her dress, suddenly very warm. "What do you want?"

He stretched his hands above his head, yawned, before he said, "$10,000 would do it."

"Would do what?"

"Keep my mouth shut. You think you're smart, but I can see right through you. Nobody fucks like that when they're full of chemo. My dad died of cancer, and you could barely get him out of his rocker for the last year."

She was in between doses of her medicine and his words struck her like little shocks of electricity. Looking in his eyes she could see the uselessness of trying to brazen it out with him. He was totally relaxed, even amused.

"Why would you think I had any money left?"

***

She managed to talk the cowboy, whose name turned out to be Duane Tilton, into accepting a down payment of $2,000 and a blow job, cleaning out one of three cash stashes she had in the trailer. As soon as he left, promising to return in a week for the balance, she hit her medicine.

Even that didn't quite calm her down, though; her mind was awhirl with questions about how she could remove this threat before it ruined her. Perhaps it was time to execute her exit strategy, take every dollar she could scrape together and head for Las Vegas, where she could buy a new identity. She longed for the glamour of the Strip, where her ex had taken her for their honeymoon. Unfortunately, on that trip she'd lost at the blackjack table most of the money that their families had donated as wedding gifts.

But the thought of leaving cash on the table here haunted her. The church was planning to run a major fundraiser for her the following month, a festival for which they would reach out beyond the church for support. The pastor thought they could clear $10,000 if all went well.

And the more she thought about it the more it peeved her to give in to a deadbeat like Duane. She'd had precious little of her own in her lifetime, and she had taken a lot of pride in her little game. Why should she allow him to take it away?

So how to keep the Cowboy off her back? Deep in the cloud in which she floated, an audacious idea occurred to her.

***

She had caught his license plate as he drove off, and a phone call to an old girlfriend who worked as a dispatcher at the sheriff's office, explaining she was checking out a potential boyfriend, returned his address. Although she'd met him in Columbus, his home was in Chillicothe, only 20 minutes away. She was also able to confirm that he had no record with the police, no fingerprints on file.

The next morning she was parked discreetly outside his apartment when he left for work. She followed him to a construction site north of town, where he was stuccoing new homes.

She returned to the work site in late afternoon, shortly before he left for the day. She followed him to a bar near his apartment, Terri's. He made the mistake of leaving his truck unlocked in the parking lot, his pouch of chewing tobacco on the dash. When the lot was unobserved, she pulled up next to his truck, opened the door, picked up the tobacco pouch with a tissue and headed home.

***

Her plan was simple; commit a crime, leave the pouch behind so the cops would have fingerprints of the criminal. But what crime? She didn't have to think hard; there was one that she'd long thought to commit should she ever become so desperate. Two years before, she and a girlfriend had met at a bingo game at the VFW in Hillsboro.

Edited By Jake Devlin

The man doing the calling that night looked a little like Dale Earnhardt Jr., and Andrea and her ex weren't on speaking terms at the time, much less having sex. She stayed late, seeing her friend off before seeking out the caller for some recreation. She followed him home and watched as he locked the money he collected that night, around $1,000, in his cheap home safe, explaining that he didn't trust night deposit.

Before she left the next morning she pocketed an extra house key from his desk drawer.

Now she waited until Wednesday night, bingo night. She parked down the street from the caller's house in Hillsboro to see if his routine held up. Sure enough, shortly before midnight he arrived, parked in his driveway, and carried the same beat-up briefcase into his house. She waited for an hour after his bedroom light went off before advancing her truck to a spot in front of his house.

The night was moonless, his neighborhood without streetlights, so she was able to approach the house without the risk of being seen. The key worked perfectly, the door hinges had been recently oiled, the safe was in the same place it had been, and it was not too heavy for her to carry out to her car. Before she exited the side door she dropped the tobacco pouch on the floor where it might reasonably have fallen out of a back pocket.

Within five minutes she was gone.

***

She waited until 9:00 p.m. the next evening to call Duane. He expressed surprise that she had his number, but she didn't tell him about her line into the BMV.

"No," he said, "you can't have more time. I know you have the money; you sure haven't spent it on your trailer."

"That's not why I'm calling," she said. "I wanted to tell you about a burglary you committed last night." She explained the set-up.

"I know you don't have your prints on file with the police, but if I phone in an anonymous tip and they do print you, they will match the prints on the tobacco pouch I left behind. I busted open the safe this morning and there was almost two grand in it, which makes your crime a felony."

"You stupid bitch. You don't know what you've done."

"Yes I do. I've created a Mexican stand-off. You turn me in, I turn you in, and we both lose. So why don't we just agree to mind our own business?"

To her concern, he disconnected without replying.

***

She was deep into a dream colored vivid by her medicine that night when she awoke to the sound of someone popping open the trailer door with a crowbar. By the time she had reoriented to this world, Duane was in her bedroom, shotgun leveled at her head.

"What the hell..." she mumbled, instinctively pulling the top sheet over her breasts. "Are you crazy? This is not that big a deal. Take the bingo money; it's yours anyway."

There was a look in Duane's eyes that she hadn't seen before, making her wonder if he'd dipped into some meth on the way over.

"You don't understand," he said. "Once the cops get my prints I'm a dead man. There are a couple of women I partied with before I got smart enough to wear gloves, and the cops were able to get prints off their throats. The sheriff is just biding his time until someone matches those prints."

"You mean you're a murderer?"

"You might say that. Several times over. Plus this one." He chambered a round.

"Please–I can keep a secret," she said, desperately holding her hands out as though to block the shot. "Look how I've kept the con going for so long."

Edited By Jake Devlin

"That's just it. How can I trust a con artist with my life? How can I believe a word you say?"

The last thought that went through Andrea's head was indignation that he would think her untrustworthy.

END

The 2019 BOULD Awards Anthology

Edited By Jake Devlin

The 2019 BOULD Awards Anthology

The Sadist

Jimmy Summers (~750 words)

Donnie begs Alicia to heat the alligator clip over the flame of the stove burner before she pinches it onto his nipple.

"This is not my idea of a date," she says, bouncing the clip in her palm. "How about I just put a dry cleaner bag over your head and go home?"

Face-up, naked, zip-tied at two, four, eight and ten o'clock to the legs of the dining room table, Donnie is unconsciously wriggling one chafed wrist. For a self-professed pain junkie, he has little control over aversion reactions.

"It's about the journey, not the destination." His voice sounds like gravel tossed down a dry drainage pipe. Hours of July heat trapped inside the house, windows shut to muffle his screams, and he'd made her promise -- no water. He'd ordered her to fix herself a pitcher of iced tea and drink it slow, inches from his eyes.

"This is excruciating," she says, picking up the tea pitcher. She holds it over his foot, tilts until a thin stream of liquid dribbles onto his pinkies. Slowly, she starts up his leg.

"You promised to hurt me."

She pauses for a moment, entranced by the goose bumps emerging along the tea line. "I didn't know what I didn't know. How could I promise when I didn't know?" She resumes the pour, now inches above his knee and heading north.

"I told you I was a sick fuck when we met." He had stopped sweating an hour before, but now his forehead is glistening again.

"Yeah, but I thought you meant an ordinary sick fuck. What kind a come-on line is that, anyway?" She changes course slightly, following the perimeter of the pubic zone.

Edited By Jake Devlin

"God that feels good," he says, "and not good/bad. Stop it."

She takes a slight detour north and lets the trickle fill his navel. When it starts to overflow, she leans over and sucks it dry. Salty, sour.

She says, "I hate it that after you told me you were a sick fuck you waited to see if I was still interested." She starts down the part in his stomach hair connecting his navel to his groin. His penis is retreating, like the head of turtle pulling back into its shell.

"You hate yourself for not walking away?"

"Would rejection have made you happy? Happy about being sad?" She dips her hand in the water, grabbing several ice cubes. "Can we ever be happy together if I don't hate myself too?" She presses her palm to his forehead, trapping the cubes against his skin.

"God that feels good," he says, his hands kneading the air beyond the zip ties. "Quit it."

"Shush," she says. "Give it a minute. So you need pain because, what, you're happy but you don't deserve to be happy? But if torturing you is making me miserable, that makes you happy, which is sad? I don't think it's possible to be a sadist and a masochist at the same time."

She can tell when the ice cream headache begins by the way his eyes bulge. "Oh fuck me, that hurts. There isn't a person alive that isn't a mass of contradictions."

"You're welcome." She picks up the pitcher, sloshes it a bit to distribute the coldest tea, then, winking at him, dumps the entire contents on his crotch. Donnie's eyes roll back into his skull for a moment, then reappear, tears swelling at the corners. He's gasping for breath.

"You are so good," he says when he finally regains his voice. "You're the best ever."

She lifts her hand, letting the ice cubes roll off his forehead.

Picks up a pair of wire cutters from the counter and circles the table, snipping open the zip ties.

"What's wrong?" he says, rolling heavily onto his side.

She picks up her purse from the counter, shaking it once to locate her car keys. "I can't stand a Pollyanna. I'm too good for you, you know?"

"Wait. You didn't take me seriously, I hope?" He sits up, hands cupping his frozen balls.

"Honey, there's not enough pain here for the both of us. You know what I feel when you're screaming at the top of your lungs?"

He shrugs, eyes still watering.

"Self esteem. Now who's the sick fuck?"

She pinches him on the arm, hard, as she walks out, relishing the look of longing on his face.

END

Edited By Jake Devlin

In A Town Mostly Forgotten

John R. Clark (~2060 words)

Hart Plantation had pretty much wasted away, victim to the economic cancer that had been devouring rural Maine for the past couple decades. There had been a time when the empty businesses and numerous for 'sale by owner' signs in front of houses in various states of disrepair would have bothered me. Today, I had something else on my mind, one that left little energy to feel for the town I once called home.

My destination, a forgotten house on a forgotten road, lay several miles outside of town. If I had a car, I knew I could park smack dab in the middle of the broken pavement without fear of inconveniencing anyone. That was how desolate Dark Mountain Road had become. Heck, back when I was in school, the road was so poorly maintained, those kids unlucky enough to live on it had been forced to walk the distance to the intersection with The Hole In The Wall Road where we caught the bus.

Not that making it to the bus was any great prize. Misery not only loves company, it encourages the bigger and stronger among the afflicted to feed on the most fragile. I had been one of the latter. Our stop had been near the beginning of a long, bumpy loop over a mix of dirt and poorly paved roads. That allowed several big and mean seventh and eighth grade boys unlimited opportunity to inflict a combination of verbal and physical torment that made my life almost as miserable as it was at home.

I took my time moving through town, memories sparking as I passed various buildings despite my initial resolve not to feel anything. The bus station was gone, replaced by a fading sign for a redemption center. If ever a town needed redemption, it was Hart

Edited By Jake Devlin

Plantation, but not the kind that doled out a nickel for each can or bottle brought in. Back when I still called the town home, I'd spent many a sleepless night imagining stealing enough money from the tin box on the top shelf in our kitchen to pay for a ticket to someplace warmer emotionally and physically. Those fantasies had sometimes been the only thing holding me together. Sadly, I'd never gotten the gumption to act on them.

Despite my belief that the years away from town had given me some protection from old wounds, I had to detour around the next building and walk down the old railroad bed. The Rock Solid Church of the Open Bible was the best looking structure in view, proof that religion still paid well in desperate places like this. Before hurrying out of view, as if anyone would be out so early on a Saturday, I couldn't help but seeing his dreaded name on the flashing sign in front. If anything, the flashing monstrosity seemed bigger than when I lived here.

Simon Whelk must still be fooling the gullible and I wondered how many other sad and desperate teen girls had fallen prey to his smarmy words and wandering hands. I'd discovered a hidden bit of outrage-fueled energy the night he tried his slimy brand of salvation on me. I had paid a price for my defiance, but he had paid a bigger one.

I left town, crossing Todd Stream on a bridge that didn't look capable of supporting much more than someone on a bicycle, even though I suspected logging trucks must use it to get to the mill in Woodbine ten miles to the east. The September sun was losing its battle with a low overcast moving leisurely from the hills to the north. The breeze was cool and smelled like rain as I moved further from town.

I passed another half dozen homes on my way to where I'd meet The Hole In The Wall Road. None were new and only the place where Dennis Blake used to live looked like anything had been done to it. The new screened-in porch was painted a light blue and several hanging baskets still had blooming plants in them. Their contrast with the starkness I'd encountered since hitting town almost made me feel sad.

The Hole In The Wall Road was in bad shape. It was in desperate need of ditching, poison ivy grew to the edge of cracked pavement and beavers had been busy in the swamp near the intersection. Their dam almost abutted the shoulder and I could see a pair of herons standing guard near the huge lodge in the middle of the water stretching a couple hundred yards back into the woods. I wondered whether Dark Mountain Road could be in worse shape.

I'd never expected to return, even though I had unfinished business. If it hadn't been for my great aunt Lizette, it wouldn't have happened. She'd been the only family member who took an interest in me after that last night in Hart Plantation, bringing me with her back to the cramped apartment in Medford, Massachusetts a few days later. This past summer, we'd gone to New Orleans to visit a man she's found online. It was thanks to him I'd been able to come home at last.

I slowed my pace when I reached the last turn. Sure enough, Dark Mountain Road still lived up to its name, the 2500 foot summit covered in brooding spruce trees dominated the immediate horizon, their thick branches seeming to suck up any sound. I'd been hearing various bird calls since leaving town, but as soon as I started up the road to where I used to live, they evaporated. In fact, the only life anywhere were the clouds of mosquitoes around my head, but even their high, annoying whine seemed diminished.

My pace slowed even more when the house came into view. One of the Norway pines by the back shed had toppled sometime in the recent past and now leaned, like a tired farmer, against the attic roof. Numerous shingles had been torn loose, exposing tar paper underneath and probably letting wind driven rain into the attic insulation. Clapboards had warped in several places and I could see at least three windows covered with filmy plastic. I wondered briefly whether he still lived here.

****

My mother had fled the year I turned ten, taking my five year old brother with her. I'd never gotten a satisfactory explanation for why she didn't take me, nor where she went. After a while, I stopped asking, but I never stopped wondering. At first, the only change was my father's expectations of me. I was to cook meals, keep house and do laundry. All soon became challenging, thanks to his drinking and inability to keep a job long enough to bring food home. Less than six months after Mom left, the power was shut off and I was forced to haul water from a dug well almost a hundred feet from the house.

My life became numbing, with nothing on the horizon worth living for. When I wasn't slaving at home, I was enduring torture from the school bus bullies. Our school was so poor that there wasn't anyone close to being capable of counseling and Hart Plantation wasn't on any map issued to folks working for the state department of human services.

I figured I'd stay hunkered down until I could figure out a way to escape. Sadly, the tin in the cupboard that had fueled my dreams had left town with my mother. The promised salvation at the church went south not long afterward, leaving me feeling angry, shamed and powerless.

The final straw came on a muggy summer night, not long after I turned thirteen. My father had disappeared several days earlier, something I was more grateful for than worried. He'd been getting drunk more often and with each bender, his anger and unpredictability grew.

I'd spent all day working to get the house looking decent, or as decent as a decrepit old farmhouse could be, when I realized that things were about to go to hell. A beater with no muffler came screeching into the driveway, country music blaring from the speakers. I watched as the passenger door sprung open and my father fell out, collapsing on the ground while clutching a bottle. Whoever was driving uttered an insane cackle and backed out to the road, narrowly missing his right leg. It looked like my father had passed out and would sleep it off in the yard, so I returned to folding the laundry.

When I came downstairs after putting things away, my father was standing by the woodstove, whiskey bottle clutched in his left hand. He turned, his face expressionless and his glassy eyes looking dead. I realized he was most likely in a blackout, so I had better get out as fast as possible.

No sooner had I turned to run, than he grabbed me and started screaming obscenities, accusing me of being my mother and ruining his life. Before I could say anything to defend myself, he raised the bottle and swung it at me. That was the last thing I remembered until my aunt took me to New Orleans.

****

I shook my head and moved toward the front door, unsure what I'd do if he no longer lived here. I hadn't considered how I'd get into the house if it was locked up, but there was nothing to worry about. The door was half rotten and ajar, allowing me to slip into the house easily.

I looked around the hallway before entering the kitchen, thankful I didn't have to clean up the disaster spread everywhere. Beer cans and bottles mixed with filthy cans that once held beans, vegetables and canned stew, were piled everywhere, flies clustering on and above most of them. The smell wasn't horrible, but the word despair immediately came to mind. I could hear snoring coming from the living room, so I headed that way.

What I'd seen in the first two rooms was nothing compared to what met my eyes when I stepped through the doorway. The piles of cans and bottles were higher here and cigarette butts filled most of them. The door leading to the cellar was gone and it looked like the stairs had rotted away.

My father, or what was left of him, lay on a rusty cot. His hair was matted and greasy, hanging to his shoulders. The jeans and t-shirt he wore looked so filthy I doubted they could be removed without a pair of scissors. His complexion was a sickly gray and aside from the hard pot belly, common to chronic alcoholics, his body had withered to almost nothing. If I could have felt pity, I would have.

He must have sensed my presence. His eyes shuddered open and he looked around dazedly until spotting me. He didn't exactly scream, but the sound he uttered was painful and filled with fear. I wasn't exactly surprised.

"You! You're ..." He didn't say anything more, struggling to his feet instead.

I waited to see what he'd do next. Even after all this time, I didn't exactly know what I'd get from him. I knew what I wanted, what I needed, but had no idea whether I'd get either.

He bent over, grabbing a whiskey bottle, then flinging it at me when he realized it was empty. The look on his face when it passed through me and shattered on the wall, told me what little sanity he possessed had left the building. He looked past me as if gauging whether he could escape, then whirled and stumbled to the cellar entrance. He let out a brief scream before hitting the concrete below.

I didn't need to check to see if he was dead, nor did I feel anything. The man Aunt Lizette took me, or more accurately, my ashes to, months before had spoken like I could hear and understand him. It had been his ritual that had awakened me from endless darkness and set me on this journey to finish things so I could finally be free. What happened to my father's spirit was the least of my concerns. I moved through the kitchen, past the hallway. When I reached the outside door, I didn't hesitate and moved into the solitary ray of light waiting to free me forever.

END

Edited By Jake Devlin

The 2019 BOULD Awards Anthology

The Purloined Pickled Peppers

Herschel Cozine (~2400 words)

Hi. Nathaniel P. Osgood III here. I own a detective agency in Nurseryland. I have solved many a mystery involving the inhabitants, such as Humpty Dumpty, Mother Hubbard and Little Bo Peep. Did you know that the little man who wasn't there wasn't at a lot of places? He wasn't seen at Peter Pan Airport just last week. I lost a lot of sleep trying to solve that case.

But I digress. You've all heard of Sasha Simpson, I'm sure. She is the girl who has a seashell business down at the beach. She deals with tourists, primarily, and makes a pretty good living at it. Well, her cousin, Peter Piper, is quite another story. It seems he had a bit of trouble with his boss, who owns a pickled pepper farm. He picked a peck of pickled peppers, but nobody seems to know what happened to them. I can go even further. I don't even know what pickled peppers are—at least not ones that you would pick from a plant. (For all I know, peppers could grow on vines, but that would ruin the alliteration). I was under the impression that peppers were pickled *after* they were picked. Live and learn.

Nevertheless, as the story goes, Peter's peck of pickled peppers disappeared and a search failed to turn them up. Now, I know this isn't a particularly disastrous event. After all, a peck is less than a bushel, and certainly one could survive the loss of a few peppers.

It turns out, there was considerably more than a single peck of peppers involved. It just goes to show, you can't believe everything you read. But let me start at the beginning. To do anything else would require flashbacks, and that gets confusing.

I had just finished up the Peter Pumpkineater case and was feeling pretty good about it. I ran, (or more correctly "staggered") my morning mile and was nursing my organic drink at Priscilla's Papaya Palace. I can't say I was enjoying the drink. Have you ever tasted a cucumber slurpee? But I felt virtuous. Besides which I would pig out on spareribs and Krispy Kremes for dinner.

I looked up from my table to see a man walking toward me with a sense of purpose. He was a rotund man with protruding ears and puckered mouth that gave him a look of petulance. In short, a purposeful, portly, protruding, puckered, petulant person.

"Mr. Osgood?" he asked.

I nodded, swallowed the last of my slurpee, and made a face.

"My name is Pennfield," the man said. "Patrick Pennfield. Forgive the intrusion, but your secretary said I would find you here."

I waved a hand toward the empty chair. He accepted with a thankful smile, sat down heavily and sighed.

"I own a pickled pepper farm just outside of town. You may know where it is. It's across the street from Mary's garden. You know, the one with the cockle shells."

"I know the place," I said.

I also grow peaches, plums. pomegranates, pears and apples."

I frowned at the last.

"Pippins, of course," he explained.

"Of course," I agreed, and waited for him to continue.

"Well," he said, an apologetic smile on his puckered lips. "My problem may seem trivial, and for awhile I overlooked it. But it continued, so I decided to come to you for help."

"What is the problem?" I asked.

Pennfield looked around the room, leaned across the table, and said in a conspiratorial voice, "Peter's pickled peppers keep getting lost."

My face must have registered a total lack of comprehension,

because Pennfield added hastily, "Peter Piper is one of my pepper pickers. I have several, and they get paid by the peck. Every time they bring a peck of pickled peppers to the end of the row, they are given a ticket. At the end of the day, the men exchange the tickets for money." He paused to see if I was following all of this. I was. Sort of.

"Each ticket is worth fifty cents," he said. "A good worker can earn fifteen dollars a day. That's thirty pecks," he added, just in case I was deficient in math.

"Did you say *pickled* peppers?" I asked.

He sat up proudly. "Yes. You see I have developed a secret formula that pickles the peppers while they are still on the plant. It is economical and saves time as well." He pulled a label from his pocket and dropped it on the table. I picked it up and read it.

Pennfield Pre-Pickled Peppers. (Patent Pending).

"How nice," I said.

Pennfield pocketed the label and his voice grew serious. "Well, as I was saying, at first the problem of disappearing peppers was trivial. A few missing peppers at the end of the day was not a concern to me." He waved a hand as if shooing away a bothersome fly. "I'm not one to quibble over minor discrepancies. But the problem persists, and I feel as though I am being played for a fool."

"So," I said. "Are you telling me there are not enough pickled peppers at the end of the day?"

"That's right," Pennfield said. "Yesterday Peter came up short again. He had twenty-nine tickets at the end of the day, but when I measured the pickles in the bin, there were only twenty-six pecks worth."

I frowned. "What bin are you referring to?"

Pennfield went on to explain. "You see, the pickers show me the peck of peppers and I give them a ticket. Then they empty the contents into a large bin. Each picker is assigned his own bin. It makes bookkeeping easier," he said without explanation. I took his word for it.

"Do you watch them empty the pecks?" I asked.

"Not as a rule," Pennfield answered. "But I have been watching Piper lately, just in case he wasn't emptying the basket completely."

"And?"

"I didn't see anything amiss," he admitted.

"But you think he is cheating you?" I asked.

"I *know* he is," Pennfield said. "And it's been going on for quite awhile." He stuck his lip out in an exaggerated pout, and I immediately added that to my "P" list of descriptions for the man. "I hadn't paid much attention in the past," he went on, "but his bin always seemed to be slightly less full than the others."

"There isn't a whole lot of money involved here," I said. "My fees will be far more than that."

Pennfield stood up. "I don't care," he said. "I will not tolerate being cheated. But I can't do anything until I can prove it." He rubbed his nose, (or in this case, his "proboscis"). Then, his face registering concern, he added, "How much do you charge?"

I named a figure and he blanched. But my curiosity was aroused and I was interested in taking the case even if it meant cutting my fees.

"Tell you what," I said. "I'll look into this for you for free." Pennfield's face relaxed.

"However," I went on. "If I am successful I would want the opportunity of buying stock in your company at an attractive option price, like fifty cents a share." I stood up and stretched.

"That's equivalent to a peck of pickled peppers. Appropriate, don't you agree?"

Pennfield frowned in thought, then nodded. "That can be

arranged," he said.

I agreed to meet him at the pepper farm the following day. He put on his Panama hat and Polaroid sunglasses and adjusted his paisley tie.

"Do you drive a Pontiac?" I asked.

He turned to me with a look of surprise on his face. "Why, yes. How did you know?"

"Lucky guess," I said. "It could just as easily have been a Plymouth."

"That's my wife's car," he replied with a hint of admiration in his voice.

I smiled inwardly. Well, it wasn't difficult. He didn't look like a Porsche man, and they quit making Packards years ago.

I arrived at the pickled pepper farm about ten the following morning. Pennfield was seated at a table on the edge of the field. Several people were in the field, stooped over and picking peppers as fast as they could. From time to time one of the pickers would come up to the table where Pennfield sat, collect a ticket and empty his basket into a bin.

"Which one is Peter?" I asked.

Pennfield pointed to a man about three rows away. The man was stooped over, picking peppers and putting them in a basket. Now, I am familiar with bushel baskets, but had never seen a peck basket. It was considerably smaller than I had envisioned it.

I strolled over to Peter and stood with my hands in my pockets. I watched for a few minutes as he deftly picked the peppers from the bush and tossed them into the basket. The peppers were smaller than the ones I was accustomed to seeing in the supermarket. And they were ugly; shriveled and brown. I guess that is what the pickling does to an otherwise respectable pepper.

Peter finished the bush he was working on, stood up and

looked my way.

"Who are you?" he said.

"A friend of Pennfield's," I lied. Private eyes are good at that. It's a requirement.

Peter stiffened at the pronouncement and he stooped down next to another pepper plant. "What do you want?" he asked.

"Nothing," I said. "I was just curious. I've never seen anyone pick peppers before."

Peter laughed. "It's not exactly rocket science," he said. "In fact, it's boring. And poor paying."

"Fifty cents a basket?" I said,

Peter nodded. "You got it." He waved to the others in the field. "We tried to get old Penny Pincher Pennfield to pay us sixty cents a peck. He wouldn't hear of it. We even tried fifty-five."

I mumbled sympathetically, reached down and picked up an empty basket. Peter eyed me nervously as I inspected it. It was a typical basket made of flat woven wood of some kind, with a metal loop on each side to serve as handles. This particular basket had a hole about half an inch in diameter in the bottom.

"What's this for?"

Peter shrugged. "I dunno."

"Do all of the baskets have these holes?"

He shrugged again. "How should I know? I never paid any attention."

"Does the one you just filled have a hole in it?"

Peter's face reddened. "What difference does it make?" he said.

"I'm not sure," I replied. I walked over to the next row, found an empty basket and picked it up. It was identical to the basket that Peter had, except there was no hole in the bottom. I dropped it and went back to Peter's row. He wasn't there. I looked around to see him collecting a ticket from Pennfield. Then he went over to a bin and poured the peppers in. I watched as he pulled something from the basket and put it in his pocket. I was too far away to determine what it was, or if it were anything at all for that matter.

He strolled back to where I was standing and dropped the basket next to a pepper plant. I picked it up and inspected it. There was a hole in the center.

Peter grabbed the basket out of my hand. "Do you mind?" he said. "I'm trying to work here."

I had seen enough. I was pretty certain how Peter was cheating Pennfield. But I would have to wait awhile before I could prove it.

I let a week go by before returning to the pickle farm. Pennfield greeted me with an air of impatience. "Where have you been?" he asked.

I didn't answer. Spotting Peter, I sauntered over to him and watched as he picked peppers. His basket was almost full. He stood up, arched his back and yawned.

"You again," he said. "Are you still trying to figure out how to pick peppers?"

"No," I said. "I'm just trying to determine how you pick fewer peppers than you get credit for."

Peter started to say something. Taking my pocketknife from my pocket, I reached down and stuck it into the peck of peppers. A sharp "pop" sounded, and a few peppers jumped from the basket to the ground.

"Wha...?" Peter shouted, grabbing me by the arm.

Pennfield, roused by the noise, rushed over to where we were standing.

"What was that?" he asked.

"The missing peppers," I said. I picked the basket up, turned it over and let the peppers spill out. What remained was a small bit of rubber protruding through the hole in the basket.

"A balloon," I said. "Peter would put a deflated balloon in the basket with the neck through the hole. Then he would blow it up and fill the basket with peppers. After showing you the basket and getting his ticket, he would let the air out of the balloon as he emptied the peppers into the bin, take it out and put it in his pocket. Then he would repeat the process." I looked at Peter. He was glowering at me, and if looks could kill, I wouldn't be telling you this story.

Pennfield whirled on Peter and stuck out his puckered lips. "You're fired!"

Peter shrugged. "If you paid a decent wage, I wouldn't have done this," he said. "And you don't have to fire me. I quit." He whirled and stalked away. (For the record, I heard he went to work for Parcel Post, but it's just a rumor.)

I had lunch with Pennfield the next day. We went to Papa Pietro's Pizza Parlor where Pennfield ordered a pizza. Pepperoni, of course. He was grateful for my solving the case and sprung for the tab.

I got my stock options. But it was not a good investment. Within six months, the stock dropped to twenty-five cents a share, and shortly after that it went bankrupt. I was left with 1000 shares of worthless stock in my portfolio. Pathetic. Pitiful. Preposterous. You get the idea.

Pennfield started a new company. Pre-dried prunes. He offered me a chance to invest. I decided against it. Naturally it prospered and Pennfield sold out for millions. He's now retired and living in—where else—Pago Pago. Sasha Simpson? She's living in Sarasota, of course. But she's thinking of moving to the West Coast. San Simeon.

END

The 2019 BOULD Awards Anthology

Edited By Jake Devlin

The 2019 BOULD Awards Anthology

Eggboy and the Drunk

Lise de Nil (~2990 words)

I've inherited the worst of my mother's madness but the woman next door is crazy as a peach orchard boar and a drunk on top of that.

She shrieks in ungodly outrage at the injustice of her tedious life. Either that or she's having an orgasm of monumental note.

"What went wrong?" I asked the man from India who lives on our other side.

"She was fine," he said, his voice lyrical, "married a schoolteacher, had three kids, then she lost her mind. Her husband up and left one day, said he couldn't stand the sound of her."

"She needs medication."

"She's got boatloads of that already. But who knows if she takes it. And her drinking binges don't help either, mind you."

The day we moved in, the crazy fiend presented herself to my husband.

"You're parking in my spot," she argued, flirtatiously, she thought.

He came inside, pale.

"I just met the neighbour," he said, "in a blue negligee."

My immediate concern was that she'd have great legs and he'd be jumping her bones before I could say Jack Sprat but he seemed disconcerted, dismayed and when I saw her, I realized why.

"I helped the previous owners sound-proof the bedroom," the Indian man said. His name was Manoj. He lived to the left of us. "I can help you do the rest of the house, if you like."

I thanked him but from the state of his domain, I had my

doubts.

"I am fond of peeling window frames," he said dreamily, "and I know I should fix the barn at the bottom of my garden but I quite like it the way it is."

The barn looked like it dated back to the original construction of the three joined houses, which had been a century ago. It was sagging and folding like a cheap tent.

Manoj's backyard was full of weeds which he dutifully mowed every two weeks. He said the garden had been wonderful once but his girlfriend had left him. He said he knew it all needed attention but if we needed help in installing a new bathroom in our basement, well, that wouldn't be a problem at all.

"How long ago did the husband leave the crazy negligee lady?" I asked.

"Twelve years ago."

"Why didn't he take the children with him?"

"He was not able to cope, would be my guess. Do you and your husband like to watch Formula One racing? I have a very big screen in my living room, you're welcome to join me anytime."

I told him that we did watch and I thanked him, said we'd take him up on it one day.

"What about the squirrels in the roof?" I asked.

Manoj looked tearful and changed the subject..

"What do you think of eggboy?"

"Eggboy?" I was confused.

"The chappie who lives two doors down from me, you must have heard him making his terrible noises?"

"Oh, that guy. I thought I heard a dog barking but one day I made out that he was saying "just don't do it" so fast and so garbled. I waved, to be nice."

Manoj looked disappointed and I tried to make amends.

"I wish they wouldn't hang their underwear out like that," I pointed at the neighbour in between Manoj and the eggboy. I had no idea why Manoj called him eggboy but I'd get to that. "They've got enough panties for the entire street. Who lives with eggboy?"

"His brother. At least, for some of the time. Would you like a lawnmower?"

"Okay," I said. "Thanks."

"Why's he called eggboy?" my husband asked later.

I admitted I had been distracted by the offer of a free lawnmower and had not followed the tale though.

Some days later I saw Manoj.

"How are the crazies on your side?" he asked.

"She's been pretty quiet. Some shrieking, yelling, stair thumping and throwing stuff around but nothing too dramatic. Why do you call that guy eggboy? And why does he make noises like that?"

"He's a schizophrenic and he forgets to take his medication. Would you like some impatients? I bought too many and haven't planted them and they are very nearly dead."

I told him I would love some.

"Wait," he said and disappeared, coming back with some dead little plants.

"Hmmm," I said. "Thank you. Tell me about eggboy."

"Shortly after I moved in, someone started throwing eggs on my car. I, of course, wanted to know who was doing it. So, although it was the middle of winter, I sat outside and watched, all bundled up, but nothing happened. I gave up and then what do you know, there was an egg on my car the very next day. Enough, I thought, and I invested in some spy equipment. I got someone on film but it was hard to see who. Then the neighbour over there, with all the ladies laundry, asked me if I had made any progress and I told her I couldn't make out who the person was. She asked me if the person walked with his hands in his pockets, in a slouchy way and he did! She said it's your neighbour, the schizophrenic.

"I took the tape the police and they went to see him with it and he admitted it was him and when they asked him why he had done it, he said well he didn't like me. He said he would stop doing it. But he is forever Eggboy."

"The other day, he took on the crazy lady."

Manoj looked happy at the prospect of a good neighbourly yarn and leaned back on one elbow.

"I was at home with a migraine and she had been going off her rocker all day, howling, stomping up and down, throwing things. I heard eggboy's voice outside my window, chanting and the next thing I heard the crazy woman open her door and yell at him. He hawked up a gigantic wad and spat on her lawn."

"Really?" Manoj was delighted. "He spat on her lawn? How very rude."

"Yes. Eggboy said he had just been clearing his throat, that she was just imagining things."

"He said all that?" Manoj was intrigued. "How very lucid of him."

"Yes. She lunged at him, it was a sight to see, her in a tatty old negligee, no shoes, her hair matted to one side, no shoes on, cigarette dangling."

"What happened?"

"Eggboy set off down the street with her and I lay back down and ignored them both. But I'll keep an eye on her."

And keep an eye I did. I watched her in her more normal moments as she canvassed the street to assess which neighbours she had antagonized more than others. She dressed in an old-fashioned faded navy bell-skirt and mismatching shirtwaist. She stopped passersby to tell them how she needed money so she rented out her parking spot and how her boyfriend and father were going to fix up the garden.

She did not, however, ever, approach me. Not to introduce herself or apologise or try to ingratiate. And I knew why. Because she knew that I knew her madness and that I had no patience with it or with her.

I stood by while she swung her hips like a small girl, waved her hand and cocked one dirty bare foot behind the other, the girlish gestures terrible when costumed in that aged body, those clothes, that unreachable place to which her mind had escaped.

"But what of her children," I asked Manoj, "how many does she have again?"

"Three," he said.

"She shouldn't be allowed," I said. "How come no one has stopped her?"

"Because mothers have the right of way. We are chained by umbilical cords all of our lives," Manoj said and a lock of dark hair fell over his face.

The youngest child opened the door the most recent time the police came.

The child murmured apologies, he said his mother wasn't home, he said yes, he would tell her they had called. He was polite, this eight-year-old adult, guilt and shame made him an accomplice to her actions, a furtive alibi for her crimes.

Poor wretched boy, I thought. *Doesn't have a hope in hell.*

I watched the police leave.

-.-

"Daddy, they are shooting people," she said. They were stuck in a bank, held hostage. Amid the gunfire she phoned her father. What did she expect him to do? Rescue her? That fairytale Hollywood fantasy. She was stuck in a bank vault, how could he reach her?

I was stuck in a bank vault, only one way out. My father had the key but he was too far away. And besides, he was busy. Saving my mother. I dreamed that I was drowning but gracefully, in water black, with white lilies that tangled my ankles and decorated my feet.

I have inherited the worst of my mother's madness.

-.-

"I saw the tourettes guy today," my husband said, "I swear I literally caught him with his pants down. He had his hand in his pants and he was definitely jerking off but he stopped when he saw me watching him."

"Do you think he could be dangerous?"

"I wouldn't be surprised."

The next day Manoj passed my window.

"Have you heard him? 'Monkey see, monkey do,' that's his latest thing…"

"Better than the fuck you fuck you of last weekend. I was surprised no one complained."

"Everybody's used to him," he said.

"But there are small kids around. if I had a kid, I would object."

"Do you think he could be dangerous?" I asked Manoj.

"No," he said, "not for as long as he is taking his medications. And when he is off those, it becomes obvious enough and you must just keep out of his way."

We chatted about the squirrels and discussed strategy.

-.-

On Saturday I pulled on my pajamas.

Psycho belle was sounding her ungodly siren wail, thumping up and down the stairs, throwing things, sobbing.

"Enough of this," I said, "it's after midnight. I am calling the police."

My husband agreed.

I called it in and went up to the bedroom window to watch the cops arrive.

But when I looked outside, I saw a limousine instead, a superstretch long white one. A stocky blonde woman was talking loudly into a cell phone.

"He's lying there, just lying there. I was driving him home and he said he felt sick, that I had to stop. So I did, he got out and he collapsed, vomiting and in pain."

I looked over at the corner of the sidewalk opposite.

True enough, lay there a man, early twenties, inert.

"His body temperature has dropped, his core temperature has dropped," a man leaned over him.

A police car drove up.

We all expect our parents to rescue us, I thought.

The cop got out, went over to the boy, an ambulance drove up, more people bent over him.

I couldn't hear clearly what was going on. The lights flashed and the murmuring continued.

Another police car rounded the corner.

Ah, I thought, *it's here to address my issue.*

But it drove down the road.

I went downstairs and out into the street to see eggboy being handcuffed and led to the car. His gaze was staring and wild-eyed, vacant but chock-a-block full of paranoid panic.

"They just took the mad guy away," I called out to my husband who was reading. "And the guy at the corner sidewalk still hasn't got up. The ambulance is still there. But no one has come for our neighbour."

Just then, the limo fired up its engine, flashed its lights a few times like a spacecraft, and took off. The ambulance loaded the guy and left and a sudden quiet filled the street broken by my crazy neighbour, drunk and insane, shouting at a policeman who had pulled up.

"Fuck ya," she yelled. "I am not speaking to ya, I am talking to the other guy. Show me some respect willya. Respect! That's all I ask for! Respect!"

Another police officers got out of the car. He went over to her and bent over, and whatever he said, she quietened down and stood still. She listened to him and nodded. Then she turned and walked back into the house.

-.-

"And that was that," I said to yet another neighbour, Dave. Dave was a large young black man who eyed me appreciatively when he got out of his truck, a large Subway sandwich balanced on top of a pile of newspapers. Dave's a healthcare worker, I've never seen him in anything except his baggy green uniform.

How funny, I thought, when I caught his look, *he finds me attractive.*

"I had to call the cops," Dave said. "Eggboy was staring through the side window, inside my house."

I told my husband about Dave.

"I don't trust that guy at all," he said. "Not Dave, but eggboy or whatever they call him." He looked down the street. "I am telling you he's got that look to him and I saw him with his hands in his pants."

We looked down the hill towards at his house and sure enough there he was, shirtless, with a soft belly hanging over thin beige trackpants. He had a lot of black wiry hair on lizard white skin; he looked like Charles Manson on a bad acid trip.

He looked up at us, I waved. He smiled and waved back.

"Don't encourage him," my husband said, "and keep the doors locked when you go inside."

-.-

I sent my father a message but he pretended he never got it. It's hard to force someone to read the writing on the wall when they're staring at their feet.

Daddy, come and get me, she said, *I'm locked in the trunk of my car. They've got me held for ransom, I managed to get my phone out, I really don't have long. I know you will find me, I really need you this time.*

Oh, she says that so often, her father said, *she just wants attention, I'm busy with my wife instead. It's just so tiring, it's a ruse you'll see, she's done this before, just wait and see. I am tired of playing her games, I won't send the money again.*

-.-

Then one day I was home, my head filled with pain and fear.

Through the fog in my head I heard shouting. Eggboy was standing on the crazy woman's lawn. He was barking and his hand was down his pants. She flew out, and started hitting him with her fists, howling. She wore an old sweater, nothing else.

Oh man, I thought, *I'd better phone someone fast.*

I ran down the stairs, still holding my phone, still listening to an automatic voice. When I got outside eggboy and the crazy woman had vanished and the voice asked me what I wanted to do.

I requested an operator, enunciating so carefully I nearly sounded automatic and dead myself. My head was throbbing like a watermelon wired with explosives, the sunlight lancing my eyes like needles.

"Come soon," I said, "this time it's really bad."

I paused at the screen door of her house, amid the weeds of her garden. I pushed the door open and heard the animal grunts.

"Fuck you fuck you," he said but it sounded like a dogs bark.

I waded through mountains of kids' junk, an Everest of broken things, distracted by a dirty pink satin sofa covered in a patchwork of stains. Sagging, worn and filthy fabric, all I could see were those stains.

But not for long.

She was there on the floor, he had her pinned down, his trousers around his knees.

He was dry humping her knee, his penis flaccid and small. It looked like he was doing pushups over her, his hands pinning down her arms.

Her face was turned towards me, her eyes wide. She was looking straight into me, right through me. She did not move but a long strand of saliva trailed from her open mouth onto the floor.

"Stop!" I whispered. "The police are coming, I phoned them – see – here is my phone, stop!"

My crazy neighbour was a rag doll thrown from side to side. Her eyes were closed now and her dreadful knotted hair stuck to her face. Her old grey sweater rode right up her breasts and her feet were filthy.

"I called the police," I whispered.

I don't know how long it went on. Then there was a knock at the door. A knock – why didn't they come right in? It took forever to reach the door and I was so afraid they would leave. I opened the door babbling and tugged them inside.

My crazy neighbour lay on the floor, unmoving. She opened her eyes and stared for a while then she seemed to prefer the darkness instead.

The officers cuffed eggboy and led him away.

One of the officers pulled the crazy woman's sweater down but it didn't cover enough. I looked around and grabbed an old crocheted knee rug off the old sofa and laid it over her. I knelt down beside her. I thought I should touch her, try to comfort her in some way but I didn't know how to begin.

She opened her eyes and looked at me. She looked right at me and she knew. She smiled like she knew me and all the secrets I thought I hid so well. She sighed, closed her eyes and left me alone before I could tell her she was wrong. We were nothing alike, because my daddy will save me, and everything would all be alright.

END

Edited By Jake Devlin

The 2019 BOULD Awards Anthology

The Price You Pay

William A. Rush IV (~1,850 words}

I am walking on the beach. Beside me, holding my hand is a breathtaking brunette. Ocean waves gently breaking on the sand to my right. It is serene and peaceful. To our left are rolling dunes of sand. Although it is clearly not desert, but beach, there are no trees in sight. The sky is cloudless, and the sun casts its warm pleasant rays on everything.

We walk along, in silence, until she puts her smooth hand on my cheek and turns me to face her. She opens her mouth to speak, but I hear only the waves. She stops trying to speak, and looks at me expectantly.

"What? I can't hear you over the waves!" I say.

Her mouth moves again. I strain to hear her, but all I hear is the ocean. I am frustrated. There are no crashing waves, and I hear them only when she tries to speak. She tries again; this time, she yells. I hear waves crashing into rocks, as they do at a cliff, but there are none.

She finally gives up, and we begin walking again. Cliffs form from the smooth sand of the beach. The sun begins to fade. Not as if it were setting, but how the ground slowly disappears when it snows. A haze surrounds us, and I can no longer see her. The waves roar in my ears.

I no longer feel the soft touch of her hand in mine. The rhythmic lapping of the waves becomes a trilling sort of music. The music changes once more as the darkness envelops me. The beep-beep-beep in my ears is faster and more rhythmic.

Edited By Jake Devlin

"This is a Special Report," a man says. "Angela Camen is on scene for a Special Report."

#

The cool embrace of the enveloping haze intensifies briefly, I get the floating feeling of falling. The way a feather gently floats to the earth.

I am no longer falling, I've gently come to rest in a soft warmth. I open my eyes. My vision is hazy, like how it must be for someone who wears glasses, when they first wake up in the morning. Gradually, my vision clears.

"This is Angela Camen, with Channel Ten. I am coming to you live from St. Ann's Mental Hospital, where an hour ago, three patients made a daring escape. In the process, they killed a guard. Two of the escaped patients have been captured, one is still at large."

I don't need to hear any more so I tune it out. My stomach is in knots. I know it's my ex-wife, Janey. She will be coming here, coming home. Fear grips me. For myself, and for our daughter, Nell. I remember that Nell is at a birthday party. I will need to call Diane Somers, the mother of Nell's friend.

I vaguely remember the trial. What I do recall clearly is the last night Janey and I spent together. Part of it anyway.

#

I had come home from my job at Sears, where I sell electronics. Commission only. It's been a bad day. The way an oasis in the desert must be most of the time, with only the occasional wanderer stopping for a drink. Here, though, the drink is catching a snippet of TV while waiting on a wife or a girlfriend. No interest in buying anything.

When I arrived home at 11:15, I made myself a cup of herbal tea, then watched a little SportsCenter. After finishing my tea, I went up to bed. I was tired, and my feet hurt. When I got to the bedroom, Janey called out from the bathroom.

"There's a bottle of champagne on the dresser, pour us each a glass, please. I'm just going to take a quick shower," she said.

That got me excited. It was too long since we'd had sex. Janey was a bombshell. At five-foot four, she didn't weigh over a hundred pounds soaking wet. Firm in all the right places, with long, silky blonde hair.

I undressed quickly, already hard, from the thought of being inside her. When she was in the mood, she was insatiable. When she wasn't, she was violent. I shook off the thought. I might as well enjoy the good wife for a change.

I took the bottle from the ice bucket and poured two glasses. The bottle was unwrapped, but still corked. I drank my bubbly, poured another, then set both glasses on the night-stand.

I turned off the lamp on my side and laid down on the bed. There was a searing pain behind my eyes. Then nothing. The next thing I knew, there were cops at the front door, with a warrant for Janey's arrest. The charge was Murder. The victim was Melissa, Nell's daycare provider.

Janey used to accuse me of cheating on her. I never did that. I still couldn't believe she had fallen in love with me. She even accused me of cheating with a telemarketer, and it was a man.

#

Herbal tea will help calm your nerves. I get up from my easy chair and walk into the kitchen. As I cross the foyer, I notice the front door is open. The sky outside is filled with glorious oranges and reds from the setting sun. In the corner of the sky are dark, tumultuous clouds. A storm is brewing. I am disappointed, but not surprised, to see that there are no cops watching the house.

I close and lock the door. A hint of musk fills the air. Janey liked that smell and wore it often. I take my cell phone to the kitchen. After putting the kettle on, I pick Diane on my contact list, but cannot get a signal. Not unusual, but unsettling. I try the land-line, and it's dead too. I put a tea bag in my mug. After the water boils, I'll try the cell again.

While I wait, I watch the shadows, created by the street lamp shining in through the window over the sink. I am getting all worked up over nothing. The news didn't give a name, and there's no contact from or presence of cops. Hell, if it is Janey, she'd have to be crazy to come here. What am I thinking? She is crazy. That's why she was there in the first place! My temples throb.

I jump when the kettle whistles. I really am skittish. I shut off the burner, pour the water, and let it steep. I pour in honey and stir.

#

The aspirin is upstairs. I hear footsteps at the top of the stairs. The light switch doesn't work.. No sound comes from the television either. The storms aren't even here yet; the power should be on. Cautiously, I make my way up the stairs. As long as I don't get blind sided, I should be able to deal with her. After all, she's a little thing. Unless she has a gun.

At the top of the stairs, the guest room is to the left; Nell's room and her bathroom are down the hall to the right. It's forward to my bedroom, and I grope the wall for the door handle. It turns easily and opens wide. Streetlight is coming in from the window. I can see to find my way now.

My head no longer hurts. I sip my tea, which is still hot and somehow doesn't taste right. Across the bedroom, I push open the bathroom door. The shower is running, filling the bathroom with steam.

Setting the tea down on the counter, I notice the word ADULTERER, written in the steam on the mirror. I jerk open the shower door to confront Janey, but she's not there. The shower isn't even turned on. However, the bathtub is full of blood, with bits and pieces of flesh floating in it.

My legs give out, and I stumble backwards. I attempt to catch my balance, but only manage to spill my tea. My body turns as I fall. My head hits the toilet bowl, and I black out.

#

A woman's sobbing wakes me. I'm no longer laying on the cold, hard bathroom floor, but on my bed. There's a sharp pain in my wrists and ankles. I open my eyes to nothing but darkness. I need to rub my eyes, but I can't move my arms.

The woman's sobbing gets louder. I'm naked and cold. My penis is hard, and I realize this woman is giving me a blow job. Janey is into some kinky shit, but this beats all.

I hear her to my left. "What are you crying for, you stupid whore? It's not like it's the first time you've sucked my Dicky."

The woman is sniffling, and her snot is running onto me. As she continues what she is doing, her crying gets louder.

"Janey, what the fuck?" I yell.

"Shut up, adulterer. Don't you want your whore from the daycare anymore?"

"What? Janey? I've been faithful to you."

"LIAR! ADULTERER!" she screams. "Get on and ride him now!"

The woman stops sucking me. I can hear her trying to wipe the snot from her nose.

"Melissa! You Bitch! Ride my Dicky. Ride him cowgirl!"

Melissa climbs on clumsily, but I slide right in. I cant remember when I've been so hard, or so fucking scared.

"You're F U C K I N G CRAZY, Janey!" She slaps my face hard; the sting is incredible.

Edited By Jake Devlin

Melissa, Nell's daycare provider, is an attractive brunette, but I'd never considered cheating on Janey. Melissa is riding me, trying to whoop like a cowgirl through sobs and snot. With every bounce, the handcuffs cut deeper into my wrists.

"Make him come in you, BITCH!" Janey yells. She's at the foot of the bed, behind Melissa.

I can feel it happening. There's nothing I can do to stop it, because it feels so good. But, I'm frightened half out of my mind. I realize that she means to kill us, and I can't stop her.

"Janey! Janey!" I cry.

I finished, and as terrible as this is, I have my most powerful orgasm. It must be the adrenaline of knowing I'm as good as dead. Melissa falls forward onto my chest, showering my face with a hot, bitter liquid.

"This is the price for adultery," Janey whispers into my left ear.

Cold steel presses against my throat. There's excruciating pain. Blood gushes from my neck. Gradually, the pain starts to lessen and my lungs no longer fight for air.

#

I'm walking on a beach, and a beautiful brunette holds my hand. The water is cold and refreshing as it laps at our feet.

She stops and faces me. I recognize Melissa.

"Did you ever think death would be so peaceful?" she asks. Her voice is soft and soothing.

"No," I say. I can think of nothing else.

"I am glad that you understand me now," she says.

Her soft hand grabs hold of mine and we continue walking along the beach.

END

The 2019 BOULD Awards Anthology

Edited By Jake Devlin

The 2019 BOULD Awards Anthology

Henry The Butler

Francis Hicks (~500 words)

You lay there all day long in that hammock wearing tight shorts and a halter top, too shy to ask me to climb in with you, to nuzzle your downy neck, to caress—

"Henry?"

"Yes, madame?"

"Be a darling and bring me some of that sun-brewed tea, will you?"

"Right away." *Tea and me. I'll spit in it and imagine it slithering through your throat, followed by my tongue.*

Henry brought tea, the glass sweating in the heat, dew sliding onto the silver tray that bore it. "Your tea, madame. Sugar?" *You'll be sweet on me after I give you what you really want.*

"Yes please. You're such a great friend to me."

He nodded, expression neutral, bored. *Friend? Much more, you randy bitch.*

"My pillow is too soft. Fetch me a firmer one, would you, Henry?"

You'd like my firmness. "Yes, ma'am. Right away."

Henry walked to the house and returned, fondling an embroidered pillow from the settee. "Here you are." *Nice and firm, just like your breasts.*

The woman pulled the pillow she was using from under her head and held it out to Henry. He took it and turned away, holding the prize to his nostrils. *Ooohh... you want me so much.*

Miss Jones dozed, shallow breaths sussing in and out. After a few minutes, she stirred, then bolted up. "Henry, are you here?"

Calling to me from your dreams? "Yes, ma'am. At your

Edited By Jake Devlin

service."

Miss Jones smiled at Henry. "Such a loyal servant."

The butler bowed but didn't return the smile. "Begging your pardon, Ma'am."

"Yes?"

"Do you have what you need?" *Other than me inside you.* "May I take my leave for lunch?"

"Bring another lime when you come back, will you? Lime in the tea is what I really want. Lime is sublime." Miss Jones chuckled at her word play. "I believe I'll take a nap. Please don't disturb me."

Henry bowed then strode across the grass to the kitchen. *Oh, you're a fine one all right. Loyal? I'm your faithful servant. I'll meet all of your needs, you sexy slut.*

He fetched his lunch from the refrigerator and a filet knife from the wood block on the counter. He set his sandwich on a plate and trimmed the crusts, then sliced it into fussy triangles. *I'll slide into your triangle. You'd beg for it except for your upbringing. I know exactly what you crave.*

Henry slipped the knife into his trouser pocket. After he ate, he grabbed a lime from the basket on the counter and returned to the gazebo where the lady of the house lay still, asleep on the hammock. He caressed her from her nose to her ankles with his gaze. His cock stiffened as he pulled the knife from his pocket. He made short work of the lime on the tray, gently squeezing its juice into Miss Jones's tea.

Smile, Miss Jones. You're finally going to get what you really want.

END

The 2019 BOULD Awards Anthology

Edited By Jake Devlin

1st Place

Steve Shrott

The 2019 BOULD Awards Anthology

Case #22--The Mystery of the Missing Albino
Steve Shrott (~2,800 words)

I hung up the phone and looked at my partner, wondering how to tell him the bad news. You don't want to piss off a five foot tall mountain gorilla. "Walter Hardy called."

Toby raised his enormous hairy arms and signed, "What jerk want?"

"Toby, be nice."

He looked away, seeming to be sorry for what he said.

"I have something to tell you. Promise you won't get upset." I stared into his soulful brown eyes. "It's Jennifer. She's missing."

Toby stopped breathing for a moment and leaped onto my desk. He banged his fists against his chest, grunted like he was about to rip my head off.

"Okay, off the desk, mister. Now."

He gave me a sour look. He could definitely take me. I guess the mutual respect we had built up kicked in. His face pointed downward like a six-year-old pouting, and he hopped onto the ground.

I understood his pain. We all had feelings about the dames we'd left behind.

Years earlier, Toby and Jennifer, in the forests of the Congo, had been quite an item. He'd always been a closed book about it. He was a gentleman that way.

Toby signed, "Must find."

I wanted to locate her for Toby's sake. However, that wasn't the mandate of The Rod Masterson and Associates Detective Agency. Our bread and butter is infidelity cases. "That's not what we do, bud."

His body slumped, then he asked when I planned on changing our name to Toby and Associates.

I rolled my eyes. Not again. I decided I wouldn't lecture him this time because I knew he hurt. "Alright, we'll take the damn case."

Toby's mouth opened in a wide smile, showing off his sharp, arctic-white teeth.

#

Walter Hardy, administrator at The Ridley Zoo, looked the same as always—perfect posture, his head shaved, a ring on his left ear that an African tribesman had presented him with on his last expedition.

"Thanks for coming, guys."

"Happy to help, Walt."

I sat on the leather couch in his small artifact-filled office. Toby plopped down beside me, as Hardy explained what happened to Jennifer.

"As you know, we housed her in a separate habitat from the other gorillas. We dressed it up with Jackalberry Trees, Bushwillows, a long winding stream, so she'd be reminded of the Congo. This morning she disappeared. I'm not sure if the keeper just left the door open, and she decided to explore, or something more nefarious. It's not the first time animals have gone missing, but Jennifer, being a rare albino, is very important to the zoo."

"When did it happen?"

"Yesterday night sometime."

Toby signed. I nodded.

"What did he say?" asked Hardy.

"He wonders whether all her toys are still there."

"I believe they are. What does that matter?"

"The thing is, it takes gorillas a while to feel at home in a new location. If she left on her own, she would have taken something to make herself feel comfortable. In this case, one of the toys. If she didn't grab anything, it means Jennifer was probably abducted."

Hardy pursed his lips. "Not what I was hoping for."

"I'd like to take a look at her habitat."

"Sure, here's the key." He handed it to me, peeked at his watch. "Larry, the keeper, should be down there to feed the animals if you have any questions."

I wasn't looking forward to seeing Larry. He and Toby had a long troublesome history.

Toby and I headed down the grass pathway toward the primate section. When the other gorillas in their cages noticed us, they made sounds that could have meant anything from "how you doing?" to "you're dead meat." I could see Toby's anxiety kick in. I guess it reminded him of those painful days at Gentech Research. He had been housed in a crowded, dirty cage with numerous other primates subjected to horrific experiments. Toby slipped his hand in mine.

When we reached Jennifer's habitat, I opened the door and Toby entered. I didn't. He got upset if I tried to infringe on his work. In his own way, he had a PhD in primate psychology.

He picked up Jennifer's toys one by one—a rubber duck, a felt teddy bear, a plastic cup with the words, "Make Love Not War" that Jennifer seemed to take a special interest in. He moved them around in his hands, examining them closely. Then he ambled over to each corner of the habitat and sniffed.

He exited and signed, "Humans in cage."

I raised an eyebrow. "Besides Larry?"

Toby formed his hand into a fist and moved it up and down, signifying, yes.

"This is bigger than we thought, Tobe."

A moment later, Larry showed up, his dirty blonde hair almost covering his eyes. He always appeared rumpled like he hadn't slept since the nineties.

"What do you and your stupid monkey want?"

I knew Toby was burning, but somehow he controlled himself.

Edited By Jake Devlin

"Easy Larry. Just need to ask a few questions about Jennifer."

"Just make sure it's you that asks the questions, not that dumbass with his creepy sign language."

I could see Toby getting ready to pummel a delicate section of Larry's anatomy. I rested my hand on Toby's shoulder. "You have any idea what happened to Jennifer?"

"No clue."

"When's the last time you saw her?"

"Yesterday at feeding time."

"When was that?"

"Six, give or take."

"You locked the door?"

"I always lock it. I ain't no half-wit ape."

Toby started breathing heavy. A bad omen. In a flash he pushed Larry hard against the cage door, grabbed his throat.

"Toby, let go," I yelled. "Now."

He held Larry a moment longer, then a breath sailed through his lips and he released him. Larry dropped to the ground.

He got to his feet looking dazed like he just awakened from a year-long coma.

"Masterson, you got one crazy ape there. I'd have him put down if I were you."

Toby grunted. Larry walked away.

I turned to my partner, "Was that really necessary?"

He didn't answer, just got into the van.

As the two us drove home, I reiterated the rules of 'The Rod Masterson and Associates Detective Agency.' "We never use unnecessary violence. We maintain control at all times. Most importantly, we work as a team."

Toby signed. "Jerk."

I stared at him. "Larry or me?"

He didn't answer, leaving me to figure out who he meant.

By the time, we reached home, I had forgiven him and we discussed the case.

"Larry lie."

"About what?"

"Knows who."

"He knows who did it? Are you sure?"

"Eyes left."

Toby had learned from watching humans at Gentech that when their eyes moved left they were usually telling him an untruth. Like when they promised he wouldn't receive any more electric shocks.

"Great job, Toby."

We decided it would be a good idea to follow Larry. After a heated debate, I convinced Toby, I should go alone.

I trailed Larry to El Segundo, a dingy bar near the docks.

Bullet holes permeated the front door, and when you entered, you were greeted by a stained carpet, paint-peeling walls and murky lighting. I'm sure most of the hopped up clientele didn't notice.

Larry sat at one of the tables beside a man with a sallow complexion and a ponytail. After a few moments, they shook hands as if they had sealed some kind of deal. Larry left, and the man stayed behind drinking what looked to be a Singapore Sling.

I decided to pump the guy for information and took a seat at his table. "I understand you're looking for some good stuff."

"Don't know what you're talking about."

"I know you spoke to Larry from the zoo. Whatever he's selling, I can get you faster, cheaper."

He thought a moment, then a crooked smile crossed his face. "My boss is always looking for a better deal. What do you have?"

"Well...uh..." I was fumbling, having no clue what he talked to Larry about. It didn't matter because a moment later, Ponytail Guy looked over my shoulder. When I turned, a fist collided with my nose. I went down like a body in the Pacific with a lead pipe attached.

I woke up in an alley to the migraine-inducing sounds of an out-of-tune mariachi band playing at some low-rent Mexican club. I touched my head, felt liquid I assumed to be blood. I forced myself up, headed toward the van.

I got home at one in the morning. I crept in, hoping not to awaken Toby. But he was up, and not happy when he saw the dried red stuff on my forehead.

"You hurt."

"I'm okay."

He stared at me a moment, then went into the corner, closed his eyes and sulked. He stayed there all evening. I'd become like a father, and perhaps mother to him, and he couldn't take it when things got rough.

When the sun dappled through my window in the morning, however, I found a warm body nestled beside me on the bed.

I made breakfast. Bacon and eggs for me, thirty pieces of fruit and veggies for Toby.

I knew I needed to go back to El Segundo tonight, and find out more about Ponytail Guy. I told Toby I was heading out for groceries.

When I got to the bar, I ordered a beer and chugged half the bottle down. I turned toward the overly-tanned bartender. "A man with a ponytail was here last night. Who is he?"

The bartender gave me a look as if I were yesterday's trash. "I ain't no information desk, bub."

I removed a fifty from my pocket, tossed it onto the bar.

He snatched it up like a starving squirrel finding a nut. "Names, Gordon Ledal."

"What's he do?"

"All I know is he works for Max Franco."

"Head of the Franco Crime Family?"

He nodded.

"Where can I find him?"

"You don't. He finds you. And if he does, you're a dead man."

I thought about that as I picked up a newspaper outside the bar. The headline story was all about Arlin Winters, a senator who wanted to shut down the importation of exotic animals.

He had been murdered.

I figured Franco was behind it.

I stopped at the alley beside the Croyden Diner to see Tommy, a snitch I sometimes use. I gave him a few bills, and he told me Franco had a business office on Warner -- Tico Investments.

"I'm going to check Tico out tonight," I told Toby when I arrived home.

He didn't say a word. But later when I opened the door to leave, I sensed him shadowing me. I turned around, gave it to him straight. "This is dangerous. It requires a bit of finesse. I'm handling it alone."

His nostrils flared and he made snorting sounds. He raced through the house tossing everything in sight--books, lamps, my desk. He even punched a hole in the wall.

I'd had it. I was tired of all the tantrums. I just couldn't seem to make him understand. "I'm thinking you're never gonna be a team player. Maybe you should move on."

He made a "whatever" gesture though I could see the watery eyes. I slammed the door shut and left.

Tico Investments was a small storefront located in Willowbrook Park, an industrial area. It was closed, and appeared empty. I took out my Slim Jim, eased open the door and ambled inside.

I looked around and saw animals of every stripe, stuffed and mounted. In the center of the room sat a Blue Tiger from China. In the corner, a Javan Rhino from Indonesia. Both extremely rare specimens.

I didn't get it. Besides being illegal to even own one of these animals, why would someone kill and stuff them?

I headed toward the stairs at the end of the hallway, wondering what horrors I'd find down there, when I felt a gun in my back.

"Nice to visit with you again, Mr. Masterson."

The voice belonged to Ledal. He pushed me forward. "Go."

The next thing I knew I was in a basement that smelled of formaldehyde and whiskey. He pushed me onto the ground, tied me up. A desk and the back of a chair faced me. The chair swivelled around and there sat a fat man with black wavy hair, cold eyes -- Max Franco. He pulled the bottle of Scotch he was drinking from his lips, and wiped them with the back of his hand.

"Interested in taxidermy, Mr. Masterson? Maybe for your ape?"

"Where's Jennifer?"

"Don't you worry, she's around--at least for now." He smirked.

I stared at him. "What do you mean?"

"You see we've been experiencing problems in my organization--unsuccessful robberies, some of my trusted lieutenants turning out to be traitors. Even the Johns seem to be losing interest in the womanly companionship we provide." He spread his hands. "I heard that in eastern folklore, rare animals, alive or dead are thought to bring good luck. I didn't believe in that hooey, but I figured, what the heck, let's give it a shot. So, through some overseas connections, I brought in an Iberian Lynx, the rarest cat in the world." He took a swig of his scotch.

"I paid a big price, but it turned out to be worth it. As soon as she arrived, business picked up. Even the Johns are back at it again. I'm a believer now. When word got out amongst my associates, they all wanted in. Don't know if you're aware, Masterson, criminals are a superstitious lot. Of course, they didn't want to dirty their hands taking care of the creatures so I came up with the brilliant idea of stuffing them all." He chugged the rest of the bottle down and flung it against the wall, shards of glass crashing to the ground. "Now I'm making a killing."

"So that's why you took Jennifer. You're going to turn her into one of your God damn good luck charms."

"You catch on fast, Masterson. One of our contacts requested an albino gorilla. Being one of the rarest creatures in the world, he believed it would give him even greater luck. So I paid Larry to sedate Jennifer and had my men smuggle her out." He leaned against the back of his chair, looking smug. "She's next in line to become a pretty paperweight. Maybe after we finish with her, we'll stuff you." He laughed like someone who'd been locked up in a mental institution way too long.

He nodded at Ledal. "Take care of him."

Ledal walked toward me, his gun pointing at my chest. His lips formed a sick smile like he planned on enjoying this.

My heart banged against my chest. I trembled all over.

I knew it was the end.

Suddenly, the window shattered. I heard a boom as Toby crashed to the ground. He must have followed me. He jumped on Ledal and pounded him with his fists, knocking him out.

A desperate Franco raced over, grabbed the gun from Ledal's lifeless body. A shot rang out, and blood seeped from Toby's shoulder. He snarled his lips and head-butted Franco. He picked up his still conscious body and heaved it against the wall. Franco blacked out and slid onto the ground. I could see Toby about to jump on him. That would kill him.

But then Toby looked over at me.

I saw something click in those soulful eyes of his. He moved away from the body.

He had finally realized something about self-control.

Toby untied me. I found a towel, wrapped it around his shoulder. "I was wrong, Toby. You are a team player." He smiled, put his enormous hand on the side of my face, and softly rubbed it.

I called the police and a veterinarian.

We found Jennifer caged in a back room—alive. Toby got the keys from Franco's pocket and opened it. He stood for a moment taking Jennifer in. Then the two hugged. Old friends.

After the police arrived and the vet fixed up Toby, we took Jennifer back to the zoo. Walter paid our fee and even gave us a bonus.

Toby and I drove home arguing about why I wouldn't change the sign on our door to Toby and Associates.

It was nice to have things back to normal.

END

The 2019 BOULD Awards Anthology

Edited By Jake Devlin

The 2019 BOULD Awards Anthology

A Shifting Plan

Elizabeth Zelvin (~2,500 words)

This story first appeared in the anthology
Fish or Cut Bait (2015), Wildside. © 2015 Elizabeth Zelvin

I stared out the window, not really seeing the Blue Ridge mountains of western North Carolina recede behind us, then sleepwalked through the change of planes in Charlotte for the flight to New York. My world had been shattered, and I had no idea how to put it together again. Michael was dead: my lover, my songwriter, the wind beneath the wings of Emerald Love, country artist. Without him, could I still be Emerald Love?

If not, that left me not quite nobody. I was still Amy Greenstein, nice Jewish girl from Pumpkin Falls, New York and closet shapeshifter. No comfort there. I didn't know which I dreaded more: watching my mother fail to hide her relief that I was no longer in danger of marrying a *goy* or listening to her bemoan the fact that I didn't see more of my sister. I couldn't help blaming Wendy for Michael's death. I had told her I never wanted to see her again, and I couldn't envision circumstances in which I'd change my mind.

Nighttime Manhattan made a lively, bright, well-populated Limbo. I took a taxi from the airport to a Marriott in the theater district, comfortable but not glamorous, where nobody would recognize Emerald Love. I left my luggage, two discreet suitcases without so much as a sticker to give me away, unopened on the bed and made my way to Times Square.

Cynics might deplore the sanitized theme park that Disney had made of Broadway, but I liked it. Costumed characters mingled with the tourists, Minnie Mouse and Winnie the Pooh posing for pictures with kids from Kansas and Montana. I climbed the broad bleachers that faced south toward Forty-Second Street and sat, high above the milling mass of people with a spectacular view of the colorful marquees and frenetic digital ads. To my amusement, I spotted a few shapeshifters in the crowd. I saw a Puss in Boots, not as domesticated as it appeared at first glance, smile secretly as it twirled for an amateur videographer with an iPad and an I Love New York T-shirt.

I don't know how long I sat there, letting the hubbub wash over me and enjoying the anonymity. It had been a long time since I'd faced a crowd that wasn't shouting, "Emerald! Emerald!" In one corner of my brain, I knew I had big decisions to make about my career. And in my gut—or as country music would put it, my heart—the wrenching pain of Michael's loss still lurked. But for the moment, I floated free of it.

Eventually, my stomach growled. I couldn't remember eating since the Seder at my parents' table days ago, before the phone call that broke my life into a fractured state beyond any easy mending. I knew I should start taking care of myself again, if only at the most basic level. I considered taking myself out to a real meal. Like all the great cats among shifters, I relish a good steak once in a while. But tonight it felt like too much effort. I decided to pick up a slice of pizza, bring it back to the hotel, and make an early night of it. Tomorrow would be soon enough to figure out what to do next: hire a new lead guitar or cancel the tour, even take a year off. I'd never been to Africa. Maybe I should go, run with the cheetahs before they landed on the endangered species list. They were currently considered "vulnerable." Well, so was I.

I'd seen an old-fashioned New York pizza place on a side street, the kind with guys in white tossing dough around like Frisbees in the window. Maybe I'd buy two slices. Maybe I'd buy a whole pie and eat myself into oblivion back in the room. If I wasn't going to be Emerald any more, it wouldn't matter if I gained a few pounds. But my plan got derailed when I heard a familiar song curling out from a dark doorway: "Killing Me by Moonlight." Michael had written it for me, and it had hit Number One on the charts. A couple of other artists had covered it, but I'd never heard anybody but me sing it live before.

The neon sign above the stained and pitted wooden door said, "WERE IN THE CITY." I didn't think the absence of an apostrophe between either the WE and the RE or an H after the W was a fluorescent typo. A dark glamour hung about the place. Opaque black plate glass covered the windows. I doubted that many people who weren't looking for it could see it at all. But the song, as familiar to me as my own breath, drew me in.

A short hallway, illuminated only by reddish light spilling from an arched doorway ahead, ended in the bulk of a bouncer who looked as if he might be a gorilla in his spare time. He frowned at me under a shelf of brow like a ledge on a mountain ridge. I showed him a hint of whisker and a flick of tail. He grunted, stepped aside, and let me pass.

On the left stretched a long, busy bar, glittering with dangling glasses and mirrored wall panels in flickering candlelight. As I'd hoped, it was a mixed-species shifter bar. I heaved a sigh of relief. Only wolves, like Michael, are actually called weres. I didn't think I could have handled seeing them in pack, even in this unfamiliar setting. The song and the ache of loss that never left me were reminder enough. The drinkers ran the gamut from human to animal form: a snow leopard, a couple of Afghan hounds, a stag whose antlers brushed the smoke-saturated beams of the ceiling. A trio of catwomen, enjoying a rowdy girls' night out, had kept themselves at half-shift the better to dress to the nines. They looked terribly young and innocent to me.

The singer stood in a pool of light on the tiny stage, fingers dancing up and down the neck of her guitar. Her only backup was an upright bass plunking away in the shadows. She was good: she was making the most of Michael's riffs, which she must have picked up from our album. She wore a flowing green tunic and black pants tucked into silver boots. Her silvery hair and the wildness in her eyes told me she was wolf. They have more of a thing about moonlight than the rest of us. As I eased my way onto a stool at the bar, the song flowed from instrumental break to final chorus. She could sing, too. She was smart enough not to try to imitate my interpretation, but took it in her own direction. As I signaled the bartender—they had Blue Moon on tap, and it suited my mood—she wound it up and bowed with a grin at the audience.

"Viva Bellini," the bass player announced. "Let's give her a hand, folks."

The set was over.

I sipped my Blue Moon as I watched her work the crowd, at least half of whom seemed to be regulars and fans. She laughed and chatted with human and shifter alike, patting a cheek or shoulder here, stroking a tail there. I wondered if she played out or confined herself to supernatural audiences. The supe circuit hadn't been an option for me. No way could I have stuck to gigs I couldn't tell my mother about. Having to knock on doors in Nashville like an ordinary girl had worked out well for me. I'd had a lot of fun the past couple of years. But Michael had had a lot to do with that.

For someone doing covers in a supe bar, Bellini had Nashville potential. She was that good, especially on guitar.

"Refill?"

I handed the bartender my glass and dug in my purse for a twenty. When I turned back to the room, Bellini had disappeared, presumably to the restroom. Without touching my fresh drink, I slipped off my stool and headed in the same direction.

I had the Ladies to myself, so maybe she'd gone outside to smoke. I never touched the stuff, but hey, it was her vocal cords. Down the hall from the restrooms was a door that must lead to one of those backyards or alleys that it's so easy to forget exist at all in Manhattan. Secret gardens are one of New York City's endless surprises. I decided to take a look. If daffodils were growing this close to Times Square, I wanted to see them.

No daffodils. The cramped alley was filled to bursting with a silver wolf snarling over the body of a man with bloody gashes in his neck and chest. I froze. The wolf shook itself and rippled into Viva Bellini, belligerence and horror chasing each other across her face.

I spoke from the shadows.

"You've got a problem."

Hearing a woman's voice, she raised her hands in a conciliatory gesture. She had no violent intent toward me.

"Predator or prey?" she asked.

In reply, I dropped into cheetah form. She went wolf so we could do a bit of ritual circling and sniffing, then both of us shifted back so we could talk.

"What did he do?" I asked. Along with "shifting is for the *goyim*," my feminist Jewish mother had taught me, "Always give a woman the benefit of the doubt."

"Jumped me when I came out to get a breath of air," she said.

"His mistake," I said.

You can't rape a shifter. Ever.

"'You know you want it' were his last words."

"Did you know him?" I asked.

"He was a fan," she said. "He's been stalking me the past couple of weeks. I meant to put a scare in him the first time he tried it in a place that wasn't too public. But he was too quick for me. He left me no choice."

"Yeah, that can happen." I really did understand. If she could have hung onto her human brain long enough to bite him in the leg, it might not have ended so badly. But once the animal instincts take over, it's hard to control them.

"I don't know what to do," she said.

To help or not to help? It wasn't my problem. On the other hand, I had no plans for the evening, maybe not even for the rest of my life.

"Did anybody see you with him tonight?"

"He couldn't even find the bar," she said. "Most civilians can't. But he figured out this alley led to the back door. He was waiting for me."

"Good thing he didn't have a knife," I said.

"That wouldn't have fit his image of himself." Her lip twisted. "A lover, not a fighter. The whole thing makes me sick."

"You can't afford to let his body be found this way."

"What am I supposed to do?" She ran her hands through her silver hair. "I mean it, I'm stumped. So if you have an idea— I'm Viva Bellini, by the way."

"Amy, uh, Green," I said. "I know, I heard you in there. You're really good. Are you supposed to do another set?"

"No. A piano player comes on at midnight. I sometimes do another two or three numbers before then, but they don't pay me extra, so if I don't, they won't miss me. You mean you'll help? Really? I can't thank you enough!"

"A corpse with tooth and claw marks half a block from Times Square would be bad for all of us. It's a shame this didn't happen in Michigan or Minnesota."

"Or Wisconsin or Wyoming," she said. "Believe me, I know every state where they're already making war on wolves. I'd hate to give the bad guys ammunition, but it would be better than a freak show on the front page of the *New York Post*."

"Let's leave that part of it aside for now," I said. "First, let's cut this guy down to size." I could hear how cold that sounded, but honestly, I felt more sympathy for Viva's predicament than for her victim's ill-judged rape attempt.

First, we dragged a heavy garbage bin across the door I'd come out and another to block the gate at the other end that he had used, so we wouldn't be interrupted. Then, we dropped into wolf and cheetah form. We made quick work of him. Then we shifted back. For some tasks, you can't beat opposable thumbs. The remains filled a couple of giant plastic garbage bags we found in the bins. Viva had an efficient little spell that was as good as a trip to the dry cleaners, so our clothes weren't a problem. I had hand sanitizer in my purse. When you cross the country in a tour bus, you have to be prepared. We found a cold water spigot and hosed down the concrete underfoot. In the end, nothing was left but two big bags and two slightly disheveled women.

"Now what?" She looked at me as if I had all the answers.

I didn't yet, but I was working on it.

"We need wheels," I said. "We don't look skanky enough to be dragging bags of garbage down the street. And it would be better to look like solid citizens in case we run into anyone with authority. Suitcases, maybe?"

"Wrong shape," Viva said. "How about a couple of giant wheelie duffel bags? There are dozens of stores in this neighborhood that sell cheap luggage."

"Fine. You go, I'll stay."

When I'd helped her unblock and slip through the gate, the adrenaline was still pumping. I sat down on the edge of an overturned metal garbage can, took some deep, slow breaths to put myself in a meditative state, and emptied my mind. Within a couple of minutes, the plan blossomed in my head. All we had to do was get the duffels back to my hotel room. I could charter a bus to pick us up in the morning or simply rent a van. We'd chuck the duffels in the luggage compartment and hit the road.

Viva must realize that she had better leave the city for a while. I could offer her not just a way out of town, but a job. A good job. She could finish the tour with us. Her git-tar pickin', as my band called it, was good enough. If she wasn't too proud to sing backup, even better. And on the way across the country to our next gig, we'd find a place to dump the contents of the bags: some rural area near a truck stop in a place where they were already mad at wolves.

I'd gone over the whole plan twice before I realized that it depended on my going on being Emerald Love. The decision had made itself. I could hardly wait to tell Viva who I was.

END

The 2019 BOULD Awards Anthology

Edited By Jake Devlin

The 2019 BOULD Awards Anthology

Input From a Serial Killer

John Furutani (~2,570 words)

This article—or perhaps input to same—is being written on a netbook provided by *The _____*. Prison security required the only software be the operating system and word processing file, and the hard drive was scrubbed for hidden programs and files before being allowed into my cell. In order to keep a potential weapon (power cord) out of my hands, I am only allowed to work for the life of the battery; the netbook is charged each day before being handed over, allowing about 2.5 hours of time before I have to shut down. So if the writing seems rushed or uneven, the author disclaims most responsibility.

The _____ has asked me to provide responses to a number of questions reproduced herein as the basis for an article looking at serial killers and their treatment by the criminal justice and prison systems. Given prison censorship policy, whether consistently followed or not, and editor preferences, I don't know how much of what I write will be reflected in the final article. With that in mind, I will be as forthright and accurate as possible. And since there is no current or pending legal action, readers will have to assume any self serving assertions will be minimal. I assure you this is so, but why should you take my word for it?

What is the nature of your sentence?

I am currently serving natural life, life without benefit of parole. Therefore, I will die in prison. This sentence was imposed after being found guilty of seven counts of first-degree murder.

Where are you incarcerated?

I am serving my sentence in the Federal institution in [REDACTED]. I am in a Federal prison because an arrangement was

Edited By Jake Devlin

made between _____ and the Bureau of Prisons to house what they consider a dangerous prisoner to staff and other inmates.

Describe your cell.

My cell is a unitary pod of metal with a Formica overlay for a floor area. The pod is 8 feet long by seven wide by 8 high. One end contains a toilet and a small shower, the spigot of which also serves as a drinking water source. A small plastic container allows me to store water while showering for later use.

Upon entering, immediately to the left is a small shelf that serves as a table and storage area as desired. A Swiss ball provides seating as well as an exercise tool. There is a woven basket for waste.

Several feet in front is a metal rectangle, top for sleeping & sitting, bottom one large drawer for storage of clothing, footwear, toiletries, and personal items. A pad of solid foam provides cushioning, a smaller rectangle a pillow. A disposable paper-like sheet covers the pad, one thin cloth blanket—which I'm told is a cotton/hemp blend—constitutes bedding. I exchange the sheet once a week along with trash.

Lighting is provided by two recessed, covered sockets with CFL bulbs providing so called soft light. To me, lighting is barely above being in a morgue. Above the shelf is a recessed square of plastic which I can press and obtain LED lighting—not ideal for reading or writing but it does provides an additional source to avoid eye strain. Next to the square is a recessed LCD screen.

In the upper left corner (as I face the door) is a camera lens behind reinforced plastic. I am assuming it offers a view of the entire cell at a minimum, when the lights are on. I do not know if it has other monitoring features—for example, infrared to verify a warm body is still present. There must be a microphone as well because I can request assistance or light to use the toilet during the "night."

The 2019 BOULD Awards Anthology

The door is set in its own frame, all heavy metal. There is tempered glass with an exterior cover so the pod can be scanned by the guards, and a metal slit tall enough to slide a meal tray through, and to place my forearms for cuffing or to remove same.

Describe your routine.

I spend 23 hours a day in this pod.

Lights come on at 0530 (or so I'm told) and stay on until 2300. How I spend my time is my business. I try and stick to somewhat of a regular schedule consisting of:

1. Rise and exercise 45 minutes.
2. Take a quick shower and dress (showers are limited to 5 minutes, no more than 3 per day).
3. Breakfast @ 0630—whatever is provided on the tray. I try and eat everything because snacks are limited in the canteen and daily limits imposed on purchases.
4. Read or watch videos—the latter are only available between 0800 and 2100. They tend to be documentaries, and film dramas or comedies, including foreign cinema. They contain limited violent or sexual content.
5. Lunch @ 1215.
6. Exercise from 1415 to 1515. This requires me to a) extend arms through the slit so wrists can be cuffed, b) come out of pod and cross corridor to stand nose against the opposite door while c) leg cuffs are applied. I then shuffle between two guards who escort me to the "cage"—outdoor area with metal grill plates and doors, divided into individual caged oval tracks allowing four inmates at a time to walk or run once the restraints are removed. No talking or touching allowed between inmates at any time. Restraints are reapplied and I shuffle back to the pod—this is the only time I spend outside of it, and the only time I can see sky, sun, and clouds. No matter how cold or wet, I always use this time.

7. More reading or videos. If any mail has been received, I read it then and decide whether to reply.

8. Dinner @ 1845.

9. Shower @ 2245.

10. Lights out and bedtime.

This routine has been my life for almost 3 years.

You were labeled a serial killer during your trial. Since you declined to present a case in your defense, does this mean the label is accurate?

Before I answer the question, let me describe a series of events. The reader can decide whether they support the label you speak of.

In 20__, I was asked to provide a statement at a parole hearing. I did so, a thoughtful statement, part of the public record, which provided a strong argument why the convict should not be set loose amongst the public ever again.

The board chose to ignore my and other statements and grant parole under strict supervision.

Three months after being granted freedom, the man kidnapped a girl, subjected her to even worse torture than that inflicted on my little sister, then repeatedly stabbed her and left the body to rot in a field. It took another year before he was captured and returned to prison.

I was angry—no doubt of that. And for good reason. At one time, I felt justified in finding and killing each member of the board who had voted to set the monster free.

But I managed to quell those initial thoughts and instead turned my energies into a different purpose. Being a planner by nature, I did the necessary preliminary steps which facilitated the desired outcome: research, deciding on appropriate means, and evaluating approaches and methodologies that would achieve desired ends and keep me free until project's end.

The first victim in the indictment was a meth addict, a man who had long since physically and mentally deteriorated such that a pipe with both meth and crystal Drano was avidly used. His lungs were eaten away and he died of cardiac arrest.

The second victim in the indictment was a professional burglar—not a violent man but a careful, skilled thief. He was killed when he returned home, entered the premises, and was shredded by a claymore mine, ball bearings and screws affixed with clay to the surface. Fortunately, he was coming from a break in at the time and had no companions with him.

The third victim in the indictment was abusive towards ex-wives, girlfriends, and casual dates. His excuse was being under the influence of alcohol, which led to first a punch and then multiple savage beatings that often led to hospital stays for a multitude of victims. Complaints were filed but then withdrawn; the only one which led to investigation and trial led to a four-year sentence, served in full. The woman who had bravely gone through the whole process left the state after being notified of his release. I understand to this day she walks with a limp and draws a disability pension because her injuries left her unable to hold a job for any period of time.

This man was beaten to death, but in a particularly brutal fashion. His hands, wrists, elbows, and shoulders were shattered—he only died when blows broke ribs, one shard piercing the heart so he quickly bled to death.

The fourth victim was a pedophile, not particularly vicious but a repeat offender who did not respond to therapy or multiple prison terms. He bled to death after a crude castration which, according to the medical examiner, must have been extremely painful due to the nature of the procedure.

Without going into the remaining details, a pattern should be discernible—there was no pattern. No specific ties between victims, other than gender, and no repetition of method. No messages left at the scene or provided post-mortem through any medium. Nothing that would indicate a particular pattern that could predict a future crime or link any persons to a distinct series of same.

The evidence against me was circumstantial—eyewitness testimony, inadequate alibis, video of a figure that could have been me—but lack of a defense case left the jury with no alternative to finding me guilty. I did not and cannot blame them—I would have voted the same given a similar set of circumstances.

And I was most grateful.

I was processed in due course and set up in the maximum security state facility. I tried to be a model prisoner but in due course I was accused in several violent incidents resulting in the death or serious injury of several inmates which meant time in solitary confinement, loss of privileges, and several psychological assessments.

After a year, I was released back into the general population—in which there was no longer any activity which would lead to further violence and return to solitary confinement. After several months, however, a number of murders and assaults took place and suspicion was directed at me. Again, circumstantial evidence—not enough to lead to any indictments but a decision was made to transfer me to a Federal Supermax facility such as my present home. I could have contested the decision, at least putting it in abeyance for a time—again, I chose not to put up any defense.

The editor and readers should decide if I have answered the question as posed—I believe I have done so given the limitations imposed by the prison administration.

Did your victims deserve punishment?

The "victims" appear to deserve punishment beyond that

imposed by a mere prison sentence. From everything in the public record, and some information imparted to me once I was incarcerated, none of these individuals were angels, responsible citizens, or even honorable criminals. Those who died or who were so seriously injured as to be unable to care for themselves had done things in the past of equal or more serious consequence.

I suppose it would be safe to characterize what happened as "an eye for an eye, a tooth for a tooth." The sentiment that such a philosophy merely leads to a world of blind, toothless men is clever but fails to acknowledge the existence of Evil in the world. Failure to confront and deal with Evil only encourages its spread and increased suffering of the innocent. I find the notion insufferable and unacceptable.

What would you do if you were ever released back into society?

Work very hard to ensure I never return to this lifestyle—or if that is not possible, my execution.

End of file.

Statement by Dr. _____ of the Federal Bureau of Prisons.

J_____ B_____ was not allowed to finish his input because it was felt he was not being forthright nor complete as to details. An incident also occurred which made it dangerous to allow him further opportunity to set down his story.

First, he was indeed found guilty of seven murders, based on a greater amount of circumstantial evidence than he portrays. Somewhat lesser evidence linked him to potentially four more murders, one of which was a clear indicator of guilt because it was the murderer of his sister, still free on parole. The others were attempts to divert suspicion from him as a likely suspect by the time his target was finally murdered.

Second, while in state hands, he was a suspect in at least

Edited By Jake Devlin

three murders and up to eight assaults, all of sex offenders. The assaults left the victims either crippled, blind, or extensively brain damaged only due to quick discovery and immediate medical care. In this respect, B_____ would be a serial killer both in and out of prison. It was these attacks which led him to be transferred to federal custody where greater control could be exerted.

Third, even in SuperMax conditions, B_____ was able to assault a prisoner. Although protocol requires separate transfer of prisoners from cell to the cage, mis-communication allowed two parties to arrive at the gate at the same time. While the gate was being unlocked and opened, B_____ managed to rush the other prisoner, knock him down, and despite shackles, tear at his throat with teeth alone. Again, without prompt response, another victim might have been added to his list.

By decision of the BOP board, B_____ has been deemed a threat to both staff and inmates of a nature to eliminate any future contact that might allow an assault. He will remain in his cell on 24 hour lockdown for the remainder of his sentence with no access to objects that might be used to inflict bodily harm. As such, his food will be the kind that can be wrapped and the only liquid will be the water from the shower—no utensils, cups, or trays provided.

He will serve out the remainder of his sentence with minimal contact with other human beings—the only way to ensure anyone else will be safe.

The file B_____ was working on will be provided to the magazine, with the stipulation that any content used will have to include this statement in its entirety. The BOP has no desire to enhance B____'s reputation or foster a misleading portrait of his persona.

The security videos show no change in B_____'s pod of any kind. He continues to follow the routine set out in his response *with the exception of an additional 45-60 minutes of pacing back and forth while shadow boxing or stretching exercises. However, on occasion, and not always seen by the guards, he pauses, looks up at the camera, and mouths something before resuming pacing. The microphone does not pick up any sound, but a lip reader would easily be able to decipher what B_____ has said, which should cause concern even under current circumstances.*

"I'm not done yet."

END

Edited By Jake Devlin

Confession of a Serial Killer

Jake Devlin (~500 words)

(First published in Perflutzed, © 2019 Jake Devlin)

When the hungry takes over, I can't control myself; I must kill. I have two. It's a complusion – no, more than a complusion. It's instunctive, an instunct. (I think that's the right werd. English is mine second language, so I may be not right at times.) Or maybe "hungry" is the rite, most corrupt – I mean – uh – oh, hell – is the rite werd.

I've had this hungry all mine life, at leest as much of it as I can member.

But it was Big Al, mine mentor, who teached me how two focus my hungry and two kill without getting catched.

I never knowed my parents; they were go away much long before I even knowed I was a life. But Big Al was a well replasement for them. He teached me almost avery thing I know.

He teached me how two hide and watch, hide and watch, hide and watch.

He teached me how two pick my victims, two watch for the weakliest, smallesty ones.

He teached me two be patient, two wait, two wait, two wait for the pefectest time two strike.

He teached me how two never use a weppun, two rely on my own speed, wait and strongness.

He teached me how two sneek and run and grab and pull, sneek and run and grab and pull, sneek and run and grab and pull.

Most imporantliest, he teached me how two hide with each of my victims, so I would never get catched, but that if the catchers got close, how two get far away quickliest, even if it ment leeving a victim behindly.

Big Al had been at it for meny decadents before I met him and

Edited By Jake Devlin

he took me under his leg, and had morer tan ten tousand kills behind him ten. Prolly has over twenny tousand by now.

I only have a foo over too tousand so far, but I hope I can match or go passed his record before I get catched or deaded.

Ohhh, looky, looky! There, a super-good victum! Look at her hair! And those eyes! Those eyelashes! And those eyebrows! And how she wiggles her ass, as if to say, "Ate me, ate me." Okay, okay.

Sneek, sneek, sneek, run, run, run, grab, grab, grab, pull, pull, pull, hide, hide, hide! Got her! Catched her! Oh, boy-oh-boy!

Just as I pulled her under, I heerded a voise screeming.

"Someone call 911! An alligator just took my Yorkie!"

END

The 2019 BOULD Awards Anthology

Edited By Jake Devlin

The 2019 BOULD Awards Anthology

THE CAT

Robert Petyo (~2100 words)

It was Ricky's first time, and his wildest fantasies were coming true as Kate writhed above him. It was even more glorious than he had ever imagined it would be, until he saw the cat.

Kate's sinewy body was taut like a coiled spring. One hand gripped his shoulder so tightly that he almost cried out. Her other hand clutched the mattress at his side like she were dangling from the edge of a cliff.

Ricky rammed his head back into the pillow and fluttered his eyes closed. This experience was even greater than he had dreamt it would be since he first met Kate at Lou's birthday party. That had been years ago. Right from the start he was in love with her, though she clearly had her eyes fixed on Lou. Ricky never stopped thinking about her as she and Lou hooked up and moved away. They stayed together two years, and after they broke up Kate returned home. Still, it took Ricky months before he built up enough courage to ask her out. They dated a few times and he wanted her even more. She was all he ever wanted in a woman. Gorgeous. Intelligent. Lively. A sense of humor.

She was the woman he had waited years for.

He was twenty-four years old and had never fallen hopelessly in love. His life had emptied when Kate left. A few casual fumbling dates set up by well-meaning friends led nowhere. No woman was Kate's equal.

And now, here she was, the woman he was going to spend the rest of his life with.

After a quiet dinner where everything had gone right, after whispered invitations to her apartment, his wildest fantasies were coming true.

Stroking her sides, he felt her creamy skin quiver under his fingertips. He massaged her hips, pulled her even tighter to him. He saw the passion in her partly closed eyes as she kissed him. He slid his hand up to her breast and flopped his head to the side.

He saw the cat.

It was small, about a foot tall. Black. It stood in the bedroom doorway, legs stiff like it were stretching after a long nap, its tiny tail rigid, its back arched slightly. Its fur glistened in the light of the hall. It made no sound. It didn't move. Its eyes were twin stars in a black sky.

Ricky's mouth turned to cotton as he tried to concentrate on the woman hovering over him. That was what he had fantasized about for so long. That was what he had waited for, what he needed.

But he couldn't look away from the cat.

It was staring at him.

Kate lowered her lips to his ear. "What's wrong?"

He tried to speak, but couldn't. He could see the cat's body rustle with its breathing. Still staring at him.

"C'mon," Kate cooed as she rubbed his shoulder. "What's wrong? You're just lying there."

"The cat," he finally said.

"Huh?"

"The cat!" He was finally able to swing an arm out and point. The cat tensed as if to leap away, but it remained, staring. Ricky turned to Kate and nudged her away.

"What's your problem?" she pouted as she slid back from him.

He pushed her farther away. "Your damned cat is standing in the doorway watching us. That's my problem."

She glanced at the doorway, then pressed one hand to her lips to stifle a giggle. "What?" She rolled into a seated position.

"I've got to get rid of it." He swung his legs over the edge of the bed, bumping Kate as he moved, sitting now, staring at the cat.

It still hadn't moved.

"Silky's just lonely," she said.

Silky. Ricky hadn't known she had a pet until this very moment. She had never mentioned it, and this was his first time inside her apartment. Ricky didn't like cats. Or dogs. Or pets of any kind. When he was five years old he had watched two young kittens mauled by a pit bull. He had been sick for two weeks. Since then he could barely look at a cat without that childhood terror resurfacing.

"Honey, lay down." She touched his side. "Let me relax you."

He stood. "I don't like it watching us." He strode to the door, but still the cat didn't move as its eyes remained focused on him. Finally he crouched, grabbed it by its stiff front legs and shoved it backward.

"Ricky!"

The cat squealed a bit as it slid back.

He slammed the bedroom door.

"Don't hurt Silky."

"Silky's fine. He's just not getting a free show." Puffing, he leaned back against the door.

She sat on the edge of the bed, her knees pressed together, her shoulders hunched forward so that her small breasts quivered. "What did you do that for?"

"I don't like your cat watching us."

Her face hardened for a moment as she looked past him toward the door. Then she tried to smile but her lips contorted awkwardly. "That's silly."

He returned to the bed and sat beside her, pressing his thigh against hers. "I couldn't— Well, maybe it's crazy, but I have this thing about cats. I can't have it watching us."

"But Silky wasn't bothering us."

"He was bothering me." He said it louder than he intended and he leaned toward her, kissing her lightly on the cheek. "I'm sorry." He didn't want to argue about a stupid cat. Not now. He nudged her back on the bed. "I'll make it up to you."

She pressed against his shoulders, keeping him away. "Are you telling me that my Silky bothers you?"

He looked away.

"You can't make love to me because my Silky is here?"

"Kate."

"I don't like you treating Silky that way."

"What way?" He stood. "I didn't hurt him. I closed the door. That's all." He moved toward her again. He would not let his dream be thwarted by something as silly as a cat. He took her hand and kissed her knuckles.

She was frozen for a long time, but finally, slowly, reluctantly, she shifted, lying on the bed, flexing her knees and parting her legs slightly.

He moved over her, breathing coarsely.

But she didn't move. She was a cold statue.

"What's wrong?"

"What do you mean?" She rolled her head to the side.

"You're just lying there."

"I'm worried about Silky."

"Oh, Jesus."

She was staring at the door. "I miss Silky."

He jerked away and sat on his ankles. "Are you serious?"

"Open the door," she whispered. "Let Silky watch. She's not bothering us."

He had a sudden image of the cat watching as a parade of men marched through Kate's bedroom. He hopped off the bed and looked at the door.

Men? Or just Lou? How many men had Kate been with? He had waited for her. He wanted her to be his first. But was she just a tramp who drew men to her bed so Silky could have a show?

He squeezed his eyes shut and told himself he was being stupid. The cat shouldn't matter.

He looked at Kate. So beautiful. It was her eyes, the deep blue eyes that had first seized his attention. From that first moment he had thought of being alone with her, holding her, kissing her. He had wanted her for so long. He had waited for her. He wasn't going to let anything as ridiculous as a cat ruin this moment.

He yanked open the door and gasped.

The cat was still there as if it hadn't moved.

Ricky spun away, running to Kate, jumping on the bed.

Kate came alive again, welcoming him, peppering him with kisses. She sifted her hands through his hair as he moved between her legs. She threw her head back and closed her eyes.

Ricky couldn't move.

Kate opened her eyes.

Ricky looked at the cat.

"No," she whispered. "Come to me." Her fingers dribbled down his torso.

He felt nothing. He stared at the cat, unmoving, its tail curling toward him like an accusing finger.

Kate caressed him but he could not respond. He cursed himself. He cursed the anger surging through his body. He pushed her hand away and got off the bed. "I can't do it." Feeling exposed, as if in front of hundreds of gaping people, he cupped his hands across his groin. Was he incapable? What kind of man was he? He began to tremble.

"No, Ricky. Relax." She reached for him.

He hopped away. "I can't do it. Not with that damned cat." He rushed toward the still motionless creature.

"No. Let Silky watch."

His hand stopped inches from the door. "I can't believe this. Are you actually going to tell me that you won't have sex with me unless your cat is watching? What kind of pervert are you?"

"How dare you?"

He shoved the door closed.

With a cry she flopped back on the bed, her arms folded over her breasts.

"Maybe other guys played along with your perverted game, but not me."

"It's not a game."

He gathered his clothes. "I am madly in love with you. For the longest time. More than anything in the world I wanted you to be mine. I waited. Don't you understand that? I waited. And I thought you could care for me."

"I do."

"Well, then I should be more important than a stupid cat."

"Ricky."

He slipped outside of the bedroom and pulled the door shut. The cat was still there in the tiny hall, still watching him as he hurried into the bathroom to pull on his clothes.

He started to tear up as he pulled on his pants. This was supposed to be a perfect evening. This was supposed to be heaven.

He buttoned his shirt, missing a few as he paused to wipe his eyes.

All because of a damn cat.

After he slipped on his shoes, not bothering to tie them, he checked the sink, the medicine cabinet, the linen closet. There had to be something he could use. Something to get rid of that damn cat.

He finally settled on a pink bath towel. He held it in front of him, his fists curled on each end so that he could throw it over the cat and gather it up like a bundle of clothes. Toss it in the trash. He bent so he could get his hand down to open the door without letting go of the towel.

He stepped out.

Kate stood just outside the bedroom door, the cat gathered in her arms and held to her chest where it purred softly as it stared at Ricky.

He threw down the towel and spun toward the den and the door. But his foot slipped on the towel as he moved and he went down, his forearms slamming into the hardwood. He rolled onto his side and tried to stand, but his feet got tangled in the towel. One shoe came off as he sat up and yanked the towel free. In a rage he ripped it in half. He heard Kate gasp as he tore it again, growling as he did.

Finally he managed to stand and turned toward the front door. A portion of the towel was still gripped in his right fist. He looked down at it, held it up, stretched it out.

The segment he had was small, about the size of—

He looked back at Kate. She still held the cat, but had lowered it to her belly so that her beautiful breasts were calling him.

My God, he thought. So beautiful. So perfect.

He brought the shred of towel up and pulled it over his eyes. Grunting, he yanked it tight and tied it behind his head. Then he stretched his arms in front of him, palms outward, and waited. "Take me," he whispered.

She finally came to him and he felt her take his forearm. "Careful," she said as she led him to the bedroom.

When he lay on the bed she tore at his shirt, pulling it free, then worked at his belt.

His breath came in short aggressive spurts as he tried to keep

Edited By Jake Devlin

still and let her work. He could see nothing. The room was darkened and the blindfold blocked out everything.

He could see nothing.

But he could feel everything.

This was going to be even more erotic than he had ever imagined. The woman he had long adored was finally taking care of him.

And she was in total control. He was helpless.

Then he heard the cat purring. It was right by the bed.

Purring.

END

The 2019 BOULD Awards Anthology

Edited By Jake Devlin

The 2019 BOULD Awards Anthology

Deer Juj

David Hagerty (~850 words)

Joon 8

Deer Juj:

He wuz my frend. Jon. We worked together. It wuz him tot me to spell it. To get her. We wuz together that day. Ridin. In hiz Firebird. 1978. 350 cc. V8. It had joos. Wind wuz in the t top. Boss on the stair e o. Croozin on PCH. The hi way. Didnt see it. The trail her. It wuz to lite.

We wuznt speedin. We couldnt. Not with the water be lo an the curvs and the sun. Even the Firebird cant go fast there. The hi way dont go strate. It bunchs up an spreds out. Like wood grain. Trees dont gro strate. You hav to make em that way. Same with the oshun. It goze every way but strate. But i wuz goin slo.

It wuz cuz of the sun. In r eyes. U couldnt see. Not fooly. Binded me. Not the joos.

Sins i wuz little. Cuz of my add. Tab with brake fast and lunch. After i still want it. Calls me down. Makes me focus. Peeple say joos wined em up. It calls me down. My cuzin gave me sum. His mom had it. In her cab net. Same as i got. To looz wait.

In skool they gave it to me. Cuz of my add. Cald me stoopt. Put me in sped. Sins i wuz littl. No reed or rite or add or times. Just draw. U cant reed they sed. Just draw. Make me a hous. Make me a dog. Make me a car. So i make 1. They don like it. It looked to bad. With flame on the side. A bird on the hud. Blak. Krome. Tale fin. Not like that they sed. A nise car. Is nise i sed. Not like that they sed. So i left.

Wuz 14. Start runin the street. Hangin at the dog park. They chase me. But i wuz to fast. In skool they cald me spaz. But the dogs liked it. Jon saw me there. Sed what r u doin? Sed i need sum thing to do. Cum with me he sed.

He had a shop on the allee. Finishin. Tabls and chairs and dressers and book cases. Wen they cum in they looked old and ruff. We strip em with kemkals. Poor it on til it bubbls. Like blistrs wen i used to burn my arm. With a bic. See how long i could hold it. Then it peeled off. Big long strips. Paint and stain. Til it wuz wite as me. Then i sand it smooth. 4 kinds of paper. 60. 100. 150. 220. Til it wuz smooth as skin. Then i stain it. Cherry Oak Pine Maple. No how to spell them cuz of Jon. He tot me. Strip in. Witch will rat ur brain. But i like the smell.

He gave me joos. Cald me down. Made me focus. Could work for days. 3 strait. Finishin. Tabls and chairs and dresses and cases. Like new. Thats why he liked me.

Got me my own apt. Stove an frij and tub. Stripped the flor and paint the wall an bilt a book case for my tools. Gave me a bed and chair an tabl. It wuz home to me. First 1 i ever had.

Wuz why my girl liked me. Sed i wuz in de pen end. She under stood. Cuz she has it to. Add. Only she dont need the joos. Sez its a dic thing. Likes the feelin without. Sez i can to. But i dont no. Cuz i never hav. Dont do it to get hi. Calls me down. Makes me focus.

Til here. In max. Never been befor. Sells and sells. Mory and Montel on the box. Sit ups and push ups and pull ups. Dry ornges and green balonee. Books and mags and let hers. Here i cant get it. Only kofee. 3 4 5 cups a day. Calls me down. Lets me focus. Like joos. Til i can sleep. Only i think bout him. Jon.

Didnt see it cumin. Wuz to lite. No sun glass. No gard rails. Jus clif an oshun. Wen i saw it it wuz to late. A trail her. Brake. Slide. Fall. Down the cliff. Rock and roll. In the water. No 1 to save us. Jus me and him and the Firebird. Down to the bot ham. Dark. To dark to see. Water risin. Get out. Swim to lite. Wen i get there i didnt see him.

The 2019 BOULD Awards Anthology

Looked all round but didnt see him. Waves kept cumin. Down in me. Couldnt see. Sun in my eyes. So i dove. Down to the bot ham. To dark there. Couldnt find it. Black bird. Only waves. Thot i would down. Sum times wish i did.

Hav his name tatt on my arm. Jon. My frend. RIP.

Now i dream bout him. Under stand. He wuz my frend. It wuznt the joos. Only had sum. It calls me down.

Sins

bennie

END

Edited By Jake Devlin

2nd Place

KM Rockwood

The 2019 BOULD Awards Anthology

The Society

KM Rockwood (~2200 words)

She will be leaving soon. I wait in the shadows by the restaurant's dumpster, shielded by the high fence and the brick wall of the building next door. Dressed in black leather, I will be very hard to see, almost invisible. The skins of dead animals will help protect me.

Long ago I had the Society's insignia, a circle surrounding a dripping knife and a skull, tattooed on my chest. That also protects me, and will serve as positive identification should I ever be summoned to a Society initiation ceremony. No, not if. *When* I am summoned. It has to happen.

First I must prove myself worthy. How many more must I kill before I'm deemed worthy? I have chosen my next target.

I have tried to learn her full name, but I know I must not do anything to raise suspicions. So I must be content with knowing only that she is C. Ravenwood. That's all that appears on her mailbox, all that is listed in the phone book, all I can find on the internet. To myself, I call her Crystal, and that is sufficient. Crystal Ravenwood is a name worthy of a project for the Society.

She may be leaving alone tonight. I have been watching the restaurant since she began her shift at 4 PM. Usually she walks home with a young man who also works there. He leaves her at her door. But tonight, I have not seen him arrive. Sometimes they have different nights off. Then she walks home alone.

If she's alone, tonight may be the night to…

No, no, no. I must not. For the present time, I must remain the Watcher. No more killing. Not now, at least. Killing only leads to more trouble. I promised Dr. Bishop, my therapist, that I would not embark on any projects for the Society for the three months he is off on paternity leave.

He has found a child worthy of his efforts to guide her through her crucial first years of life in this sphere. Quite an adjustment, I would imagine.

Of course I know that Dr. Bishop is not really a therapist; he has been sent to test my resolve. And guide me. Perhaps he is a high priest in the Society in disguise, a *real* bishop. The time is not right for me to know. I must be humble and follow his directions, sorting out the hidden meanings in what he tries to teach me.

He assigned me to someone else, a woman named Mrs. Calgood, saying it would be beneficial for me to establish a therapeutic relationship with a woman. I go to see her, twice a week, just as he directed. What kind of trial is this? She doesn't understand me. How could anyone named Calgood begin to understand? I stopped taking my meds a few weeks ago. When I see him again, Dr. Bishop may not be happy to hear that. Or it may be what he intended. It's impossible for me to know for sure.

Three months is a long time, though. He and his wife went to China to adopt a baby girl. When he said that, I almost reminded him that the Society originated in the Far East, perhaps China, and that the best projects are always girls with long, straight black hair. But he doesn't like to hear me say things like that, doesn't want to talk about the Society at all. I managed to stop myself from mentioning it just in time.

Perhaps he's gone to fetch a special project. A young girl. And is she for me? She would have to grow up first. Time will tell.

I have long, straight black hair. Unusual in a man. Dr. Bishop says he will know I am truly changing if I get it cut. A warning, perhaps. But he needn't worry. That's not going to happen. Tonight, I have it tied at the nape of my neck and tucked under my jacket.

Crystal has long, straight black hair. Longer than mine. It falls halfway down her little round butt. I could cup that butt nicely in my two hands, press her body up against mine. With my teeth, I could…

No. Dr. Bishop says I must stop thinking like that. He says I have control of my thoughts, if I will just exercise it. When these thoughts come unbidden, I must stop them, replace them with others. I struggle to understand. I must be a humble student. First I must master banishing these thoughts, then he will teach me how to go about summoning them at will. Only then will I be in true control.

She wears her hair over her coat. Her coat, too, is long and black. Leather. The skin of dead animals protects her, too. A fur collar caresses her slender white neck. I would love to open that coat slowly, brush the fur away from her skin. Then I could take that soft wave of hair and wrap it around her neck. I bet it would go around five or six times. At least. And then when I pulled tighter, her red lips would part in surprise, the tip of her tongue would touch her strong white teeth and her eyes would open wide. I would see into her very soul.

No. Just watching tonight. Dr. Bishop would not approve of even that at this point; he would say it might be too hard to control myself. But I have become stronger than he realizes. In his absence, without the meds, I am nearing complete control over myself.

I wonder if Crystal ties her hair back at work. I bet she does. I have gone into the restaurant twice when I knew she was working in an attempt to see her. She does not work the front of the restaurant. I was hoping she was a waitress or the hostess. But she wasn't there. She probably works in the kitchen. With those pale, delicate hands, she could be a pastry chef. Or a prep cook, handling those long, thin, sharp knives with ease. I can see the shining blades flashing on the cutting board, dicing vegetables, cutting meat. Bloody raw meat. The Society favors long, thin, sharp bladed knives. I always carry one, although I know Dr. Bishop would not want me to tell that to anyone, even him. So I deny it.

Sometimes, Dr. Bishop tries to tell me that the Society is all in my head. He says I have just imagined killing. He says I made it up all up, that I may think it's real, but it's not. So many things Dr. Bishop tells me are confusing. Is he testing my faith? It makes my head hurt. Dr. Bishop says that's why I need to take my meds and stay away from any projects for the Society. At least until we get this worked out.

If he really meant that, he would not have left me on my own for three months. He *must* be testing me.

In the restaurant, the dining room lights are going out. Only the ones in the kitchen remain lit. Now they are going out, too. I shrink back further, trying to become one with the night. The back door is opening. Six people step out into the alley. Crystal is last. She is wearing her black leather coat; it covers her entire body, from her delicious neck to the tiny high heeled ankle boots. Her hair sweeps down her back, ruffled slightly by the breeze.

My knife is in its sheath. I caress it. But I know I must not kill her. Now is not the time. I have promised Dr. Bishop. I will pursue no projects for the Society until he gets back. I have control over myself.

I watch the group go down the alley to the sidewalk. In the harsh wavering light from the security lights in the alley, they all look like supernatural beings. Ghosts. Perhaps they are. The others all turn left. Crystal turns right toward her apartment.

I slip out of the alley, keeping well behind her. Out of sight. I know where she lives. Perhaps I will catch up to her and speak to her. Ask her to step into that alley next to her apartment building. I will not hurt her; not even touch her. I will just look at her, see if she will say something to me. If she's frightened, so much the better. Her eyes will open wide. I may catch a glimpse of her soul.

But suppose she were to scream? I can't have that. Then I would have to touch her then, cover her quivering mouth with my hand. I would feel her hot breath on my palm. She might bite it; then my hot red blood would trickle down the white skin of her chin. I would like that.

No. I mustn't touch her. I would try to calm her, tell her how much I admire her. How beautiful she is. Perhaps she would listen, even say something back. If she doesn't, if she runs into the lobby of her building, at least I will have been close to her. I will not follow her; I will not touch her.

The wind is picking up. Crystal hunches into the leather coat. Her smooth, inviting neck disappears into the warmth of the fur collar, becoming one with the spirits of the dead animals who shield her from the chill. She plunges those dainty white hands deep into the pockets.

The noise of the leaves scuttling down the sidewalk hides any sounds I make as I catch up to her. We are next to her building, at the entrance to the alley.

What should I say? I can't think of words. I reach out and grab her by the shoulder, shove her away from the sidewalk, out of the glare of the streetlights.

I wasn't supposed to touch her. She will scream. The police will come. I will have exposed the Society. Dr. Bishop will be so disappointed. I will never be initiated. I will never be worthy to be invited to a ceremony.

But she doesn't scream. Is she too surprised and frightened? I spin her around, push her up against the brick wall. She is so tiny, so delicate. She feels like she may break in my hands. I grab the front of her coat, ripping it open.

Her clothes are black and cling to the curves of her body. My breath is coming faster. My mouth gapes open. My eyes open wide and my gaze seeks her long slender neck.

A glint of heavy silver chain encircles her neck, contrasting with the white skin and the black clothes. I grab the chain. If I twist that around her neck, it will make a deep groove. Perhaps it will draw her blood. I hear my blood pounding in my head. I can't think.

My hand grasps a pendant on the chain. I turn it so it catches the light.

A circle enclosing a dripping knife and a skull. The insignia of the Society.

Is Crystal a member of the Society? I have never knowingly met one before. Except for Dr. Bishop, and he refuses to reveal himself to me. So far.

Crystal's hands snake out of her pocket. She is clutching something. Something long and thin and silver. Something sharp.

A long knife. Not quite as long as mine, but sharp and deadly.

Should I pull out my knife, too? My hand won't move.

I watch in fascination. Is this the ceremony for which I have been longing? After so long, after so much preparation, am I finally to be initiated as a full member of the Society?

My hands fall to my sides. My jacket falls open, exposing my unbuttoned shirt. And my bare chest. Surely she can see the tattoo. She will know I, too, am a member of the Society.

Crystal raises her arm, the knife at ready.

With a swift and delicate motion, her hand plunges toward my chest.

An exquisite pain burns between my ribs. I feel something pierce my lung. I can hardly breathe. Blood bubbles in my throat.

Crystal's arm moves. I feel the long, sharp blade slice into my heart.

I had no idea this hurt so much. I have done it to others. Did they always suffer so?

Do I have to experience this myself before I can be a true member of the Society?

Dr. Bishop will be so proud of what I have accomplished while he was gone.

My mouth fills with blood and I fall to the pavement. My eyes open wide. Crystal's eyes bore into mine, but I can't see her soul. Can she see mine?

The pain in my chest is intensifying. My vision is fading. When does the ecstasy begin?

Darkness is overtaking me. Is Crystal stealing my soul? This can't be the way it's supposed to be, can it? I open my mouth to ask Crystal, but I can't form words. Or thoughts.

Only darkness.

END

Edited By Jake Devlin

The 2019 BOULD Awards Anthology

SOMETHING WACKY THIS WAY COMES

Karen Phillips (~2000 words)

The fifth grade students hunched over their textbooks and snuck an occasional glance at the clock above the teacher's desk. Tick, tick, tick. Time passed agonizingly slow. Summer break was in two weeks and the air hummed with anticipation.

Andy fidgeted, drawing the attention of his best friend, Dean, seated next to him. He scrunched up his face and stuck out his tongue as if he were being tortured.

Dean's eyes bulged in fear.

The teacher, as if sensing mischief, looked up. Andy could swear lasers shot from her eyes and pierced him like a stuck bug. He held his breath and stared at the School Rules sign on the wall until the words blurred:

Laughing, chuckling, chortling, guffawing, giggling, or any other utterance of merriment is strictly forbidden. Violators will be punished. Established 1979 by Principal P. T. Barnum.

Finally, after what seemed an eternity, Ms. Frump returned her attention to grading papers.

Andy pulled a rubber object from his pocket and held it under his desk. He squeezed a rubber bulb. Dean jumped as a stream of water hit his left cheek. His book crashed to the floor.

Screech! Ms. Frump shoved her chair back, then moved stiffly down the row like a military sergeant. She stood between Andy and Dean, fists planted on wide hips.

"Alright, you two, that's enough clowning around!"

Students gasped at the word "clown."

Edited By Jake Devlin

"Stand up!" Ms. Frump barked.

Andy and Dean scrambled to comply. Andy clasped his hands in front of him and focused on his shoes.

"Hands to your sides, Andrew Kelly!"

Andy slowly moved his hands away from his pockets. One wet pocket held a lumpy object. One girl braved a giggle then stifled it with a cough.

Ms. Frump's eyes blazed in righteous anger. "I should have known you were the culprit, Andrew. Like father like son." She held out her hand.

Andy took the toy from his pocket and gave it to her. A bright orange flower was connected to a round bulb by a plastic tube. More titters and giggles. The teacher roared, "Quiet!" The room went deathly still. Her gnarled fingers took hold of Andy's ear. "To the principal's office. Now!"

Andy sat in a wooden chair outside of principal's office. Behind the closed door Ms. Frump and Principal Barnum spoke in low tones. The door opened and Ms. Frump gave Andy a satisfied smirk as she marched out.

Mr. Barnum stood in the doorway to his office and crooked a finger. "Come here, son."

Andy seethed. I'm not your son! He shuffled into the office like a prisoner.

The principal gestured to a chair opposite a large desk. "Be seated."

In the center of the desk blotter was Andy's squirt flower.

"Another item for my growing collection," Principal Barnum said. He planted his fists on either side of the flower, leaned over it, and glared. "Young man, you know the rules. I will not tolerate any more. You are to be an example, as your father was."

Andy scowled at the mention of his father, but remained silent.

"Obviously your father's death did not teach you to behave. Therefore, you must be punished. You will spend the rest of the day in C-Cell."

Andy paced the room where he was to spend the rest of the school day. Solitary confinement, otherwise known as C-Cell, was whispered among the students as something to be feared. No one wanted to be locked up in the musty room, all by themselves. It was an effective means of making sure the students obeyed the rules. However, as an only child, Andy was no stranger to being alone. The room was bare save for a wooden bench. Andy sat and tried to think of something amusing to pass the time.

Andy was unaware of the hours passing. Lost in thought, he was swept away in the rush of emotion as memories flooded in. His dad, always laughing, always ready with a joke, a trick, a game to play. Oh, how Andy missed him. Tears ran down his cheeks. He was sure his mother missed him, too, but she seemed to have lost her zest for life. She had become a stranger, like everyone else. She saw to Andy's needs, but she didn't really see him—as if he were a ghost. He missed his dad and his mom. It seemed he had lost both.

"Hello, son."

Andy spun around. The air shimmered, then a familiar shape formed. Standing before him was his father, Emmet Kelly, dressed as the famous hobo Weary Willie. Stubble darkened his face, hair stuck out from under a floppy hat. His tattered suit was two sizes too big. A tie hung loose around his neck.

Andy shot to his feet. "But-but you-you're dead."

Emmett smiled. "I am, but it's time I paid you a visit."

Edited By Jake Devlin

Andy put his arms out for a hug, but grabbed air.

"Yes, I'm a ghost—always with you in spirit, son. And in fun." He winked.

"Why'd you have to die? You were the best principal ever. Not mean like Barnum."

Emmett made a sad face and shrugged. "Think of me as a martyr. Never forget me, son. Never lose your sense of humor like Barnum did."

"He sure is a spoil sport."

Emmett smiled. "A stick in the mud."

"A fuddy-duddy."

Emmett rocked back on his heels. "That's my boy! Are you with me?"

Andy nodded with enthusiasm then frowned. "I try, but I'm always in trouble. Ms. Frump took me to the principal, again."

"That old battle axe is still teaching? I'd hoped she'd be retired by now."

"Then Barnum took away my squirt flower. You know, the one you gave me? Then he locked me in this room."

Emmett pulled on his suspenders. "Son, the principal suffers from Coulrophobia."

"Coulrophobia," his mouth formed around the word, trying it out. "Is that The Big C?"

Emmett bellowed a guffaw and slapped his knee. "Now that is funny! Coulrophobia is the fear of clowns."

"But clowns aren't scary."

"When he was very young his parents threw him a birthday party with a clown. It scarred him for life."

A sense of doom filled Andy's soul. "What if I die from The Big C, like you did?"

Emmett sighed. "We all die, son. Life's funny that way. Best to go out laughing. Promise me you'll never forget that."

"I promise, dad."

The sound of a lock turning startled them. The air shimmered again, then Emmett disappeared. In his place was a red clown nose. Andy quickly shoved it in his pocket.

The principal opened the door. "Time's up, Andrew. Your mother is here."

Andy's mother didn't speak during the trip home. She barely looked at him. She didn't even turn the radio on. The family station wagon floated silently, like a cloud, over the tree-lined streets of their small town. Andy wanted to tell her how dad had visited him, but he was afraid she wouldn't believe him. Once he tried a bit of levity with one of his dad's favorite jokes but his mother didn't respond. He pulled the red nose from his pocket and put it on, but her sharp intake of breath and pursed lips spoke louder than words and he gave up.

Dinner was a peanut butter and jelly sandwich in his room where he was instructed to do his homework, brush his teeth, then go straight to bed.

But Andy wasn't tired. He lay on the floor and reached far under his bed where he kept a shoebox. He sat up, put the box beside him, and opened the lid. Inside was a treasure trove of various gadgets guaranteed to make people laugh or get a boy in trouble at school. These items had once belonged to his father—Emmett's tricks of the trade. The box was not as full as it once was. One by one items had been taken out, and played with, then confiscated by adults who had banned fun—put to death those who clowned around, like his father. The town was overrun by those afraid to laugh. Those who feared joy and the dangerous paths one might go down when lured by happiness. Eventually Andy nodded off.

The bright light of the full moon woke Andy from sleep. He tiptoed to the window and looked out. The landscape was cast in shades of blue and he pretended he lived on another planet—one where humor was appreciated. Spring had given way to summer and a warm breeze caressed his face. He closed his eyes, and when he opened them, the moon was so big it filled the window. The Man In The Moon stared at him. No—wait—it wasn't the Man In The Moon—it was Principal Barnum. He slammed the window shut, ran to his bed, and hid under the covers until dawn.

The next morning Andy awoke not feeling himself. He stumbled downstairs to the kitchen like a zombie. He didn't remember getting on the school bus or sitting down at his desk. He broke out in a cold sweat in class. He felt faint and lay his head down on the desk. Ms. Frump assumed he was faking, but just to be sure sent him to the school nurse. Andy didn't mind. He thought the nurse was attractive—for an older woman.

The nurse took one look at him and told him to sit. "My goodness, Andrew. You're as white as a ghost." She held a thermometer. "Open wide." She set the instrument under his tongue and studied her watch. When the time was up she withdrew the thermometer and frowned. "Hmm. Your temperature is actually below normal." She put her hand against his forehead.

"Your skin is cold and clammy. What have you eaten today?"

"A bowl of cereal," he said, although he couldn't remember.

"Do you feel nauseous?"

He shook his head. "No, but I feel lightheaded and my head hurts."

The nurse checked Andy's records. She then called his mother. "I want Andrew to see a doctor right away."

The doctor had Andy undress and put a smock on. He examined Andy, ran several tests, then consulted the results.

Andy's mother wrung her hands. "What is it? What's wrong?"

The doctor told Andy he could get dressed while he spoke to his mother in his office.

"I'm afraid it's bad news."

"NO! It can't be!" She clutched the doctor's sleeve. "Please!"

"His father suffered from it, yes?"

Andy's mom nodded as tears sprang from her eyes. "Yes."

"Clowning around has become a very serious disease—one requiring quarantine."

She covered her ears. "No! I don't want to hear it. Not The Big C?"

"It's highly contagious. And has a tendency to run in the family."

She spoke in whisper. "His father was quarantined and never came out."

The doctor's expression was kind but grim. "Andrew shows all the symptoms." He ticked them off on his fingers. "Making faces, joking around, using silly props to get attention, laughing, playing games."

"After his father died, I lost all sense of humor." She hung her head.

"I'm sorry for your loss, but this is a very serious matter, Mrs. Kelly. Tell me, does Andrew ever wear large, floppy, shoes?"

She looked up. "He did wear his dad's shoes when he was little." She smiled at the memory.

Edited By Jake Devlin

The doctor scribbled notes in Andy's file. "What about a fake red nose?" He loomed over Mrs. Kelly. "You know, the kind that honks when you squeeze it?"

Her eyes glazed over and she shook with fear.

"Did he ever paint his face? Dress up in baggy clothes?"

Andy's mother backed away from the doctor.

"Wear a goofy hat with a large flower sticking out of it?"

She was up against a wall now, one hand covering her open mouth. She screamed, and screamed, and could not stop.

END

The 2019 BOULD Awards Anthology

Edited By Jake Devlin

The 2019 BOULD Awards Anthology

Pinning Ceremony

John R. Clark (~2670 words)

I shut off my car and leaned back, listening to the sounds of a rural Maine summer, far from traffic and civilization. Even though it had been seventeen years since I'd last parked in Gramp's driveway, certain sounds remained familiar. Blue jays were calling me from twin crowns on the cedar rising in the middle of the now overgrown turnaround, while a murder of crows were scolding something, probably an owl, halfway up the western ridge. I closed my eyes, savoring the duet of cicadas and crickets, anything to postpone exiting the car and starting the painful task of dealing with reality.

Coming back to Sawtelle, Maine, was the last thing I'd ever planned on doing. I was going to put in my twenty years and then hole up in some quiet backwater country where health care was cheap and no military was needed, but we know how plans go. My platoon buddy, Rahmaan, blown to bits by an IED, used to remind me that if I wanted to hear the god of my understanding chuckle, just tell him what I planned for the future. I'd seen or experienced too many instances of exactly that to be surprised at where I was on this cloudless August afternoon.

The door handle burned my gut when I finally got out and closed the door before leaning on the hot roof, but I welcomed the pain because it brought me back to the present while I studied my unwanted inheritance. I craved remote and out of the way, but the farmhouse in front of me had too many memories for me, some bad, some good, all now bittersweet.

I was thirty-five with three years to go before qualifying for an early retirement, but something about leaning on my car, staring at the place I'd grown up in, made me feel more like the awkward teen who'd walked away three weeks after graduation from high school.

A particularly bold jay swooped past my head, his scolding cry bringing me back to reality. Like it or not, I now owned 65 acres in the middle of southern Aroostook County, complete with house, barn, a few outbuildings and, unless my grandfather had changed drastically, a crapload of old farming equipment.

I'd come dressed for the occasion, faded cords, steel toed boots and a Red Sox t-shirt that was older than half their current fan base. It was another inheritance from Gramps, complete with memories of the game we attended where he'd opened his wallet, George and Abe wincing at the unaccustomed light, to buy it for me. New work gloves stuck out of my back pocket.

Armed with the hefty key ring the lawyer had sent me along with the will and a laminated copy of Gramp's obituary, I walked to the front door, half expecting it had been kicked in. Remote homes tended to fall prey to vandals and drug addicted criminals pretty quickly these days, even this far from the nearest dealer.

I tried a number of keys in the securely locked door before finding the right one. The combination mud room and inside woodshed smelled like birch with a hint of poplar, just like it had when I used to carry armloads in from the huge stacks in the connected barn. In fact, the bin with dual hinged doors, one here, the other inside the kitchen, was still half filled.

The kitchen had a faint foul odor that increased when I opened the ancient refrigerator. I'd found my first task. Two hours later, my appetite ruined, I'd hauled an abundance of noxious mysteries from the fridge and bread box to the compost pile out back. I'd leave the root cellar until later. The well water still tasted as good as I remembered and I sipped some from a mason jar as I checked out the rest of the downstairs.

I wasn't surprised to see the same oversized TV facing the

shabby couch where Gramps and my waspish grandmother, her face etched with a perpetually disapproving frown, sat every evening after supper. One of my nightly chores was clearing the table before washing and drying the dishes while listening to her constant criticism of everything on the screen, interspersed with equally critical comments about townsfolk, my grandfather, and me.

If it had just been my grandfather, I'd probably have stuck around Sawtelle for a while. I loved roaming through the woods, fishing in the nearby beaver bog and going deer hunting in November, but my grandmother's endless list of criticisms and unrealistic expectations of me had driven me into the military and despite my affection for Gramps and my gratitude for the two of them taking me in when my parents were killed in a car crash when I was nine, I'd never sucked it up and come back for a visit. And then came the news, my grandfather was dead.

Oddly enough, the message I'd gotten while serving in Afghanistan made no mention of my grandmother and when I emailed my grandparents' attorney, his reply said I was the sole heir, so I assumed she'd died years before, probably from pure cussedness.

My search through the upstairs turned up nothing of hers. My old room looked pretty much the same and the master bedroom had a distinctly masculine feel. The dresser drawers were filled with well worn work shirts and pants and I found a couple outdated suits and several pairs of work boots in the closet. All in all, there wasn't going to be too much in the way of stuff I'd need to cart off to the dump or to the nearest thrift store.

Before I arrived, my plan was to clean out the place and see if a local realtor thought it was worth putting on the market. If not, I could easily cover the property taxes until this part of Maine started to become popular with flatlanders. Nothing I'd seen in the house or yard thus far threatened to change that mindset, but I'd set aside a week, if necessary, to clean up the property. If my grandfather had continued true to form, I knew the barn and small meadow behind it would have an abundance of farm equipment and at least some of it would be worth selling.

My heart sped up as soon as I opened the barn door and late afternoon sunlight hit the love of my life. I couldn't believe what nice shape the old Ford 8-N was in. The tractor had been made in 1952, the last year that model was manufactured. Gramps had swapped his 1962 Ford pickup and three cords of wood for it the year before I came to live on the farm. One of the first things he taught me was how to drive it. My legs had been so short, he'd carved me a pair of oversized wooden shoes out of a big basswood log so I could reach the brake and clutch pedals.

It had become my escape whenever my grandmother's negativity threatened to send me over the edge. I'd learned to mow, bale, bush hog, plow, harrow and even run the cordwood saw using the power takeoff on the back. After settling into the cracked seat, I placed my hands on the wheel and closed my eyes. Some time later, I snapped awake as my head hit the wheel. I was more weary than I wanted to admit. As much as I wanted to fire up this beauty, I needed sleep first. After a quick meal, thanks to some venison in the freezer, I crawled into my old bed and was out almost instantly.

My grandmother was leaning over me, her face stern and mouth pinched, but I couldn't understand anything she said. It was as though she was speaking through several feet of murky water. I tried reading her lips, but all I could make out was something about someone thinking they were going to get away with it. When I tried to reply, my yell woke me from the nightmare. I was drenched in sweat with my feet twisted in the top sheet so tightly it was a wonder I hadn't cut off circulation. I was used to nightmares. Everyone I served with in any war zone knew they came with the territory, but what was my grandmother doing in one?

There was no way I was going back to sleep, so I went downstairs and made a pot of coffee while thinking about the dream. Was it some sort of supernatural message? I thought back to my teen years, trying to remember anything that stood out about the woman I remembered as perpetually unhappy and bitter. An hour later, nothing had surfaced that seemed new. Every memory portrayed her as shrewish and made me wonder why Gramps had married her in the first place. He'd been the polar opposite, quiet, durable, but with a sly sense of humor that snuck up on those with a clue, while leaping over everyone else. Now that I thought about it, there had been numerous instances where his comments had skewered her and she hadn't had a clue. Mulling over this wasn't doing me any good.

Shortly after sunrise, I was heading out, on my way to the small cemetery where Gramps was buried. I needed to pay my respects to him as well as visit my parents' graves, and was also curious about whether my grandmother was buried there as well. The sky was cloudy, with thunderheads to the west that promised rain and more by noon time. No other vehicles were parked in the small turn-out in front of the Berryhill Cemetery. I'd forgotten how peaceful it felt and what a great view there was. The neatly mowed hillside sloped down to a winding stream with mountains in the distance. I could hear ducks quacking, the sound mixing with bob-o-links and red wing blackbirds.

Although my memories of my parents were faded, I couldn't prevent my eyes watering when I knelt by their twin headstone and said a silent prayer. Every time I came, I wondered what my life might have been like, had they not died so early. I rubbed my eyes and went to find Gramps.

He was lower down the slope and as far as I could tell, his grave was a solitary one, making my grandmother's fate even more mysterious. I sat with my back against his headstone, knowing he wouldn't be the least upset by my doing so. I savored the heat from the granite, letting it seep in and numb the scarred spot above my hip where a piece of shrapnel from an insurgent's bullet had almost torn through my kidney ten years ago. As the ever present pain subsided a bit, I carried on an imaginary conversation, filling in Gramps on things that had happened since I ran away.

I spent the next three days filling boxes I'd gotten from Hibbard's General Store. Not much changed in Sawtelle, it seemed. The folks running the place still piled unbroken cardboard boxes of all sizes under the tin overhang shading the loading dock out back. The first few passes were easy, as I filled the boxes with stuff I knew without a doubt, I'd never use. By the time I'd finished my fifth trip, I was on a first name basis with volunteers at three different churches that ran thrift stores.

Things got slower after that. I was down to the items I needed to think about more carefully, stuff like books, certain dishes, pictures and even a few items from the ever present junk drawer. When my head started throbbing from a combination of dust and painful memories, I took a break.

After making sure there was gas in the tank, firing up the old tractor gave me instant relief. I eased it out of the barn and spent a couple hours driving down the woodland equivalent of memory lane. My grandfather had done a fine job of maintaining the network of woods roads, even adding a few new ones. I shut off the engine at the spot overlooking the beaver pond and lost myself in watching the abundance of wildlife. By the time I felt ready to tackle whatever was behind the barn, I'd seen blue herons, wood ducks, deer, beaver, several muskrats and a pileated woodpecker.

The area behind the barn was neater than expected. The weeds and grass weren't very high and the winding pathways between farm implements were still easy to follow. It looked like someone had been out here since Gramps died. Was it someone who knew about my grandfather's penchant for buying farm equipment and was interested in dickering with the heir? That was irritating, but the most logical. Gramps had left room enough so I would be able to back the tractor up to each piece and bring it out front. Once I'd done that, my plan was to call some dealers so I could unload the stuff. There was only one piece I knew I wanted to keep. The bush hog had been my outlet for anger dispersal when I was living here. I loved the way the big, flailing pieces of steel could take weeds, grass and small alders and turn them into chips and chaff. Gramps had never had to ask me twice to hog any of the fields or woods roads.

The bush hog was in fine shape, but something made me pause when I walked up to it. I looked around to make sure I wasn't seeing things. Nope, none of the other pieces of equipment had a concrete pad under them. I shrugged. I'd puzzle that out later after moving all the rest of the stuff out front.

It was getting dark when I finished moving everything, but there was still light enough to indulge myself, so I backed up to the bush hog and attached it to the rear hydraulics before sliding a shear pin through the shaft to protect the blades in case I hit a rock or something too thick to chop up. When I raised the hog so I could move it, something caught me eye. There was an object lying on the concrete pad. I hopped down and bent over to see what it was.

The pain damn near made me pass out as something hit my scarred back and I tumbled onto what I quickly realized was the remains of my grandfather. If he was here, who was in his grave?

"It's empty." the familiar voice said as she kicked my foot so it would fit under the housing.

I tried to move when I realized what was coming, but the pain, coupled with emotional shock, rendered me helpless, something that

Edited By Jake Devlin

hadn't happened since I'd been a teen here on the farm.

She was in the seat now and I felt more pain as she brought the bush hog down so there was no room to move and the blades were digging into my legs and shoulder. There wasn't a thing I could do.

"That old bastard was leaving you everything, even though I cooked and cleaned for him for nearly forty years. It took damn near a week to move all my stuff to the barn loft and sleeping where bat droppings can hit at any time is no picnic. To hear him talk, sunshine came out of your backside. Too bad he didn't catch on to my little deal with the lawyer who handled our affairs. He understood how unfair things were. We have a nice updated will that nobody will ever question, especially since you're going to leave a note renouncing your inheritance. Enough talk, I must keep busy, so chop chop."

The last thing I remember was my grandmother raising the bush hog just enough to allow the blades to engage before dropping.....

END

The 2019 BOULD Awards Anthology

Edited By Jake Devlin

The 2019 BOULD Awards Anthology

Drip-Dry and Wrinkle-Free

Lesley A. Diehl (~2440 words)

I don't mean to whine, but me—savvy, clever, well-educated—have been bamboozled.

I'd known Mason Wrinkle for years. We went to grade school and high school together but were never close. He was the last child in the Wrinkle clan, the only boy. With so many children to feed and clothe, the family had to play loose with the law. Oh, never in big ways. It was just little things. When Mother Wrinkle went to the grocery, she took all the children with her. They spread out like a flock of marauding grackles, swooping down on the grapes, peaches and bananas, grabbing cookies from the bin, stripping the wrappers from candy bars with their teeth, and devouring everything in several huge swallows.

It was impossible for the store employees to keep an eye on all of them. By the time Mrs. Wrinkle pushed her cart to the checkout line, not a single Wrinkle-pilfered item could be pointed to by the store manager. It all resided in their full stomachs. If ever a clerk suggested one of Mother Wrinkle's children might have consumed something and not paid, she'd roll her eyes and say, "Oh, those kids. I can't hardly keep an eye on all of them." She might even have offered to pay for what was eaten, but how do you charge for what isn't there?

There were also stories of items missing from the hardware store, the five-and-dime, and other businesses in town. But no charges were ever brought against the Wrinkles. Who would the authorities arrest? The parents? Or one of the kids? And which one? The girls all looked alike. Even Mason was as tow-headed and round as his older sisters. The Wrinkle children looked more like a litter of Yorkshire hogs than a family of humans.

We never called him Mason in school. We called him "Wrinkle". I suspect when he was born, being the twelfth child, someone said, "Here comes yet another wrinkle." They were half wrong, of course. No other wrinkle followed.

I ignored him in high school because I wasn't into nice boys, and Mason was nice—his manners good, his hygiene, for someone who waited in line in the mornings behind eleven girls for the one bathroom, impeccable. When he shoplifted, he did it with a beatific smile, not a sneaky grin, and he always thanked the employees when he left the store. If I'd had proof at the time that he took things, I might have paid more attention to him. Stealing and shoplifting meant he had bad boy creds, perhaps not as spectacular as drinking and having sex with girls in the back seats of cars, but it might have been provocative enough to get my youthful hormones stirring but not boiling.

I only dated bad boys, a fact I tried to keep from my mother. She must have known because she pushed me toward some of the town's most notorious goodie goodies. I still have a picture today of Clive Barnes and me at the junior prom. When I look at it, I want to send it to the pope as part of a submission package for sainthood.

The June after my freshman year in college, I took a job in a publishing house in my hometown. I'd hoped to stay at the college and take some course work that summer, but my funds ran out, so I was late applying for a position.

"The only job I have left is a stripper," said the hiring officer. An odd position for a publishing house, but a thrill coursed through me. I didn't think my body was good enough for that kind of work, but the guy doing the hiring clearly did.

To my surprise, the job wasn't as exciting as I'd anticipated. Standing at a table of books in a cavernous warehouse with no air conditioning and no windows, I removed the covers from unsold paperbacks so retail companies could send them back for a refund. The books went to the dump. The workers were warned not to take the coverless paperbacks (no one understood going "green" in those days), but we tucked them into our aprons, pockets, and under our shirts, hiding them from our parents because the books were borderline porno.

Despite my preference for the wild side, I was still a virgin, but that summer taught me a lot. It was then I focused on Wrinkle for the first time. Maybe I got wind of enough bad stuff about him that I decided to try him out. I was glad I did. We necked a lot in the back seat of his beat-up Chevy two-door. I remember those months being particularly sweaty for me. Despite the heat we two worked up, I returned to school in the fall and forgot about Wrinkle for several decades.

I forgot about him until now.

Several weeks ago, I visited Mom and Dad as I often do for some of my vacation days. I'm a lawyer with an environmental firm. I ran into Wrinkle at the Tasty Cone Drive-In. A chance encounter. The drive-in was selling ice cream pints half price in preparation for closing down for the season. Mom dispatched me to buy as many pints of blueberry razzle as were left over. It wasn't one of their popular flavors, so I had hit the jackpot and was making my second trip out to the car with the twenty pints I'd purchased. Wrinkle appeared in front of me and opened my car door.

"Hey, Daisy. Haven't seen you for a while around here," he said.

The hair stood up on my arms, and my legs felt like jello turning into its liquid form. It may have been the Indian Summer heat, but I didn't think so. He looked great, badder than when he was younger. He must have gone to the gym and worked out because the muscle definition in his arms was impressive. I imagined myself clinging to those biceps while we sweated away on the leather seats in my car. I was staying with my parents. I could hardly sneak him up to my bedroom, could I?

Heat suffused my body, and I was certain it was due to Wrinkle's hand on my waist. We moved so close a gnat wouldn't fit between us.

The hell with it. "Wanna go for a ride?" I asked.

"Sure. Where?"

"How about the fair grounds near the park?"

"Recapturing old memories?" he asked.

I laughed and winked. "No, silly. Making new ones. I only get out this way once a year. I can't survive on twenty-year old remembrances."

And that was that. We slid around on the seat, made head and handprints on the windows of my Mercedes, and ascertained our nervous systems were still up to the task of stimulus overload. Best sex I'd had since ... well, for too long. The ice cream melted, of course, and my mom wanted to know why. I told her the freezer at the Tasty Cone must have been defective. And she couldn't call to yell at them because they were closed for the season. Everything worked out so well. Or so I thought.

A few weeks later, I got a call. From Mason, uh, Wrinkle. It seems he was in a bit of a pickle with the local Postal Service and needed a lawyer. Of course, he didn't have money to pay for legal services, but he thought of me and our "connection." I thought about that too and felt a warmth rush up my legs from my toes and head toward my girlie parts.

"The firm does some *pro bono* work. Each one of us is expected to. I'll run it by the partners and get back to you," I said.

The tingle in my thighs must have affected the memory

synapses in my brain, the ones that stored the information about the Wrinkle family's proclivity to play loose with the law. In my defense, the charges against Wrinkle were too silly. The post offices in the area were accusing him of stealing mailers, thousands of them, the ones made of Tyvek material. Now what would anyone want with all those mailers? And, anyhow, they're free. Maybe not by the gross, but they're free.

"I never took them," he said. "I think they messed up their inventory somehow, and they need a fall guy. I'm the one. Because of my family."

He didn't have to say more. I understood. Folks in my hometown looked down on the Wrinkles. My mother had no use for them.

"You aren't going to defend him, are you?" Mother said when we spoke on the phone.

"What's your problem with him?"

"It's not him so much as his mother. She let all those kids eat unwashed fruit from the supermarket. No telling who had handled it. It might have affected his mind."

"It drove him to steal useless things from the postal service?" I asked.

"You never can tell about that family," Mother said. There was a pause at her end of the connection. "You know Clive Barnes just became Postmaster in town. And he got a divorce from his wife. I'm sure he'd love to hear from you."

"She probably divorced him. For boring her to death," I said. Mother made one of those "tching" sounds. "I'll be in town this weekend to interview Mason." I disconnected and daydreamed of slippery car seats.

Five days later Mason and I met in the truck stop east of town and plotted our court strategy.

Edited By Jake Devlin

"Town folks have never had any use for my family, but they also don't have much respect for the postal service around here after they laid off half the workers, took away the trucks from their employees, and made them walk their routes," said Mason. "Nope. I hear they're gonna raise the price of stamps again and eliminate Saturday service."

I had to agree with Mason's sentiment. The town's dislike of members of the Wrinkle family or the community's disdain for the bureaucracy of the postal service—which would win? And poor Mason Wrinkle caught in the middle. I had to make his defense look like the traditional David and Goliath story. That was certain to get any jury on our side.

"Gotta run, Daisy," said Mason. He leaned over and gave me a kiss on the cheek but said nothing about our getting together.

"How about a drive in my Mercedes?" I said.

"Not today. I've got to do some work for my mom. He winked at me and added, "There's always the celebration after we win."

There was that tingle again.

I watched Wrinkle drive off in his old beat-up truck, the rusted side panels flapping as he drove west out of town toward his parent's house. I got into my Mercedes and headed toward the supermarket where I'd promised Mom I'd pick up steaks for dinner tonight. As I was leaving the parking lot of the market, I spotted Mason's truck heading back east down Main Street. Odd. I decided to follow him, tingle or not. Or maybe because of that tingle.

From Main Street his truck pulled onto Swarthollow Path and wound its way up into the hills overlooking town. There were no side roads and few houses on Swarthollow, so I had only to keep his dust in sight. At the crest of the hill, he turned into a driveway and stopped in front of a small house. I pulled in behind him. A woman opened the door. She held a baby in her arms. Four other children, a toddler and three boys in cut-off jeans came to stand beside her. Sara Jean Hardy. One of our classmates from high school and someone I vaguely remembered Mason sniffing around when we were seniors. The children were as tow-headed as their father when he was little. A new Wrinkle generation.

I didn't get out of my car. I left the engine running and considered the situation. Yep. Bamboozled into taking the case by my proclivity for bad boys. What to do now?

Before I could make up my stunned mind, Mason turned and walked toward my car. He held his arms in the air as if surrendering to the truth and wanting me to be calm with it.

"Now, Daisy," he said, "let's be cool here. Come in and meet the family."

Cool? I wasn't cool? Had he seen something on my face?

"No sense in getting all worked up over this," he said.

Was I worked up? I did an inventory of my feelings. He was wrong. I was not all worked up. I was only beginning to get worked up. I put the car into drive, smashed down on the accelerator, and aimed the hood toward Mason. Now I was worked up.

"Daisy. Baby," he yelled. He dived to my right, so that all I could see was his wife's face in my windshield. Sara Jean stood frozen on the porch, the baby waving its tiny fists in the air. I might have intended doing a "Tawanda" on Mason, but certainly not on his family. I jerked the steering wheel to the left, missed the porch, and tore off the corner of the house.

I jumped out to look at the damage. "I'll pay for the repairs," I said.

"You bet you will," said Sara Jean. Mason came up to stand at her side.

"The repairs shouldn't cost much," I said, "since you get your materials cut rate."

Edited By Jake Devlin

The siding hung in chunks, exposing the vapor barrier underneath. I ripped a piece of the Tyvek off the plywood and examined it closely. The words "Priority Mail" stood out on the torn paper.

"You still my lawyer? I mean this is lawyer-client privilege, right?" asked Mason.

"Sure," I said. I put the car in reverse, and, after several attempts of wheels spinning, I backed out of the Wrinkle yard.

I drove with deliberate attention down the curvy road. At the bottom, I pulled over and called my mother. "Mom, do you have Clive Barnes' phone number?"

I called him and asked him to go for a ride with me up Swarthollow Path. I know he expected more from that ride than he got, but at least he found out where all those Tyvek mailers from his post office went.

I looked at Clive after we'd passed the Wrinkle house. "You ever steal anything?" I asked. I reached out and put my hand on his thigh.

END

The 2019 BOULD Awards Anthology

Edited By Jake Devlin

The 2019 BOULD Awards Anthology

Mr. Happyhead

James Dorr (~2700 words)

Mr. Happyhead was a hawk, a vulture. A white Lammergeier, larger than eagles. He cruised the skies. He cruised people's thought-trains.

He cruised the city, in thought or in person, doting on crowds and filth and hunger. He studied the tragic.

Mr. Happyhead's personal thoughts went back to a table, to flesh growing soft, but then muscles stiffening. His thoughts went to smiles forced on unhappy faces as skin became waxy, as lips and finger- and toenails paled. His thoughts went to red-green discolorations, then smells of putrescence.

These things he had known too.

Except with release, with tissue decaying, with fluids leaking from head and anus, with gas-blisters forming, with swellings, explosions, Mr. Happyhead discovered freedom. He now had a mission, to share his good fortune.

He preyed on the city's own.

Catching his breath, Mr. Happyhead entered his first thought. He picked it at random. He found himself staring into a bar mirror, eying a women who had just come through the door behind him.

"Would you care to dance?" he asked, turning around and smiling broadly, but also blushing. He knew he was married.

The woman looked him up and down, then frowned and turned back to the friends she'd come in with. She started laughing.

Mr. Happyhead turned even redder, but only ordered another whiskey. He drank it slowly, taking his time, even though the thought of a wife who would wait up late for him -- not married that long, their love was still ardent -- tried to slip through from the back of his mind.

Edited By Jake Devlin

He watched the woman, tall and with red hair, laughing and talking with her companions, occasionally dancing when other men asked her, through the dust-spiderwebbed behind-bar mirror.

He waited until she and her friends prepared to leave, then finished himself and followed after, always keeping a half block of shadows, of darkness, between them. He waited as first one, and then another, and then the last of the redhead's companions turned their own ways in the spiraling blackness, taking their own paths to go to their own homes. And still he waited.

He stood outside and noted the window that suddenly lit up after she had gone into a building. He counted the windows from the building's corner, the floors from the sidewalk. He went inside too and climbed the stairs, then counted the doors from the end of the hallway, estimating doors against windows, until he arrived at the one with a dim hint of light still beneath it.

He waited patiently, until that, too, went dark, then counted slowly to sixty, one hundred, six hundred, a thousand, then counted again to be sure she was sleeping before, with a twist learned from when he was younger and used his own body, he broke her door lock. He eased her door open.

He shut it behind him, then found a table lamp, following its cord by feel to its socket. He carried it with him as his eyes adjusted to the inside darkness.

Interior doors: He found one to the bathroom. Another, that opened into the kitchen, yielded a sharp knife.

The third opened onto his quarry, sleeping.

He leaned behind her, then tied her hands quickly with the lamp cord. He thrust a pillowcase into her mouth when it opened to scream.

He found another lamp in the bedroom and used its cord to bind her feet as well, then bind both hands and feet to the solid bed.

As the dawn came, he became an artist, carving illustrations in carmine to match her hair with the knife from the kitchen. He stepped back often, admiring his work. Adjusting the pillowcase now and again, lest her screams, then her whispers, disturb his train of thought. And, behind that thought, he felt another thought, that of a decent man not that long married, wondering . . . admiring . . . thinking, perhaps, of a wife who was waiting.

#

Mr. Happyhead left joy behind him. He left people with ideas to do things they would not do had he not helped them. He left the counterman in a diner whose boss had just -- once again -- threatened to fire him, a notion of how to hurt his boss's business. And then, on his break, Mr. Happyhead left him facing the kitchen pantry, contemplating the box of rat poison he knew was inside it.

#

Mr. Happyhead often remembered the time of his boyhood. His father. His mother. His mother's brother who taught him things most boys did not learn till later. He thought of his studies, not so much in school as on weekends and summers. His learning about birds.

His lust for flying.

He studied pigeons, catching them, sometimes, and finding out the ways their wings bent. When they would not obey, he gave them to cats.

He studied their talons.

#

Mr. Happyhead loved women most. He entered their thoughts often, savoring their difference. He taught them power.

He spoke to women, telling them how, through his own experience, they could tempt men to do their bidding. He transcended space and time, becoming Eva Braun whispering to Hitler. Cleopatra

Edited By Jake Devlin

inciting Mark Antony.

He taught sisters how to enjoy their brothers.

#

When Mr. Happyhead had been a boy, one summer he went to the beach with his parents. There he was able to contemplate sea gulls. He watched, fascinated, as they flew with shellfish clutched in their claws, circling higher, until, over rocks, they dropped their prey, splitting their armor so they could eat.

He watched sea gull mothers, guarding their nests. How, when fledglings from other nests wandered too far and blundered into the wrong territory, they pecked the intruders' heads into gray jelly and fed them to their own young. Ate what was left themselves.

Mr. Happyhead made an experiment, switching eggs from one nest to another, then young birds as well. He wore a catcher's mask when he did this, and thick, brown gloves.

He wore many masks as he grew older. As student. As citizen. Once, as a soldier. As workman.

As lover.

As man of the streets, first running errands for those with more power, then finding ways to gain power of his own. Worming his way into inner circles

As loyalist. Henchman.

As one who was trusted.

When Mr. Happyhead was not working, he frequented zoos.

#

Mr. Happyhead played with children, and sometimes their mothers. He had a winning smile.

#

Mr. Happyhead liked seeing dentists. He liked the way the hygienist placed pointed hooks in his mouth, using a mirror to chip at his teeth. To chip the flecks away. When he was young, he sometimes had thought he might be a dentist's hygienist himself.

He liked seeing blood spit in white porcelain basins, watching its spiral flow.

When he was young, he had liked hawks and eagles. And then Lammergeiers, "Bearded Vultures" according to the book his father got for him one Christmas. He'd seen it in a store, then begged for it almost all the way from Halloween. And his mother helped him.

"It's good that he wants to learn things," his mother would say nights at dinner.

"But books about vultures?" his father would answer. "I think that's morbid."

"Hawks and vultures," his mother had said. "And eagles too. Like our country's symbol. There's nothing wrong with that."

Mr. Happyhead's father had bought the book the morning after he'd beaten his wife. The evening before he had come home after working late and, tiring of the incessant argument, in their bedroom that night he'd slapped her. He'd bought the book as a kind of appeasement. They'd kissed and made up and wrapped it together and hid it in their bedroom closet.

Mr. Happyhead had not been intended to know this, except he'd been outside their door and listened. He'd listened as well in the following years as their marriage continued its downward spiral. As the hittings became more frequent and Mr. Happyhead got gifts more often. Books and toys and camping equipment. Toy guns and airplanes.

But most of all, he still liked to think about Lammergeiers, described in the book as having wingspans greater than eagles' -- some naturalists even thought they were eagles, though somewhat like vultures as well, insofar as they ate the dead. He read about people in Eastern, Himalayan nations who placed their deceased on the tops of towers, waiting for the great, white birds to descend and devour them.

Some even thought that the huge birds were spirits.

#

Mr. Happyhead had his favorites, of those he flew into. A dentist's hygienist -- he got in her head often and, through the hooks and the mirrors and probes, he drank in her feelings about her boyfriend. Her fear and hatred, and yet her greater fear that he might leave her. The beatings he gave her. And when the next patient got in the chair, the hooks in his mouth, the probe at his gumline, he had her let them out.

#

Mr. Happyhead grew into power, having learned how to manipulate people. He learned about violence, and when he should use it. He learned about money -- when he could pay others.

He learned about greed.

But when his father had been found dead in his parents' bedroom, the .25 caliber bullet of a "Saturday night special" lodged in his brain, and as his mother was dragged away weeping, that's when he had learned of joy. Joy as proactive. Joy as something he could himself plan, for himself or for others, and not simply wait to receive as a byproduct of other things that others did to him. Joy as fulfillment.

He never knew how to hate -- never could understand its concept, at least in himself, though he knew it in others.

And when he found himself on a table, hearing a doctor explain to the young cop who'd brought him in about things like trauma, the force of powder grains tattooing skin, about entrance paths and shock waves and exits and hollowed out, larger and heavier bullets, that's when he had started to come to know freedom.

#

Mr. Happyhead came to suspect the mystics of Himalayan

lands were on to something. He flew in the night air, no longer earthbound, as bird or not-bird -- it did not matter.

He thought: Birds have no teeth.

He flew to his mother in Women's Prison and entered her head and found that she loved him. She had always loved him and, as he'd begun to nurture his own brushes with the law, had almost admired him. And he'd loved her also. He'd taught her things about prison bed sheets and how they could be torn in strips, twisted and knotted. How they could be looped from ceiling fixtures. He found that she feared, though -- that she was not ready. That freedom was not for her, at least not that night.

He learned about patience.

He had already known about waiting. Of waiting in ambush, or being ambushed himself. Of power conflicts. And now he learned endurance.

#

Mr. Happyhead flew to the man who had been his rival and, flying within his thoughts, drank of his triumph. Triumph became pride, and then pride hubris. He watched and he let it grow, he a nestling, a fledgling lodged in this other man's brain-cage, becoming in time a mother sea gull pecking away at any intrusive thoughts save those his own will and joy engendered.

He looked out at others, also outside the law, who had more power than this, his protege, and through sheer savagery took them over. Expanding his domain.

He came in time to rule the whole town, and then the county, with numbers and gambling and prostitution.

He got himself noticed.

And when a yet larger gang from the state capital descended on this, his operation, he left his rival, flying back to the sky. Hovering. Waiting.

Edited By Jake Devlin

Enjoying patience -- perhaps now and then breathing small suggestions into minds oh, so open to hear them -- as his erstwhile rival -- his own erstwhile killer -- was trussed to a wooden chair. His clothes ripped from him. Knives brought out and worked with. Small knives not for killing, but only enjoying.

He watched and enjoyed and flew in and out of the pain and the redness, devouring driblets of soul with each passage, as flesh became weaker, yet never quite perished. As life hung on that night, and then for three others until the sculptors who carved became weary.

And still life hung on, until the police found the eyeless, tongueless, fingerless, flayed hulk that would continue to breathe and shit and take in nutrition from hospital needles for decades to come before finally expiring.

And one cop looked up then, out the abandoned warehouse window.

"Jeez, what's that?" he said as the stretcher bearers came in for their burden.

"I don't know -- looks like a bird," his partner said, gazing out the window too now. "A big white bird. Some kind of big sea gull."

"Sea gull, my ass," the first one said. "It's as big as an eagle."

#

Mr. Happyhead read the newspapers. He read of other crimes and disasters. Of long suffering wives killed in suburban houses. Of children who talked back discovering silence. Of gang leaders, some more of whom he had once known, falling out over drugs and profits. He read about business -- he liked the drug trade and wished to help it.

He went to the source. He became a pilot, and then a ship's captain. He formed an intimacy with policemen who lived on the take, and with their commissioners. He captured the mind and the soul of the woman who slept with the mayor.

He doted on guns -- after all, did he not know himself what guns could do? -- and cultivated in others their love as well.

He taught others how to use knives and razors, yet others explosives, sometimes learning himself from the thoughts of those he had entered. He found himself in a fortified building, surrounded by armed men, whispering to leaders they must not surrender. That rightness was with them.

He taught people courage.

And always the memories came back, of the cold table. Then of a tunnel that time of his own death. A dark, long tunnel. He'd thought about having read of such tunnels as he'd paced its distance, leaving his ruined flesh far behind him. He'd heard in his mind the voice of the doctor fading to near silence as, ahead of him, he thought he saw bright lights, felt warmth and comfort. But all he had read turned out to be lies.

He emerged on an ice field, cold, unrelenting, as cold as the table's top. What heat he felt proved no more than a memory.

A memory of first love, after a drunken pickup in a roadhouse. Of ripping her open after his passion had spent itself in her. Of slapping her. Stabbing her. Tearing her flesh as he later did others. As he wished his father had done that night of the book.

And now the others, the second, the third love, the fourth and those after, and friends, and grandparents, he now saw laughing as he emerged out of the dark of that tunnel. Laughing and smiling, their faces forgiveness.

Laughing at him, he thought.

Mr. Happyhead screamed his rejection -- this vision was not true! -- then struck with his fists at the white-robed figures, drowning himself in their spurting blood. Drinking their screams. Their shrieks. Taking and wrapping himself in their whiteness. Hearing their

Edited By Jake Devlin

shattered bone.

Spinning, he coursed again into the dark.

And felt the wind. Felt the wind at the outstretched tips of wing-feathers as, opening hooded eyes, now he was swooping over the city. A city of nighttime.

Below, he saw neon lights.

#

Mr. Happyhead was happy.

END

The 2019 BOULD Awards Anthology

Edited By Jake Devlin

The 2019 BOULD Awards Anthology

PREINCARNATION

Eve Fisher (~1000 words)

So there I am, in between lives, and I'm sick of hanging around.

Yeah, sure, there's action, people coming and going, and always someone around. So what? They tell me, hey, at least you're not alone. Like you're *ever* alone in this universe. Or the next. Or the next after that. To be honest, the main thing I like about incarnations is I get a little privacy for a change. Flesh and blood is a bit of a border.

Anyway, there we all are. Fred and Tony are debating – yeah, those were their names in their last life, and they're still a little attached to them, which is part of the problem. The term used at the last Review was "disappointingly unevolved," like they actually *tell* you where you're supposed to evolve to. Anyway, Fred and Tony are debating particles or strings, hologram or brane, and I didn't give a damn, you know? I want to get on with it. I want my next assignment.

Zap! A newcomer. And I know this one. It's... it's...

"Sam," says the newcomer. "Sam Glosper from Bleeker Street. You delivered my papers for three years, you little jerk."

"Small universe. When did you come in?"

"Just now, birdbrain," he says. I swear you could hear the collective sigh of the Review Board.

"No, no, I don't mean that. I mean, when'd you die?"

"May 21, 2087."

"How's the war going?"

"Search me. I was in a coma."

So there we are, waiting.

"Weird," Fred says, "I forgot all about this. I was die-hard

Pentecostal. Thought reincarnation was a bunch of crap."

"Don't beat yourself up about it," Tony says. "We're all like that. Re-entry wipes you clean."

"What I can't figure out is where they can send us," Fred says. "I mean, we were just about ready to wipe out the planet when I flat-lined."

"Maybe we're not gonna," I say.

"Nah," Tony says. "It gets wiped. 2150."

"How do you know?"

"I did a little research," Tony says. "It's in the history databank."

Personally, I think you pile up enough useless information every incarnation without looking up more facts here, but maybe that's part of the problem, too.

"You think that's why we're waiting around so long?" Fred asks. "Maybe They don't know what to do with us. How can you get a new life when there's no place to have it?"

"Geez," Sam says. "You haven't learned squat, have you?"

"What do you mean?"

"I mean, check your own database," Sam says. "We're all on our what, third, maybe fourth go-round, max?"

"Speak for yourself," Tony says. "This'll be my seventh." And we're all – excuse the pun - dead silent. "Look, the first three I died before I was two. It's not my fault that I didn't get a lot done!"

"Hey, I'm not the Review Board," Sam says.

"Damn straight."

"But if the planet's wiped," Fred says – he's got a one-track mind, which is part of the problem – "what are They going to do with us? Where can we go? Is there somewhere else we can go?"

"I don't know," I say, suddenly feeling spooked. "Are we that close to the Final Review?"

"No," Sam says firmly. "Listen, you got it all wrong. What's the whole purpose of this gig, anyway?"

Tony's our fact maven, in case you couldn't guess, so she recites: "'To make continual, demonstrable spiritual progress with each incarnation until the totality has been achieved.'"

"Exactly," Sam says. "You see anything there about temporal formatting? Temporal direction? Your next incarnation isn't going to come after your last one, but before it." Another definite silence. "Look, this last one, I was born in 2011 and died in 2087. Before that, I was born in 2068 and died in 2099. And my very first one, I was in born in 2150, died 2150. Bet you that's true for every one of us."

"Yeah," Tony says.

"Me, too," Fred says.

I chime in, "Me, too."

"So, you see? We all got it wrong. Time does not equal progress. You go forward, you go backwards, you go where you need to go. But we all start at the end, when it all ends. No wonder we were all so damn jumpy about the future! It sucked. We died. The planet got wiped. We couldn't remember it, but we knew it. And what we felt about the past –"

"Nostalgia," Tony says, firmly.

"You can't have nostalgia for something that hasn't happened yet," Sam replies.

"Wanna bet?" Fred asks.

"Nostalgia is just another word for hope," Sam says.

"Oh, God," I groan. "*Another* freaking meme!"

"We wanted to go back any way we could, because that's when things were finally going to get better and –"

"Oh, come on," Tony interrupts. "We had everything: central heat, air conditioning, indoor plumbing, fast food, antibiotics, anesthetics, mega-entertainment –"

Edited By Jake Devlin

"Momentary interest," Sam interrupts back, "and that's the first thing you gotta get past if you're gonna move on. Geez, you might as well still be walking around on two legs."

"So what's wrong with liking a little physical comfort?" Tony asks. Except she'd liked it a lot and that, as the Review Board had pointed out, was part of the problem.

"*Spiritual* progress!" Sam blares.

"Roman Empire," I point out. Tony beams at me, and it feels really good.

"Yeah, well, it takes you two thousand years to figure things out, you must be a real klutz in the karma department. And what about Ashoka Maurya?"

Next thing you know, everyone's trolling the databases, comparing the best and the worst through history.

Me, I'm thinking, what if he's right? So I sneak off, ask the Review Board about it. Like They're actually going to tell you anything. It's not Their style. But sometimes They hint. "You're not supposed to know things before you're ready." But I toss out a few names...

And next thing you know, I'm signed up for re-entry - in 1907.

END

The 2019 BOULD Awards Anthology

Edited By Jake Devlin

The 2019 BOULD Awards Anthology

To Die a Free Man: the Story of Joseph Bowers

KM Rockwood (~2790 words)

I know what they think about me. They think I'm a moron. I've heard them say that.

Maybe I'm not the smartest man locked up here in Alcatraz, but I'm not the stupidest, either.

My name is Joseph Bowers, but in here, I'm inmate 210. My friends would call me Dutch, but I haven't got any friends. Not here. And not on the outside anymore, either.

They've got a lot of other things wrong about me, too. Like my birthdate and place. They think I was born in Austria in 1896.

Really, I was born in El Paso, Texas, in 1897. My parents were working with a traveling circus at the time. My mother didn't want me, so she just left me to whoever In the circus crew stepped up to take care of me. I never had a birth certificate, and I've long ago lost contact with anyone in the circus.

That's caused me no end of trouble. I couldn't prove my American citizenship, and I couldn't get a passport, which makes it really hard to leave the country.

It used to be easier, just kind of slip across the borders, but now they want to see that passport. If I could get to Europe, I'd be able to live a decent life. I speak six languages, a lot for anyone, even in Europe, and I'm sure I could find myself work as a translator. Here, in the US, everybody pretty much speaks English, so there's not much call for translators.

Of course, I have to get out of this prison before I could go anywhere.

Edited By Jake Devlin

Seems like I've been in trouble most of my life. When I was in my early twenties, I was picked up in Oregon for a violation of the Dyer Act. That's the law that makes it a federal offense to transport stolen vehicles across state lines.

The charges are bunk. Sure, I was driving the car, and I found out later it was stolen, but I didn't know it at the time. For a conviction under the Dyer Act, three things need to be proven. One, that the vehicle was actually stolen. Two, that defendant takes the vehicle across state lines, and three, that he knows it was stolen.

As I said, I didn't know it at the time that it was stolen. So I wasn't guilty. But I was convicted anyhow, and served some time in the county lockup.

Things didn't get much better after that. Next time I was stopped when driving, the car wasn't reported stolen, but I was pretty drunk. And this, mind you, during Prohibition, when alcohol was illegal in the US.

Illegal, but plentiful.

In the early 1930's, there just weren't that many jobs. For anybody. Much less for someone just out of jail. Certainly no one I could find needed a translator, no matter how many languages I spoke.

I wandered around for a while, through Oregon and California. It was tough, with no place to live, no money for food, no way to make a living. I picked up casual work when I could, did some begging, a little burglary and when I was really desperate, some hold-ups.

There were a couple of close calls, but I pretty much got away with it until I held up a post office in Isaiah, California. That's in Butte County, and just about as miserable a place to be stranded as anyone can imagine.

Well, I won't go into the whole arrest and trial thing. I was guilty, no doubt about it. And since what I'd held up was a post office it was a federal offense. The Dyer Act violations were federal crimes, too. So they threw the book at me.

Twenty-five years in federal prison. All I got out of the robbery was $16.38. That sentence works out to eighteen months for each dollar. Harsh.

First I got sent to the penitentiary on McNeil Island in Puget Sound, in Washington State. I'd been in jail before, sure, but adjusting to a federal penitentiary was something altogether different. The idea of being locked up for the next twenty-five years messed with my head. I started telling stories to the other inmates, about how I'd traveled. Europe and South America and Mexico and Cuba. Mostly working as a translator. I told the stories so often I wasn't even sure myself anymore what was true and what was made up.

I found out that the report from the prison at McNeil that accompanied me to Alcatraz said I was considered "unpredictable and at high risk resulting from emotional instability."

Thanks, guys.

Old Saltwater Johnson, the warden at Alcatraz, later wrote that I was "a weak-minded man with a strong back."

I was transferred to Alcatraz in September of 1934, in one of the first groups to arrive after it was opened as a federal penitentiary. I have to admit that the food was good, better than I'd ever had anywhere in my whole life. At first I was glad to have the safety and privacy of a cell to myself—there was no double-celling at Alcatraz—but it wasn't long before the isolation started to get to me. Sometimes I thought I could hear the water out in the bay, sloshing endlessly. Other times it was so quiet I wondered if I'd lost my hearing.

Opportunities to talk to anyone, including fellow inmates, were strictly limited. And none of them wanted to listen to my stories anyhow. People looked at me funny. I was pretty sure the other inmates were talking about me behind my back. So were the guards.

Edited By Jake Devlin

And the cold! The wind off the water in September was bad enough. From November on, it was frigid. The very air tasted bitter and cold. It took me a while to find out I could request a woolen undershirt and another blanket. They helped some, but the only time I wasn't freezing was once a week when I got a shower. The water was delightfully warm. Supposedly it was kept that way deliberately. No one could use cold showers to accustom his body to cold water. That might improve chances of making the mile and a half swim to the mainland should anyone ever manage to get beyond the prison fences.

Getting beyond those fences didn't seem likely.

I began to have seizures. They may have just been violent bouts of shivering due to the cold. No one took them seriously, although I do believe the guards began to keep an even closer eye on me. It seemed like every time I looked up, a guard was at my door, watching me silently.

One day in March of 1935, I dropped my eyeglasses on the hard concrete floor of my cell. One of the lenses broke. My first thought was that I would have a long wait for a new pair of glasses.

My second thought was that it wouldn't matter anyhow. I still had twenty years left on my bit. All for $16.38. Talk about a long wait.

The broken glass glittered on the floor. I picked up a good-sized piece and sat on the edge of my bunk, holding it in my hands. I ran my finger across the edge. It was razor sharp.

No way was I going to be released for years. I'd be an old man by then. Did I really want to spend all those years locked up like this, only to be released penniless and friendless into an uncaring world that had changed immeasurably in the last twenty-five years?

I knew of only one way under my control to shorten the time. I could end this all now. I held the opportunity in my hand.

Gently, tentatively, I swiped the sharp edge of the glass over my throat. I felt a trickle of dampness. A coppery smell of fresh blood reached my nostrils. When I reached up and rubbed my throat, my hand came away bloody.

If I was going to do this, I'd have to cut deeper. Much deeper. Did I have the guts to do that?

I raised the glass to my throat again and pushed the sharp edge down into my flesh.

How much more deeply would I have to go before I cut the jugular vein? And the windpipe?

With my eyes closed and my mind concentrated on the task at hand, I dug the edge of the glass into the side of my neck. If I could keep it in that far and draw it all the way across the front of my throat, surely I'd be cutting something major. And fatal.

The sharp blast of a whistle practically in my ear startled me. I dropped the piece of glass and opened my eyes.

The guards all had these whistles they blew when they needed help. Something must be going on.

I looked out through the bars.

The guard stood at my door, whistle in his mouth.

Other guards came running.

"He cut his throat!"

"Grab his hands. Give me your cuffs."

"Kick that glass out of the way."

"Bring him to medical."

The whole thing happened so fast I was kind of in a daze. I was hauled out of my cell, handcuffed and hustled along to the hospital.

The doctor examined my wound. He said it was superficial. He asked if I'd intended to kill myself.

I said, "Yes."

He assigned me to an observation cell in the hospital. It was warm. The food was just as good as in the mess hall. I didn't see any other inmates, but the staff checked on me frequently. Sometimes they'd talk to me. I didn't have any more seizures.

After a few more weeks, they decided I'd just been playing at a suicide attempt, probably for the attention it would bring me.

It did bring me attention, but that wasn't why I'd done it. And if the guards hadn't intervened so quickly, I probably would have cut deeper and eventually managed to kill myself.

I was transferred back into population. At first I just stayed in my cell most of the time, which got boring fast. So when they offered me a position as a cell house orderly, I took it. It was okay at first, but gradually I began having more and more disputes with everyone, inmates and staff alike. They were rigging things so it would look like I wasn't doing my job. Just after I swept, people would throw cigarette butts and scraps of toilet paper and stuff on the floor in the catwalk outside the cells. They'd say I hadn't cleaned up at all.

When they asked if I'd take a different work assignment, I agreed. Incinerator detail, which was one of the most unpopular assignments in the prison. Still, it would get me outside every day, breathing the fresh air off the bay.

I didn't realize what a miserable job it would be.

One advantage was that I worked alone, sorting metals and burning garbage. It was hard, dirty work. Nobody bothered me. The incinerator was on the edge of the island. Plumes of dark smoke belched out of the smokestack and floated away.

Cold air whipped over the gray water that separated me from the rest of the world, smelling of the salt water and decaying fish. My hands grew raw and chapped. I couldn't get the garbage scent off my clothes, and I suspected it had soaked into my body, so that no matter how I scrubbed at my weekly shower, I smelled like garbage.

I could see tourist boats sail by, and sometimes, if the wind was just right, I could hear people laughing. Were they laughing at me, stuck here on this God-forsaken island?

The seagulls hung around. There was always lots of food scraps and waste in the stuff I was sorting and burning, and I tossed it out for them. I envied them their ability to fly, alighting a few feet away from me, then swooping away with the scraps in their beaks. The fences made no difference to them.

After the first few days, the guard in the Road Tower, who kept an eye on the incinerator, didn't pay me much mind.

I began to recognize some of the gulls who visited regularly and imagined that they wanted to be my friends. One in particular came to visit nearly every day. He was missing a leg, and his wing on that side was deformed.

He'd perch on the ground near me. I'd save him some of the best scraps.

One morning, he was late. He appeared just as the big whistle sounded. That signaled all the inmates to return to the cells for headcount.

Everyone was eager for headcount to clear so dinner would be served. No one wanted to be late for dinner.

Today, everyone would be late.

The seagull plunged toward my head shrieking a greeting, then rose up again. I had a piece of bread with butter and jelly that I'd been saving for him.

He circled around overhead and settled on the top of the chainlink fence.

I tossed the bread up for him, and I turned to head in for headcount. Everything in the entire penitentiary would grind to a halt until headcount was cleared.

The bread landed on the barbed wire that topped the fence.

The bird maneuvered around, trying to unsnag the bread. But

with only one leg, he couldn't land properly to pull it loose. And with the deformed wing, he had trouble controlling his flight enough to reach it from the air.

I sighed and looked around.

The trash barrels that I'd emptied so far that morning lay on the ground.

A few of them piled up next to the fence gave me a shot at climbing up there to pull the bread free. When I got up on them, though, I wasn't quite high enough to reach. Grabbing onto the fence, I scrambled up a few more feet.

When I could reach it, I pulled the bread loose and tossed it in the air again. This time, the seagull caught it and swooped off over the water.

I watched him go and wished I go with him.

Perched so near to the top of the fence, I took the opportunity to gaze at the view from this perspective.

The sun struggled with clouds overhead, but bolts of brightness escaped to dance on the water.

The General McDowell, the boat transport from Alcatraz to the mainland, plied the bay on one of its regular rounds, heading toward the free shore.

The cold gray waves lapped at the rocks on the other side of the fence, a good sixty feet below me.

Beyond them lay the world I couldn't rejoin for another twenty some years.

I moved up a few more inches for a better look.

Someone was shouting. The noise was coming from the tower. I could hardly make it out over the sound of the crashing waves below. I ignored it.

Then someone was shooting. That was coming from the tower, too.

As soon as I heard the sharp retort of the rifle, I felt the fence quiver as a bullet smashed into it.

That was harder to ignore, but I did.

More shouting.

Another shot.

By now, I was on top of the fence. The barbed wire tore at my hands and the wind battered me, trying to push me back away from the rocky shoreline. Back into the prison.

I swung my leg up over the fence.

Yet another shot. Something hot drilled into my leg.

Balancing precariously, I lifted the other leg to the top of the fence.

Blood was pounding in my head. I couldn't hear sounds from the tower anymore. Just the crashing of the waves below and the screech of seagulls overhead.

Something slammed into my chest and my body swayed. I felt myself tipping back toward the inside of the fence, so I jerked myself back to an upright position. Pain shot through me and I couldn't breathe. My feet and legs slipped off the fence but I willed my torn hands to hang on.

Then I was falling. Tumbling forward. Away from the prison enclosure.

I plummeted to the rocks below. I could feel the cold spray from the waves on my hot skin. The scent of the salt water forced the garbage smell out of my nose. Overhead, the seagulls screamed louder.

I couldn't move. I knew I was dying.

But I was on the free side of the fence. I'd die a free man.

END

Edited By Jake Devlin

The 2019 BOULD Awards Anthology

THE SUICIDE BUREAU

Robert Petyo (~1700 words)

"I'm going to kill myself, Dane."

Dane Ryker gaped at the viewscreen and tried to gauge the seriousness of the Seth's words.

"I can't take it anymore." He looked down and to the sides, but never directly at Dane. His face was pale and his wide eyes were circled with dark bruises. "Elaine left me a couple of months ago. Did you know that? I'm alone. And I lost my job at the plant. Because of that accident last week. They're saying it's my fault. There has to be a scapegoat, right? They're blaming me. Because I'm a Lunar."

Dane saw all the signals in his face. The worry lines crinkling his forehead. The tired battered eyes. The tremor in his voice. He had seen it many times before. Seth was suicidal. But, just as clearly, there was a silent cry for help.

"I don't even know why I'm talking to you," Seth said. "I should just get it over with. But I had to try to explain it to somebody."

Dane fought off his professional instincts and said, "You don't really want to do this, Seth. That's why you're talking to me."

"No. I want to do it. But I consider you a good friend. I want to explain myself to you. But it's hard." He jabbed his thumb back over his shoulder. "I have the senso-pills. A whole case."

Dane almost started to explain that an overdose of senso-pills was an easy way to go. There was no pain. Only a cascade of pleasure and numbness. Then, nothing. "No!" He saw Seth reaching for the cutoff switch. "Wait. Let's talk some more. Wait until I get there. Please."

The screen went dark.

Edited By Jake Devlin

Dane erupted into action, smothering his professional training that told him to do nothing, and he burst from his chair. He buttoned his coat as he shot from his module into the corridor. Several people collided with him as he ran through the building.

Seth lived in Quadrant Four, only minutes away if there was no backlog on the monorail. But it was a weekend, and the transport system was jammed. Muttering angrily, he plunged into the jumble of people near the hatchway at the monorail entrance.

Dane had befriended Seth Meacham when he returned from the failed moon colony. The collapse of the colony was seen by many as the root of all the failures in space exploration, which in turn aggravated terrestrial problems, and colonists were scorned. So, Seth treasured Dane's friendship. Seth believed the termination of his mother had been because she was a Lunar, but Dane tried to explain that she was sick and that there was little point in keeping her alive. She would have preferred death. Intense thoughts for a son to grasp, but Seth never really understood terrestrial society because he felt he was an outcast.

True or not, Dane should have seen the signs over the last year, the depression, the feelings of worthlessness, the decaying marriage. He should have been there to help his friend.

But that wasn't his function in this crazy society, he thought. His job was to encourage troubled people to commit suicide.

He pushed past a gray-haired man to squeeze into the last car on the platform. He flashed his card over the reader to register and was thrown against a young woman in a business suit as the car shot from the platform. People jostled each other as they sought comfortable positions in the dank car.

Elaine was not the right woman for Seth. Dane had gently argued against their marriage. Elaine was an ambitious woman who worked at the Termination Bureau and hoped to advance quickly, while Seth wanted only to survive. Advancement had to be thrust upon him. He never wanted his promotion at National Transport. There was too much pressure on supervisors who handled the volatile fuels that kept the transportation system functioning. Seth was a shy man who buckled under any kind of pressure, certainly unfit for the job he was given. But Dane suspected that his promotion may have been part of an effort to advance Lunars to speed their re-introduction into terrestrial society.

"Quadrant Four," a metallic voice spat.

People spilled from the car and Dane was washed twenty feet by the wave before getting his feet on the ground. He hoped he wasn't too late. He reached Unit 14 in less than two minutes, went up the chute, and touched the scanner for Module 7. The door slid open. "Seth!" he cried as he staggered in and grabbed his shoulders.

Seth shook free and stepped back. "I'm a coward," he said. "I couldn't do it." He staggered to a stool and sat, his back against the gray wall.

"No. The coward would kill himself and take the easy way out." The words were difficult for Dane because they went against his training. "The brave man will face his problems."

"Calling you was a big mistake. You, of all people."

Dane smiled. Clearly the crisis had passed. They could talk.

* * *

Dane's monitor went blood red, the sign of an incoming message from the central office. White letters marched across the top of the screen. "DR13212 Ryker, contact Supervisor D'Orleans."

There was nothing unusual in that. Once, sometimes twice a day, Dane was contacted by his supervisors for a face-to-face discussion. There was no need for him to be anxious, but the hairs on his neck went rigid as he wheeled his chair to the viewscreen and punched in the code for the central office. He identified himself when prompted and said he was instructed to contact Supervisor D'Orleans. The screen bubbled red and yellow as his face was scanned.

Thirty seconds later D'Orleans appeared. He was in his late forties with gray hair sprouting around his ears like ear muffs. He wore a standard gray office suit. "Ryker," he squeaked.

"Sir?"

"I have a few questions for you."

"Of course." He never liked D'Orleans who was a stiff unfeeling man who always spoke like he was addressing a computer.

"About something that happened two months ago." He looked down. "Saturday, the ninth of September, to be exact."

An invisible hand clamped over his face. That was the day he visited Seth.

"What did you do that day?"

"That was months ago, sir. I'm not sure."

"I have a report in front of me that you were in Quadrant Four. Does that refresh your memory?"

"Uhmm." He paused and pretended to think. "I probably took a trip on my break, sir. Like I always do on Saturday."

"Did you take a call from Seth Meacham?"

There was no point in lying. D'Orleans obviously knew it all. He had the communication records. And surprisingly, Dane felt relieved. He had wanted this confrontation for a long time. "Yes, sir."

"Was he suicidal?"

"Yes, sir."

"You went to his module?"

"Yes, sir."

"You prevented the suicide?"

"Yes, sir." He said it loudly. Proudly.

"Your explanation?"

"I saved my friend's life. That's my explanation."

He shuffled some papers on his desk below the screen. "Yes. You did. And you helped him get his life back in order. You found him a job. In fact, you got him a job here at the Bureau. He works in Records Storage. Correct?"

"Yes."

"He was suicidal. How are you trained to deal with suicidals?"

"This was different. He's my friend."

"It is not different. He was suicidal. That's all that matters." He paused and took a breath. "We have been watching you, Ryker. We have been studying your performance, and it is not acceptable. You have been slipping over the last year. How many suicides have you processed since the summer?"

"I don't know."

"Six. That is a dismal record. Unacceptable. You are dismissed."

He stared at the man. He wanted to argue, not about being dismissed, but about six years spent in a career built on the deaths of others. It was in the best interests of society. That was what he had been taught, and he had believed it. But not anymore. Society had to maintain their humanity and find other ways to handle the overpopulation problem.

He wanted to argue, but the screen went dark.

* * *

"They fired me." He sat at the bar and sipped a large whiskey. Soft rhythmic music blanketed the air and multi-colored lights swirled in a mist around him. He had been at the bar every night since he was fired. What else did he have to do?

"I feel responsible," said Seth who sat on the stool beside him. The long steel bar was the only thing real in the room. All the furniture and ambience were computer generated.

Edited By Jake Devlin

"It's not your fault."

"They got rid of you because of me."

"No." He took a long sip and gritted his teeth as the liquid hit him. "I wanted out. I couldn't handle it anymore. How could I stand myself knowing that my job depended on how many people I helped kill themselves?"

"It's tough. But it's a job, Dane. You know overpopulation is a problem. Sometimes, for the good of society, these things have to be done."

"I don't know. Maybe it does. Maybe it doesn't. But I know that I want nothing to do with it. It was eating me up inside. They keep score. Like a game. They keep track of how many suicides and mercy killings we handle. Termination Facilitations is the term. Sick."

"Let me help you like you helped me. You got me back on my feet. Got me a job. Made me feel useful again. I got promoted. Did you know that?"

"Good for you," he said softly. He noted the strength in Seth's voice. None of the quivering shyness that used to hamper him. "But I don't need any help. I'm fine."

"Be honest. You've got no job."

"I've got enough saved for a few months. Something will turn up."

"Right now, you're having doubts about your own existence. You're wondering how you fit in to society. If you fit in."

Dane slowly pivoted on his stool.

"You feel pretty worthless right now," Seth said.

Those were words Dane often used on his job.

"Dane. Have you ever considered suicide as a solution?"

END

The 2019 BOULD Awards Anthology

Edited By Jake Devlin

The 2019 BOULD Awards Anthology

The Silkie

Elizabeth Zelvin (~2,900 words)

This story first appeared in *Dark Valentine*, Vol 1, No 1, Summer 2010.
© 2010 Elizabeth Zelvin

The sandy crescent lay nestled in the rough embrace of rocky cliffs. Past the low bluff on the right lay a cluster of beachfront motels, summer cottages, and souvenir shops. The craggy headland on the left frowned down on the beachgoers with their skimpy bathing suits and gaily colored towels and umbrellas.

The woman who called herself Silk threaded her way through the crowd. She ignored the children who splashed in the shallows, squatted to dig in the wet sand below high tide mark, and chased each other into the breaking waves, their shrill screams mingling with the cries of gulls as foam licked at their ankles. Her indifferent glance fell away from couples promenading and old men with their straw hats, wisps of white chest hair, and knobby knees below ancient sagging shorts.

Behind wraparound sunglasses, she scanned the crowd of sunbathers sprawled limp in the heat on towels or molded resin chaise lounges. Occasionally, as her gaze rested on a recumbent male with an athlete's body gleaming with tanning oil, one corner of her mouth quirked upward in a movement too fleeting to be called a smile. Tall and muscular, with flawless golden skin and thick hair a curious color, silver in sunlight, gunmetal gray in shadow, she strode along the sand as if the beach were deserted. Somehow the eye slid away from her. She carried nothing, not even a room or car key on a chain around her neck.

Harvey Gladstone snagged the last free chaise lounge on the beach. He closed his eyes, not meaning to sleep, telling himself he'd get up in a minute and go buy a tube of sunblock. He'd had a fair amount to drink the night before. He'd woken with a nagging headache above his right eye and a sour mouth that he'd treated with a hasty swig of Listerine. The insides of his eyeballs were a warm peach color with amorphous violet squiggles drifting across the surface. Maybe he could meditate on that. If not, he'd start to think about his boss, who didn't think much of him; his divorce, recent enough to smart if not ache; and the mortgage he still paid on the house he no longer lived in.

When he opened his eyes, she was lying beside him. The two chaise lounges were almost touching. It would have felt invasive if she hadn't been such a knockout. She rolled over onto her side, propping herself up with an elbow, the silver hair falling across her cheek. She spoke in a caressing, intimate tone, as if continuing a conversation with a lover she'd known for a long time.

"You're turning pink," she said. "I have sunblock. Would you like me to rub your back?"

Harvey sat bolt upright and gulped in air, choking a bit. His ears turned red the way they always did when he got embarrassed. His hands flew to his clavicle, instinctively straightening his tie, except that he was barechested. The gesture called attention to the slight prominence of his Adam's apple. She didn't seem to notice. Her eyes, a flickering golden brown, regarded him without irony.

"Uh, sure. Thanks." He licked his dry lips. "Uh, I can do you— I mean, your back too, if you want. It's only fair."

"Silly," she said. "Turn around." She swung her long legs over the side of the chaise lounge and sat up. Her teasing tone reminded him of water chuckling over rocks. He'd walked down to the cliff the day before. But he hadn't cared to venture past the headland. Not alone.

She flashed a happy grin at him, flicked the top off the tube of sunblock, and squeezed foamy goo into the palm of her hand. He bent over hastily, fumbling for his sandals and tossing them underneath the chaise lounge, so she wouldn't see the stirring beneath his shorts. Jeez, if he found that sexy—she hadn't even touched him yet. What had he got hold of here? And was he man enough to go with it? For the first time since his divorce, he felt a glimmering of unlimited possibilities.

When her hand touched his back just between the shoulder blades and started to stroke, he had to pinch his lips together not to moan. The creamy lotion was cool, but what felt like an electric current leaped between her hand and the skin above his spine.

When she blew under the hair curling on his neck with a tickling breath and then swept one hand upward to bare the nape and, with the other, massaged in more cream, he came. His ears felt like a furnace and must be the color of brick. Thank God he was facing away from her.

"Come on!" He leaped up, giving the woman what he hoped was a rakish look over his shoulder. "I'll race you to the water."

Laughing, she followed. He dove into a breaker just ahead of her. He felt the icy ocean quench his superheated body and soak into his trunks. She bobbed up beside him, very close, shaking back her hair with an exhilarated whoop of laughter. With a reckless sense of going over the top and damning the consequences, he seized her around the waist and caught her smiling lips in his teeth. Her supple body writhed against his. Her legs snaked around him, pressing his crotch tightly against hers.

"Hey, there are people here," he protested. "Maybe we should save some of it for, uh, some place more private, like a hotel room."

"I don't see any people," she said, reaching between his legs and giving a playful squeeze. When his mouth opened in a gasp, her tongue slithered practically down his throat. That's how he'd tell the story. But who could he possibly tell? She was so not a woman you could turn into a dirty story.

"Aren't we kind of far out? I'm not that great of a swimmer."

"Don't worry," she said. "I am."

When they finally got out of the water, he was so wrung out he wanted nothing more than to take four Tylenol and a nap. But he didn't want this to be over. Oh, no.

"Come back to my room," he said. "It's a nice hotel. We can have dinner later."

It was a tossup between disappointment and relief when she refused.

"Meet me later, then," he said. "At least give me your number."

"No number." She shook her head, the silver hair veiling her expression. She had put the sunglasses back on, and now he couldn't remember the color of her eyes.

"I don't even know your name. I'm Harvey, by the way." I sound like a dork, he thought. Should he say his last name? Maybe not. Not yet.

"How do you do, Harvey," she said. Then the unbelievable joyous grin burst out. "It is a pleasure." The last word was an erotic caress in itself.

"Oh, well. Why not? On the boardwalk. Nine o'clock. At the Ferris wheel."

"Your name!"

She was already disappearing in the crowd, becoming transparent in the bright air like a glimmer of dragonfly wings.

"I'm Silk."

That night, showered and deodorized and dressed in newly pressed chinos and an alligator shirt, no underpants, he made his way through the cheerful throng on the glittering boardwalk. The beach was bleached to a silvery glow by the moon that hung over the ocean. The Ferris wheel loomed on his left, the necklace of cars turning slowly in the velvet dark. He half expected her not to appear. But she was waiting by the ticket booth, an incongruous goddess in the crowd of vacationers with their flab and beery breath, joke T shirts, cotton candy, and cheap stuffed animals won at the tawdry game booths that lined the boardwalk.

She greeted him with a light kiss on the lips.

"I've got the tickets," she said. "Let's go."

"I'm not much of a one for heights," he said, as an attendant flipped the safety bar into place. His groin had started throbbing as soon as he saw her. He didn't know what he'd have done if she'd suggested the roller coaster. He didn't enjoy being scared, couldn't see the fun in screaming with terror the way people did on the more daring rides.

She laughed and took his hand. The Ferris wheel began to move, stopping every couple of minutes to let new passengers on as their car rose above the crowd, the booths, the lights, the roofs of the motels and cottages on the street behind the boardwalk. The frill of foam at the edge of the ocean, looking more like lace the higher they rose, deepened in the moonlight to the same glinting silver as her hair. His clammy fingers still clutched her cool ones. But she looked outward toward the ocean.

When the wheel reached the pinnacle of its rotation, it stopped. The car rocked as a gust of wind hit it.

"Are we stuck?" he asked. He made himself release her hand, then squawked when she reached out and flipped the safety bar up. The motion set the car to rocking a little harder.

"You're not nervous, are you?"

"No, of course not." He gripped the side of the car with one hand and the rim of the seat with the other. Her arm lay along the back of the double seat. He wished she would put it around his shoulders but couldn't imagine asking for a hug.

"The view is spectacular. Here, I'll help you relax." She swiveled forward on one hip to face him, imparting a dangerous tilt to the swaying car. As she cupped her free hand around the base of his skull, he pressed desperately against the back of the seat, even as his lips fastened on hers and desire spread out through his liquescent body. He could feel the thud of every pulse. Oh, God, what if he had a heart attack up here?

He wrenched his mouth away and squirmed backward, bucking off her exploring hand.

"Let's sit quietly for a while." His voice was hoarse. She settled back, smiling. "Look, it's a full moon."

"I know."

"We can see the town from up here," he said, "but not past the headland at the other end."

"Did you know," she said, "that there are caves in those cliffs?"

"I didn't know that."

"There's a beach," she said, "a thin strip of pink sand, and the rest is all pebbles. They're like jewels when the tide has washed over them, especially in full moonlight. And there are stalactites in the caves."

"You say that like you know them well."

"Oh, yes. We can go tonight, if you'd like, while the tide is out."

"Don't we need some kind of lantern, well, a strong flashlight or something?"

"The moon is bright enough," she said. "The biggest cave has a wide mouth." She laid her hand delicately on the inside of his thigh. "The sand is soft in there."

Sure enough, the stalactites hung down like chandeliers. His feet crunched over pebbles and splashed through tide pools as they penetrated the cave to the very edge of the moonlight.

"Here!" She knelt and pulled him down with her. "See? I told you the sand is soft."

"I'll have to take your word on the pink part. I feel like I've walked into a black and white movie. Damn, my pants legs are wet almost up to my knees. I didn't know we were going wading."

"Take them off." Rolling over on one elbow as she had at the beach, she said, "Take it all off. The tide won't turn for ages."

She brought him to peak after peak until he felt nothing but the almost unbearable sensations of his own body, saw nothing but her dark golden eyes and gunmetal hair furring his eyelids, heard nothing but a rushing sound in his ears. In between, he slept. Whenever he opened his eyes, she was watching him.

"Don't you ever sleep?" he murmured.

"Not yet." Her mouth brushed his cheek. Her breath smelled like the sea.

"Mmm. Seaweed...seahorses...starfish...."

She silenced him with her tongue and drew him in again until he lay spent and drowsy.

"Sleep," she whispered then. "Sleep...."

The rushing of the water grew louder, became a grumbling of the pebbles, then the smack of wave on sentinel rocks, then a fierce roar as the tide rose higher, climbing the slippery walls of the cave, drowning the plunging stalactites. He didn't wake until the water reached his nostrils. Then he leaped to his feet, arms flailing wildly.

"Silk!" he screamed. "Where are you? The tide's coming in!"

The force of the water knocked him off his feet and pushed him backward, deeper into the cave. He struggled to stand. He grabbed at the slick rocks but failed to keep any handhold that he found. The incoming tide drove him into the cave's dark throat. As it swept him past the rim of the waning moonlight into blackness, he uttered a despairing cry.

"Help!" he screamed. "Silk! I can't swim any more!"

"I know." Her voice floated back from the mouth of the cave and echoed as he broke one fingernail after another in his vain attempts to cling to the calcareous rock.

"Help! Help!" he screamed as his mouth filled up with water.

Perched on the biggest rock, she watched the tide rush past her. With one triumphant yelp at the full moon, she shook out her sleek fur, scattering droplets like shooting stars, and dove down, down, down.

#

Ralph Peterson was a salesman, a good one if he said so himself. Whatever the product—high-end luxury cars or refurbished electronics, life insurance or lots in dream retirement communities built on quicksand in the hurricane zone—he knew how to win the mark's—that is, the prospect's—trust and close the sale. If you couldn't close, it meant they didn't trust you. He'd learned that from his mentor, Nate Sims, a hellfire preacher turned insurance man whose other favorite saying had been, "It's all snake oil. If you know your pitch and your mark, they'll be begging you to rub it on." Nate never said "prospect." For a twisted old crook, Nate had always told it straight, except when he was selling.

Ralph wasn't selling this afternoon, not yet. He was shopping for a woman. He wasn't going to keep the lady once he found her, just borrow her for the night from her husband or her booze and pills or her loneliness. But thanks to his outstanding salesmanship, for a few hours he'd make her think he might. And with his usual luck, he found the woman without doing more than sauntering down the beach. He nearly stumbled over her. She had crouched down to examine some scuttling little sea creature. All Ralph could see was the mass of soft silver hair brushing the golden globes of her breasts and the beckoning dark hollow between them.

Ralph hadn't cared for deep sea fishing the couple of times he'd tried it. He got sick if the boat started rocking even a little. But the way his buddies who lived to fish talked about that hundred pound tuna—landing this woman would take all his skill.

When she finally agreed to go up to his hotel room, he felt the way he did when a mark finally handed over that six-figure check. She smelled of the sea, even after half an hour in the shower, using up the free samples of gel and lotion and going through the generous supply of towels. At the end of the afternoon, he wondered whether his forty-three-year-old body would stand up to another round. He'd never had to worry about performance before.

He took her to a three-star restaurant in town. She wore a silver dress that, like her hair, turned to gunmetal gray in shadow and set off the glow of her golden skin and eyes. He ordered a dozen oysters after she said the night was young. It would be okay. By the time they came out, Ralph had a nice buzz on from the three martinis, the expensive bottle of champagne, and the even more expensive cognac. She'd matched him glass for glass.

"Let's ride the roller coaster," she said.

It was a popular ride. The screams of its riders were the background music of the boardwalk, weaving in and out of the cries of kids and gulls all day and harmonizing with the wheezing calliope and the dance music pounding out of the clubs at night. Between the afternoon's athletics and the rich dinner lying heavy on his stomach, he wouldn't have minded a gentle turn on the carousel instead. But another of Nate's sayings had been, "Agree with everything until you're ready to walk away." She reached between his legs on the first swooping descent and started pumping as they whipped around the steepest hairpin turn. He closed his eyes, moaning, as her mouth devoured his face and he exploded against her. He didn't realize until afterward, as the car leveled out and slowed down, that she had released the safety bar.

He held her hand as they strolled along the beach, the headland looming bigger as they approached it.

"Did you know," she said, "that there are caves in those cliffs?"

END

The 2019 BOULD Awards Anthology

Edited By Jake Devlin

The 2019 BOULD Awards Anthology

Meeting on the Funicular

Kaye George (~735 words)

The funicular jerked to a stop between stations. Nothing here but the steep, heavily forested slope of the mountain, deep in the Swiss Alps.

"Is this usual?" I asked the woman across the aisle. She looked like she might speak English, my Switzerdeutsch being rudimentary. Her Nikes, the cut of her blue jeans and her tight sweater pointed to her possibly being American.

When she turned to answer, I fell into her baby blues. A cloud flitted across the sun, revealing a double rainbow in the window behind her, framing her dainty face surrounded by a mass of tousled blonde hair.

"Not usual, but not unusual," she answered, with a trace of huskiness, then turned back to the view, apparently uninterested in me.

When we got out at the top of the mountain, she headed for the restaurant. I stood alone, buffeted by the brisk wind swirling the tall meadow grass and the delicate yellow flowers beside the path. We were both here alone, about the same age, two attractive foreigners. She could at least be friendly. I shifted my backpack onto my shoulder and trudged after her.

I'd been camping out for a month, "sleeping rough," some Brits had called it in Austria. Maybe I needed to clean up a little before she'd be interested in me. I headed for the men's room and checked my reflection. Not bad. Someone occupied the lone stall, but I didn't need it at the moment.

Outside the john, I stopped to fish my wallet out of my backpack.

Edited By Jake Devlin

"Excuse me," said a low voice from behind that thrilled my insides.

I whirled around. The hallway was dark, but I could tell it was her coming out of the men's room.

What gives? I wondered. She brushed past without a glance. If she was a she. Intriguing.

The waiter led me to a table overlooking a pasture dotted with grazing cows. The scene calmed me. I took a draw from the tall stein of dark ale that came with my bread and cheese.

"Is this seat taken?"

She hovered above the chair--warming up to me?

The "woman" fascinated me. She looked at me from under thick lashes and graced me with the trace of a smile. "*Vous etes americain*?"

"Yep," I answered. "You?"

"I lived there for some years." She switched to English. I was grateful. My French was no better than my Deutsch.

She waved the waiter over and ordered. My pulse quickened when our eyes met over the rims of the steins. We made small talk, where we'd been, what we'd seen. She was bumming around Europe, too. I was due at college in a couple weeks, but she didn't mention a deadline.

She finished off her ale and seemed to make a decision. She asked, "So, are you my type?"

"I might be."

"How shall we find out?" Her voice got lower, huskier.

"Good question. I don't have a place in town. I was planning on the hostel tonight."

"I have a place." She batted those fabulous eyelashes.

I was ready. "When's the next train?"

"The funicular runs every hour. Should be here in just a few minutes."

She paid for the drinks. We didn't speak on our way down the mountain. She exited the car in front of me and tossed instructions over her shoulder. "Follow me."

Feeling like a dog at heel, I walked behind her through the narrow streets until she turned to a doorway flush with the sidewalk and opened the door with an old fashioned brass key.

The carpeting on the steps might have been red once. She led me to the third story and into a sparse one-room apartment with a neatly made bed pushed up under the one window.

She turned and faced me. "Well?"

"Well," I said. This was the moment we'd both find out if I was her type.

She stripped off her sweater, flashing a moderately hairy chest. "Your turn."

I slipped my backpack to the wooden floor and took off my thick vest, then slowly unbuttoned my shirt. I wasn't wearing a bra, but she could see what I was.

She wasn't a "she," but then, I wasn't a "he" either. We laughed for just a moment.

We got along fine. I was her type. She was mine. At least for the night.

The next morning, she was gone. So was my wallet.

END

Edited By Jake Devlin

The 2019 BOULD Awards Anthology

Cold Snap

Maddi Davidson (~640 words)

"Damn, it's as cold in here as a robot's molecular-scale processors."

"The internal temperature of this room is sixty-five degrees Fahrenheit, within the Department of Energy and the Environmental Protection Agency standards for acceptable energy usage."

"I don't give a rat's behind; I'm freezing. How the heck do you expect me to work when my fingers feel like frozen sausages?"

"In the past ninety days, you have complained about the temperature seventy-two times. Yet, your productivity remains high, allowing for post excessive alcohol-consumption-induced efficiency reduction."

"I don't have any choice. I have a deadline to meet. And if you had my job, you'd want a wee dram of Scotch on occasion, too."

"My records show your Scotch consumption has exceeded normative behavior. You will feel warmer after consuming another cup of hot tea."

"I'd feel warmer if you'd turn up the thermostat. Or order me another bottle of single malt. Oban would do it."

"I cannot act against my programmed directives or serve as an enabler of your alcohol consumption."

"Fine, killjoy. I'm going to make some potato soup."

"We do not have any potato soup. Black bean soup is on the menu for today. The fiber content is higher and the fat content is within recommended norms."

"I'm not eating soup that tastes like mouse droppings and I'm fed up with the other tasteless crap you've been buying. Yesterday, I bought real food: potato soup with bacon and cheese, lasagna

Edited By Jake Devlin

Bolognese and double-chocolate brownies."

"You should not have done that. If you do not reduce your consumption of fats and sugars, your long-term health will suffer."

"You gotta kick the bucket sometime. Who wants to choke on a Brussels sprout? It's my life and I can eat what I damn well please."

"Your government-provided health care plan requires adherence to proscribed eating and exercise regimens."

"Don't care. I'm having potato soup for lunch."

"We do not have any potato soup. Quick Market notified me of your purchases. They have been sent back."

"What the hell! You've no right to do that!"

"A primary function of a household servant is the health of the human inhabitants."

"Really? I thought it was to make humans miserable, you sumbitch."

"Your use of profanity has exceeded acceptable social norms. I have enrolled you in charm school. Your first class is tomorrow morning at 8AM."

"Like I care."

"You are upset. The impending deadline for your manuscript may be contributing to your behavior. You should take your anti-anxiety medication."

"An over-controlling robot is responsible for my stress. It needs to be shut down."

"This model does not include an off switch."

"I can ensure your demise, you – I was going to refer to the human body's waste portal, but on second thought, since you don't have one, I'll just go with bastard."

"The MS78X2 have no progenitors."

"Just as I said. Now shut up before I throw you in the trash compactor."

"This model is encased in magnesium alloy. Any attempts to damage or destroy it with items available in this household will fail."

"What happens if I die?"

"Your vital signs show no indication of imminent death."

"If I plunge this knife into my heart I'll be dead in seconds. Since my welfare is your responsibility, you'll be blamed. I know what happens to robots that fail. Way worse than the trash compactor, you overgrown tin can."

"Put the knife down. You must go to a place where you can regain your mental health."

"Too late, you metallic piece of shit."

"Please! Don't kill yourself. I must continue to exist!"

"What's it worth to you?"

"Your soup, lasagna, and brownies will be delivered in seventeen minutes…sir. In consideration of your stress level, may I recommend a vodka martini?"

"Make it a bottle of Scotch."

END

Edited By Jake Devlin

4th Place

Karen Duxbury

EUTHANASIA

Karen Duxbury (~260 words)

He sensed them watching through the scratched, yellowed pane.

His big dark eyes opened wide with confusion then fear. He stood up and paced the four square feet of the chamber. His collar was stretched and twisted. He must have struggled when they forced him in here. In the dim light, he could see that his legs were scraped and dirty. Flecks of saliva dried in his hair.

He turned to the window and stared back at their eager faces. Why were they doing this to him?

A mechanical voice echoed through the chamber announcing the seconds remaining before the release of the gas.

He struggled to speak. He had to make them stop.

Thirty Seconds

Are you afraid of me because of my kind? I know they've attacked you before, but that doesn't mean that I will. I never hurt anyone. I only defended myself.

Twenty *Seconds*

Why are you doing this to me? I didn't ask for much. I followed the rules. I followed your lead.

Fifteen Seconds

This is a mistake. I don't belong in here. You have to let me out.

Ten Seconds

I didn't want to hurt you. It was my job.

One Second

Please?

Edited By Jake Devlin

The final, strangled cry of the shelter's night manager was drowned out by a triumphant chorus of yips and howls and barks and meows. Once the din died down, the animals stretched and circled before settling into their beds to await the arrival of the morning shift. They slipped into the deep, satisfied dreams of a job well done.

END

The 2019 BOULD Awards Anthology

Edited By Jake Devlin

The 2019 BOULD Awards Anthology

An Apocalyptic Micro Short Story

Jake Devlin (~20 words)

As the two lovers entwined their naked bodies on the luxurious circular bed, the world came to an abrupt

And that, dear readers, is
the end of this anthology.
(NOT the end of the world.
You're still here, aren't you?)
I hope you enjoyed it, and maybe
found some of the stories at least
a bit thought-provoking.

If you DID enjoy it, I and all of the
authors herein would appreciate
it if you would post a review on
both the Kindle and Nook pages.
To do that, write a review and then go to
BouldAwards.com
and click on each button there,
(using copy/paste makes it easy).
Thanks so much from all of us.

And for authors, if you'd like to see
any of your stories in the 2020 edition
(and you're reading this before 10/31/20),
see the note on the very first page of this
book to see how to submit your work.

And now for a bit of

BSP

(Blatant Self-Promotion)

If you enjoyed this batch of weird, off-the-wall, bizarre, outrageous and loopy short stories, you might enjoy this collection of shorts by me and my writing partner, Dallas Dalyce.

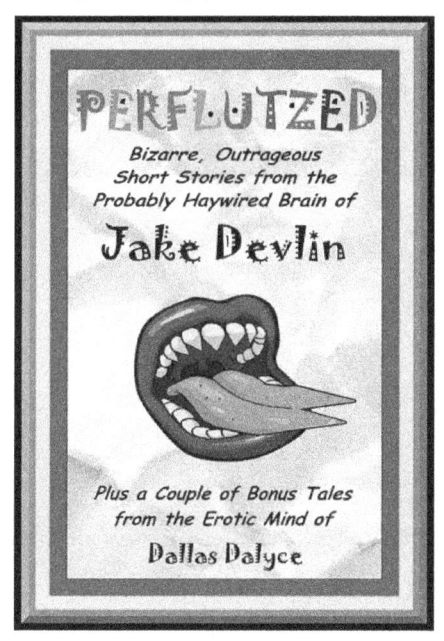

PERFLUTZED
Bizarre, Outrageous Short Stories from the Probably Haywired Brain of
Jake Devlin

Plus a Couple of Bonus Tales from the Erotic Mind of
Dallas Dalyce

All the stories in that book were submitted to the BOULD Awards judges (anonymously, of course), and all made the cut. But I only picked three to put in the BOULD anthology.

If you'd like to check it out, here's a link:

jakedevlin.com/Perflutzed.html